THE

BASTARD

CITIZEN

From the Author

By

Funom Theophilus Makama

18/02/2021

First Published in December, 2019
Second Edition, published in January, 2021 by
FeedARead Publishing

British Library C.I.P.

A CIP catalogue record for this title is available from the British Library.

Dedicated to all the hard working Nigerians,
trying to make it through the right means.

When death knocks at the door, the doctor is looked upon as a God.
When he accepts the challenge, he is looked upon as an Angel.
When he cures the patient, he is looked upon as a common person.
When he asks for his fee, he becomes the devil.

All names, characters and incidents portrayed in this novel are fictitious. Any resemblance to any person, living or dead, is purely coincidental.

Clinical consultations and the taking of medical histories are concisely summarized to keep the plots timely and intriguing.

PROLOGUE

Just the second week of operations, the doctor is already having a heavy work load as patients keep trooping into his facility. The one week free medical services he rendered has been a successful strategy as the good news of his expertise spread so fast within the community to the joy of the locals.

It's 2pm and the doctor has reviewed every patient admitted, after his clinic session. He holds a brief meeting with his nurses in his office and 25 minutes into it, there is a knock on his door, "who's it?" He asks, "It is me sir, Angela." His receptionist replies and continues, "Sir, there is an emergency; you need to come to the reception." "Okay Angela, thank you and inform the accompanying relatives that we will be right there." Angela leaves, while he dismisses the Nurses to go back to their stations and get the new case ready for him.

In no time, a new file is brought to his desk, he reviews it and takes note of the vitals of the patient, some of which are so bad that he re-examines the patient to be sure of the accuracy of the values registered when he sees her. He leaves his office with his portable 'laptop-like' Ultrasound machine, goes to the patient in the Female ward and assesses her pregnancy, while two women, obviously related to her, stand aside, "who can I talk to?" He asks, facing the direction of the women. "You fit talk to us, doctor," they answer in pidgin English in a chorus as one of them, genuflects.

"She get hypertension before?" The woman in red traditional attire immediately replies, "we no know o, but e be like say she dey always complain of headache every time." He nods his head and asks again, while the nurses enter with items to set up intravenous fluids for her, "sugar nko? She dey suffer from sugar problem?" The second woman on blue and white shakes her head several times, "we no know doctor."

"Where her husband dey?"

"Him dey Porthacourt," the one in blue and white answers.

"She don get belle before?"

"Yes doctor, but she bin get two miscarriages and in between them, one pikin die inside belle when e reach 8 months."

He takes the folder and takes some notes, asking more questions in the process. After about 7 minutes of doing so; he refocuses on the women. "So I fit talk to the two of wunna abi?" The women say "no" and immediately, the one in the red attire dashes out, to return after about a minute with an elderly man, who greets the doctor as soon as he enters the ward "good afternoon my doctor."

"Good afternoon sir, please introduce yourself sir."

"I am Mr. Philemon, the elder brother to her husband, so feel free to tell me anything doctor."

"Thank you Mr. Philemon. Your sister in-law is carrying a high risk pregnancy. She has had two miscarriages and a still birth before. Her blood pressure is currently at 210/100mmHg and her blood glucose level is also high, at 19.8mmol/L. And above all these, she is carrying a twin gestation….." The man interrupts, "sorry doctor, what do you mean by a twin gestation?" The doctor smiles, "it means she will be giving birth to twins."

"Ehhhh!" The three relatives scream as the woman in blue and white laments "but doctor, we don do scan three times since she carry belle, them no show us twins o!" He smiles and opens his portable ultrasound machine once again, pours some gel on her abdomen and begins to move the transducer on it, and in the process, shows them major convincing features of a twin gestation, explaining in the simplest of terms for them to understand. 7 minutes after, he stops, switches off the device and cleans the woman's abdomen. "So as I was saying, this is a high risk pregnancy and she will need immediate surgery to save her life first, and that of her babies. Their heart rates are currently high, 165 and 173 beats per minute, which means, they are distressed and since they've reach 35 weeks already, I think the right thing to do is to save them all. So, if we must act, now is the time to do so, as we are already resuscitating her."

The elderly man comes close to the doctor "but sir, we do not want C/S o! We don't do C/S in our family and no matter the issue our wives face, they always overcome them and give birth to bouncing babies. Six out of my nine children supposed to be born through surgery, if we had followed our Doctor, but I insisted as of that time, and see it now; they are all alive and grown. Please doctor, what is the sex of the twins?"
"They are both boys." He replies the man which attracts a loud reaction from the three relatives, after which, he continues the conversation, "Sir, with all due respect, I envy your faith, your belief and

stance. But what worked for your wife may not necessarily work for your sister in-law. Besides, your wife's pregnancy may not be as complicated as this. The two circumstances, I'm sure are very different and should not be compared, so please sir, consider the health and life of this woman and allow us intervene immediately."

"My Doctor, we refused three hospitals before coming here o, because we've heard so much about you, just in a week of operations. Please, be different from the rest and do your best without cutting her skin." The doctor gets really sad, "Sir, thank you for your kind words and the trust you have for me already, but I'm afraid, that will be the best and also the least I can do for her. If you are not willing to allow us do the best we can, you can then make this hospital the fourth one in your rejection list."

"Ah Doctor! No! Since all of you seem to be saying the same thing, then please give me some time to consult with the other male relatives outside and also speak to our brother, her husband, through the phone."

"Good! But we do not have much time, Sir. If this woman convulses, we may lose one or some or all three of them. Please, don't hesitate. I'll be waiting in my office. As soon as you've made a decision, let my nurses know so that we commence immediate preparations after you consent."

The doctor leaves the ward to his office and just immediately, the elderly man, Mr. Philemon leaves too, but in about 15 seconds, a man in expensive clothing, from neck to his feet, who carries a large bible walks into the ward to much of the excitement of the two women. "I am here with the power of the holy ghost. When the lord says, no one dares object......." The two women submissively oblige to his strong worded proclamations. "I have seen it, I have heard the lord speak, himself, just as the Hebrew women gave birth, so shall you..." He lays his right hand on her abdomen as he fidgets vertically with eyes forcefully closed and head facing up. "I say you, Mrs. Rebecca will be counted among the Hebrew women of our generation. The lord has blessed this family that you are married to and with the spirit of natural birth; you shall overcome, because by the virtue of a permanent and godly union, you have possessed it. So your time has come to be a part of their glorious history of victorious births. Who is he to stand against the words of the lord? Who is he to spit on the power of the most high?" He speaks with authority, dishing out commands with gross insensitivity to the environment he is. He then faces the women as he continues to exert his authority, "tell that elderly man who just left here, I speak to him right now, his presence shall represent the spirit of this family; his words shall speak life to her bones, her muscles and the babies. He should never leave her sight again until victory is sure. She will give birth, she is already on the way, so let him come back and be the pillar of her victory. The battle ground has been taken over and the devil is already overwhelmed." The woman in red attire rushes out to inform the man as the other woman pour out appreciations to the man of God and to Jesus.

Meanwhile, Nurse Onyinye quickly runs to the doctor's office just in time to inform him of the recent development and when he comes out, he meets the man of God at the reception, about to leave the premises. "Are you the pastor who is here to see Mrs. Rebecca, my patient?" The man of God pauses and faces him in a sheer display of arrogance, "yes, I am he! Anything the problem?"

"Yes! What have you done? This woman needs help and you came to lie to them all?"

"How dare you accuse the lord falsely?"

"And since when have you become the lord?"

"I am his mouthpiece, young Man. Leave spiritual matters to those in the spirit and stick to your clinical matters."

"And who said the clinical matters aren't spiritual too? Who gave us the knowledge of medicine? Is it the devil?"

"Doctor, I will not argue spiritual matters with you. I operate in the supernatural and the one who sent me is above all supernatural beings and elements, so I get it if you do not understand what is going on here." The doctor gets furious, looking up the ceiling and his two hands rested on both sides of his waist as his body shakes. "As a doctor, I am also a minister. Jesus Christ healed the sick, so his manifestation is also made a reality through my knowledge and skill. He has revealed unto us this marvelous craft, blessing man with the miracle of understanding on how to bring life to the dying and restore wholeness to the weak. For a woman in such a situation to be convinced by you not to be helped is rather unfortunate. You are surely not from God; you are, as a matter of fact, a wicked soul; a misleading agent and the mouthpiece of yourself and yourself alone. If this woman refuses this surgery and anything happens to her or her babies, their blood will be on your head. As the high priest of this facility and a minister called to manifest his power through medicine, I have spoken. Get out of my sight!" The man of God drops his Bible on one of the white plastic chairs in the reception hall and begins yelling, "Me! Me, His Holiness Comodos Festus Obidozor Ph.D, you call me wicked? Do you know who you are talking to? If I raise my hands to the heavens and lay a curse on you......." The doctor interrupts "Get out of my sight! Raise which hands? Curse who? Security! Come and take this agent of deceit out of this place before I transfer the aggression on you. MONSTER!" The relatives outside hear the altercation, prompting Mr. Philemon to quickly enter the reception, even before the security man comes in. He waits for the man of God to be escorted out before speaking, "Oga doctor! E no reach like this nah! Anyway, we've come to a decision and we will not allow her undergo any surgery. We will take her home because we know what to do." The doctor gets really sad and convinces him one more time. "Sir, with all due respect, your family isn't Hebrew. You have no link to the Hebrew women, you guys are not related in any way to them and for the fact your wives have been successful in having uncomplicated vaginal births does not mean, every case will be like theirs...."

Mr. Philemon interrupts, 'God forbid! Doctor, say no more please, we are leaving. We have paid your balance, so we can go. No matter how we explain this to you, you will not understand. It is our way of life, our spiritual heritage and ancestral strength. Since they do not teach you people these mysteries in medical school, I totally understand you, if you refuse to understand me. I have signed our 'leave against medical advice' so can we go?" Reluctantly, the doctor nods his head in agreement. The man quickly goes inside as Onyinye, one of the nurses, gently removes all intravenous assesses for the patient to be taken away.

XXXXXXXXXXXXXXXXXXXXXXXXXXXX

It's 6:30pm of the same day and the doctor just finishes his evening rounds, writing his final report in his office when Nurse Medinat knocks and enters his office. "Sir, there is a man hiding behind the building. He is outside, near your office window. I asked him what the problem was and he said he wants to see you, only you. I spoke to Nurse Fatimat and Hajarat but he threw stones at them when they tried coming close to him." The doctor gets surprised, "what exactly is going on?" She panics a little, "I swear sir, I have no idea. And the man seems to be in pains, please Sir, try and check him yourself." "Okay Medinat, calm down, I think everything is fine. I will go and see what is happening." He finishes his paper work and goes outside to the hospital's backyard. "Can I help you sir?" "Yes doctor, my stomach bites seriously. I feel so much sharp pains and heat inside. This is the first time it is happening to me. I just came back from Zaria and as soon as I arrived home, the pain started and increased in severity. I have taken Buscopan, Ampiclox, Flagyl, Paracetamol and even Magnesium transillicate but the pain keeps worsening."

"So, you need to go inside and follow our normal protocol. I will attend to you as soon as you get our card and a folder is created for you."

"No doctor, please I want this to be discrete. I am ready to pay any amount, just treat me secretly. And let only the fair nurse who first saw me be the extra hand that will attend to me. I want no other person."

"I am sorry sir, I cannot do that, you have to….." The man interrupts, "even if it is 100,000 naira sir, I will pay. Please, take me to your amenity ward through the backdoor if there is one; isolate me there, I should be the only one there please; whatever it is, I will pay." As he talks, his agony increases, shown by a sharp scream and a strong hold of his stomach with his arms, then he falls to the ground.

The doctor quickly runs inside, speaks to Medinat to open one of the locked back doors. She quickly does as told while he takes a wheel chair, resisting all attempts to be helped, from the other nurses and he goes to the backyard. He struggles to lift the man up, but eventually does, placing him in a sitting position on the wheel chair before wheeling him through the back door, into the Amenity ward.

Medinat's shift has just ended, so he speaks to her and also to her dad through the phone to let her stay for the night because of the new patient. After negotiating with her dad, he finds out from her if she is able to stay back and afterwards, she assures him; he allows her to have a 2-hour break so that she can return to take care of the man. Through the 2 hours of break, the doctor solely handles every need associated with the man. He creates a folder for him, gets a new card and asks a few more questions as the man answers in severe pains. The doctor instructs the nurses present to set the tray for intravenous assess but collects it outside the door and administer some fluid to him.

"So doctor, what is wrong with me? Is it ulcer?" The man asks.

"For now, let's say you have dyspepsia or dyspeptic syndrome, but we will keep Gastric ulcer in view. Once you undergo an endoscopy, we will confirm if it is ulcer or not."

"I understand you doctor, but why now? Why at this my age?"

"Well, there is nothing abnormal about having ulcer at your age and from your answers to my questions, it is clear you do not eat food the way you ought to and the few times you do, your meals are usually spicey. You also have persistent heart burn for a few years now and with a family history of heart burn from your mother and three out of your five other siblings, I think there is a hereditary link. I just gave you the magic drug-Omeprazole, intravenously, so in no time, you will be fine. I will get the tablets for you and prescribe how you should be taking them. Your preferred Nurse is Medinat and she will be here soon to continue monitoring you; if there is no more issue for the next 2 hours, we may discharge you."

"Thank you very much doctor. Are you sure five thousand five hundred naira is enough? Here is twenty thousand naira more. The doctor smiles, "no need for that sir, just make sure you are fine, you eat well and take your drugs as advised. See you in the clinic in a week's time." The doctor leaves the ward.

Within the compound is parked his car and just as he is about entering to leave, a white Mercedes Matic car enters in speed. The doctor quickly comes out as the doors open and Mrs. Rebecca is hurriedly carried in an unconscious state into the hospital. The doctor stands annoyed as relatives come straight to him to kneel and beg for his prompt intervention. The two women who were present earlier also come along but Mr. Philemon, the elderly brother in-law is absent. They beg him to do the surgery and in fact, one of them immediately drops 150,000 naira on the ground, right in front of him. He does not speak a word to them as he walks through them into the Hospital. She is taken straight to the theatre, while he goes into his office to take his portable ultrasound machine once more. He assesses her abdomen, getting angry from every observation he makes and shaking his head in pity as he analyzes the images from its screen. Mrs. Rebecca is now between life and death with her only proof of life being the heavily-laboured breathing she suffers. He comes out to inform them of the demise of the twins and explains to them the need for an emergency surgery to boost her chances of survival. He inquires about the number of times she convulsed after leaving the hospital in the afternoon and some say 'two', some say 'three', others 'four', another person 'five'. He asks after Elder Philemon and one of the women replies, still in agony, "he is busy, he said he isn't coming." He shakes his head, leaving their midst to save the woman. He orders one of the nurses to take the money they drop on the floor, and then, he calls his laboratory scientist to group and cross match the patient's blood. As soon as she is set and three pints of blood are made available, he enters to perform the surgery. The two dead fetuses are eventually brought out, cleaned and weighed by an extra assistant and then dropped carefully in a carton box already provided. 37 minutes later, the surgery is over and the woman is taken to the recovery room, still on blood transfusion. He writes his operation notes and the dead fetuses are presented to the relatives outside the reception, who react with increased wailing and weeping but he cares less as he enters his car and zooms off. The Nurses are up and doing, closely monitoring the woman postoperatively but 2 hours later, she gives up. He is alerted through the phone, he returns, confirms her dead and then certifies. The hospital vicinity is now marred with so much weeping as sorrow clouds the environment but he shows not an iota of emotions or concern, ignoring the atmosphere damped with strong emotions as he immediately leaves after performing his duty. The corpse too is taken away as soon as he leaves.

Just when absolute calmness is restored within the hospital premises, the man with dyspepsia sneaks out through the back door, tip-toeing his way to the Gate and finally, leaving the hospital premises. The next time nurse Medinat goes to check on him, she notices his absence and his escape, proven by the incompletely closed back door. She locks it and writes her report.

XXXXXXXXXXXXXXXXXXXXXXXXXXXX

It's now two days after this eventful day and the doctor comes unusually late to work due to domestic issues needing his attention. As usual, he follows through the back to avoid being seen by the patient, entering into his office and calling out for Nurse Onyinye. She enters and greets, "good morning sir."

"Good morning Onyinye, how are you?"

"I am fine sir."

"So, how many patients do we have for clinic today?"

"48 sir."

"Any new patient?"

"Yes sir, 35 of them."

"He screams "35!" And then, readjusts his position, "let's get to work then, please call Medinat for me, on your way out."

"Okay sir." She leaves and almost immediately, there is a knock on the door and Medinat enters on his invitation. "Good morning sir."

"Good morning Medinat, how are you?"

"Fine sir."

"I forgot to ask you, do you know that strange man of dyspepsia who came two days ago, the day the mother of the twins died?" Medinat bursts into laughter for 7 seconds, "Sorry Sir, that man is a doctor o!" He looks at her in surprise, "a doctor? I don't understand."

"Not a real doctor anyway, but he is one of these quacks around. His highest level of education is a diploma in religious reconciliation sir."

"I see! And how did he manage to become a doctor?"

"Sir, you will soon know how this place operates. That man learnt from somebody who is also a quack and after 4 years, he opened his own clinic. He doesn't treat people o. What he does is to wash people's systems."

"Incredible! How does he do that?"

"Honestly sir, I don't know, but that is just his specialty and if you see how people troop into his clinic ehh!"

"Really?" He screams as he shows more interest in the conversation, "you don't say!"

"I swear down sir. There is no day, you won't see at least 15 people waiting for him and I heard he charges between 15,000 to 30,000 naira."

"What!" For washing people's systems?"

"Yes sir!"

"No wonder, he wasn't bold enough to face all of you. He was trying to protect his identity since he could not wash his, to prevent dyspepsia." Medinat laughs and he continues, "it is okay Medinat, you can go now and let the first patient come in." She leaves and after 10 seconds, the door opens. He raises his head in shock and instantly becomes dumb founded as anger grows inside of him to be well expressed on his face.

"Good morning doctor." He refuses answering. The man comes in with a little girl who is around the age of 7. "Doctor, I say good morning now! Answer me please." The doctor stares at him and looks down, flipping through the empty folder. "I am so sorry doctor, if that is what you want to hear from me. Whatever has happened is the will of God." The doctor instantly stares at the man in rage, "will of God you say?"

"Okay, doctor, let the past stay in the past, please attend to my daughter, she is really sick, we need your help."

"Oh! So the lord did not tell you anything pertaining your daughter, most holiness Comodos Festus Obidozor? Where are your matters of the spirit? What happened to your ability to hear God? Are you no longer his mouthpiece?"

"Like I have earlier told you, God's ways are not our ways……" The doctor interrupts, "will you shut up or I send you out of this place. Don't just annoy me this morning, don't dare! You are lucky I am not as heartless as you are, and I owe it as a responsibility to attend to patients come what may and irrespective of how devilish their fathers are…." The man quickly cuts in, "Ah Doctor! My daughter is here now! Take it easy; know how you talk to me in her presence."

"I do not bloody care Mr. Man, you have gone away with a terrible thing you did, but know it this day that the blood of 3 souls is on your head now."

"It's okay doctor, can you please attend to us now?"

The doctor looks at him angrily, "so you know the relevance of medicine in the life of your family but lie against God, as you gamble with people's lives just to exact your 'so-called' spiritual relevance? Don't worry; your deeds will catch up with you soon. So what is your daughter's problem?"

CHAPTER 1

Omega Medical Centre is an averagely equipped health centre situated on the ground floor of a three-storey commercial building with its first to third floors still uncompleted. It is located in the middle belt region of Nigeria and in a municipal of 85,000 inhabitants of different tribes and religions which sadly suffers from a very poor healthcare system both in infrastructure and manpower, giving room for quackery to thrive. Ever since Omega Medical Centre, popularly known as OMC started operations, about 8 months now, a lot of patients have been trooping in, especially after knowing the person in charge is actually a Doctor who, additionally, acquired his training abroad. Though at this time, the economic situation of the country is bad with a huge uncertainty of the future which is a major factor for patronage and as well as patients' attitude towards the doctor and his staff.

During his ward round, one evening, the doctor gives his usual consultation to a family, "I'm happy with his improvement."

"Thank you doctor," the mother of the recuperating child appreciates.

"In the meantime, continue the treatment to completion please. Don't skip even a dose of medication."

"Okay, sir."

"After four weeks, come for another checkup so that we examine his progress."

The doctor looks up a calendar and counts, "11th! On the 11th of next month, you'll come back to see me."

"Thank you very much, doctor." This time, it's the child's father who appreciates. "That does not mean you'll sit back at home in the event of an emergency," the doctor warns as he plays with the boy and then the parents stand up and leave.

Another parent knocks and comes in. This time, it's a father and his eight year old son who comes in with a penile erection.

"Good morning, doctor."

"Good morning... Mr. Bassey, I suppose?" he reads from the folder as the man replies, "exactly sir. Ubong Bassey. Here is my son." The man introduces his son, smiling in confidence. The doctor notices a frontal bossing on the fore-head of the boy and his inability to stand erect without showing some signs of pain distress. Another observable feature is the boy's penile erection which never comes down since he entered the consultation room. The doctor widens his gaze as he looks at the father.

"For how long has he been erect like this?" He asks.

The man laughs, "my strong boy has been like this for about three hours now. I've gone to another clinic and they gave me vitamin B complex and one white and yellow capsule, assuring me that he is fine and he is never too early or too quick to becoming a man; proving that my son is great and strong."

"What!" The doctor exclaims, standing up. "Do you know what you are doing? This is an emergency." The doctor runs out of his office, calls for a quick set up for a cavernous aspiration and comes back in.

"But doctor, I'm only here because he's complaining of pain due to the erection which I still consider as normal," the father protests and continues, "you know, once in a while I take Viagra to perform and my manhood down there stays erect even after my performance. Its long stay can cause pain which I feel is the same for my son."

"Mr. Bassey, is your son not a sickle cell disease patient?"

"I don't know doctor."

"How often does he fall ill?"

"He falls ill almost on a weekly basis, doctor."

"What about falling seriously ill?"

"Yes sir, it happens like once or twice in a month for the past 6 months now."

"And even with all these events, you did not deduce that there's more to just a regular illnesses?"

"We've been going to a clinic, the one called Majestic Healers and they've been treating him for malaria and typhoid all the time."

"Do you know your genotype?"

"No doctor. What's that?"

"That means you don't even know your wife's?"

"I don't, doctor."

"But it is a pre-wedding requirement these days, so how come you don't even know?" "We wedded in the traditional way and only that way sir."

"How many children do you have?"

"Three of them, doctor."

"Are the others always falling ill as regularly as Ubong?"

"No, sir."

"Mr. Bassey, your son clearly presents with signs of sickle cell anaemia. You can see how yellow his eyes are. He's so weak and obviously, his knee and toe joints hurt a lot. This erection is what we call priapism and it occurs in sickle cell disease patients, especially young boys like him. My nurses are setting up the procedure room now, while my laboratory scientist will take his blood samples for investigations. We will drain some blood out of his penis right away to resolve the protracted erection. This is an emergency and I want you to fully understand the situation we are in right now. The longer the erection, the more he stands a chance of becoming impotent for life. Do you understand what I'm saying?"

The man jumps up immediately, "Doctor, please help my son. Help him, please." Before the doctor responds, the man drops to the floor, screaming. The doctor goes after him to encourage him. "Stop this, Mr. Bassey. What's wrong with you? This is not the end. The situation will be salvaged, this I assure you. Please stop this and man up."

The man acts crazy as he repeats "Majestic healers have killed me o." The doctor convinces him to sign a consent form and, immediately after, the nurses come in to notify him who alerts the security officer to take Mr. Bassey out of his office, to the reception where the other relatives are.

The doctor takes the boy to the procedure room and as soon as his father is with the others, pandemonium breaks out when he tells them of the situation. The ward attendant and even the receptionist get busy as they try to make the place calm while comforting them. After about 30 minutes, the doctor comes out while the nurses take the boy, who has already unleashed a two-litre bowl of urine, to the ward. The boy's parents immediately rush to the office as the doctor enters, "sit down please. I believe she is his mother, right?" The woman falls to her knees, "yes doctor, but please tell me the truth. Is my son okay?"

"Yes madam, he is okay. He will be fine. Don't worry."

"But doctor, why blood? Is this case that serious?" The father asks.

"Erection is a blood activity, not a muscular one. What makes a man erect is the blood filling of the penile vessels."

"Oh, okay. But, how is he now, doctor?"

"He's fine, but fast asleep. Please don't panic. For now, let's have a serious chat. I'm still surprised you know nothing about the genotype and sickle cell anaemia."

"Doctor, I have heard about it. It is an ancestral curse. Nobody in my family has it. My one time neighbour in Jos, when I was working with the Nasco Company, lost all four children because of this sickness. In fact, I packed immediately so that the curse would not follow me. Look at it now, it truly has followed me."

The man laments while the doctor takes his time to properly educate and counsel them on the illness.

"I will kill those people. All they do is just deceive us and collect our money," the man shows so much anger.

"Calm down, Mr. Bassey. Now is not the time for this. Just calm down, we've come to the rescue, so it isn't a fait accompli. Just ensure that everyone in the house knows his or her genotype now, since we have confirmed that of Ubong. We will continue to observe him within the next twenty-four hours. We will also give him some medication, one of which will restrict blood flow to the penis, to avoid any immediate reoccurrence. We call it a vasoconstrictor. If the vessels are constricted," he demonstrates using his left index finger and thumb as they form a circle, "…they will not allow for adequate blood flow, hence, a reduced amount of blood to the penis."

Nurse Miriam comes in. "Sir, you didn't indicate the promethazine dosage."

The doctor collects the folder, "Sorry about that, it's still 25mg to be used, which is half the bottle." He makes the correction and hands the folder over to the Nurse and she leaves.

The doctor faces the parents who are now calm. "So, any questions for me?" He asks.

"No, doctor. But are you sure he will be fine?"

The doctor smiles, "Yes, Mr. Bassey, so far as priapism is concerned, I am very sure. Nevertheless, we will still run further tests to see if we can commence additional treatment. His joints are weak and very painful. He's suffering from severe fatigue, as you can see. He cannot cry, even though he wants to. So, we will definitely keep him for more assessments but one thing is sure, he needs blood, at least 3 pints. Please tell the other relatives that the situation is now under control. This is a hospital and there are other patients in need of the tranquility. Please go and talk to them."

"Okay doctor, we will do so," Mr. Bassey assures, while his wife genuflects to a degree that the right knee is almost touching the ground, "thank you very much doctor. You're a God-sent. Please take good care of my boy."

The doctor stands up, "Don't worry Mrs. Bassey, he's in good hands by the special grace of God." The couple goes out for the next patient to come in. They take the other relatives outside and the man begins ranting in his local dialect while they stimulate him to more anger. After speaking aggressively, he enters his car and leaves.

XXXXXXXXXXXXXXXXXXXXXXXXXXXX

Meanwhile, outside a popular bar which is situated in the heart of town are four men who carouse the afternoon to everyone's notice, including passers-by. Alhaji Abdulfatai Mohammed, popularly called "Dr. Abdul" or "Presido", is the president of the clinics association of the town, who is with other colleagues; Mr. Lookman Suleiman, also known as Sule, his vice; Mr. Innocent Peter, the secretary; and Mr. Audu Paul, the treasurer. They create an isolated occasion, not minding the immediate environment as bottles both empty and filled in different capacities litter their surroundings. "Peter", the president calls, "I saw a fine chick in your place the other day. What was she doing there?"

Peter smiles, "Mr. Presido, she hawks bread o."

"Supaninlah!" The president exclaims in shock as Peter continues, "I bought all the loaves of bread she had, gave her extra cash and asked her to follow me."

"So you mean, such a fine chick so fair and ripe hawks bread? You're a lucky man o. It's been long I tasted fresh bush meat like that. Second hand products are what are chasing me about, right now," the president comments as everyone else laughs, then Sule resumes the conversation, "and my sharp guy here just seized the opportunity. You are a bad guy o! This is the true definition of a bread winner."

They laugh again while he shakes Peter's hand, the rest sipping their drinks. "That girl can cure depression o. Forget these hawkers you see on the road. They're not just bad, they've decayed. That girl made me scatter my table and break one of my windows," Peter explains, and Audu continues, "So you did it in your office? What about your nurses?" Everyone laughs as the president picks up from there, "Which nurses? The ones we've all done royal rumble with? Audu, you're the only one fucking up o. You see, there's one of them with the long neck, what's that her name again?"

"Kudirat" Peter answers as the president continues.

"Yes! Kudirat, sweet girl, that one has been eyeing you o!" Sule cuts in immediately. "Oh presido! You've also noticed?"

"Yes, of course. I be bad guy nah! I bad pass devil." They laugh again and then he continues, "who observes the way her body was springing like rubber band when Audu touched her while sending her for an errand?" Sule and Peter scream on top of their voices for about twenty seconds.

"Mr. Audu, stop dulling o! It's not as if you're a saint either. I caught you, two months ago doing it inside your incinerator with your lab scientist."

Sule and Peter, at this point are intoxicated in laughter. The president continues, "news is everywhere about how you've pounced on three half-sisters, each, the daughter of a different wife to Mallam Usman." Sule and Peter's laughter get louder and the president continues, "so, no need to form holy-holy for us here o!" Audu gets into an anodyne mood, "you're right, Presido. I just don't want complexity in my escapades. I feel everyone's nurses are his territory."

"Come on Audu!" The president pats his back. "Life is not that serious. Once you've slept with more than one woman, you've already attracted complexity into your sexual life. One extra woman is enough to cause serious havoc, don't you know that? There's love in sharing and the four of us have opened the forum for trans-border trade…"

Peter cuts in, "ECOWAS." Sule adds, "EU, Schengen. Or you think we've not already tasted your women?" Audu opens his eyes wide as he focuses on the president while the rest continue laughing.

"Oh yes! Don't look at me like that, you are not married to them, remember? I handled three of them at once some months ago. You're very lucky o!" Peter and Sule are still in laughter as the president continues. "I hope they're as hard working as they are in bed. My heart and lungs almost had an exchange of location that day."

Sule mocks, "Presido, presido! When you carry three at once, why won't your body organs shift? In fact, you're lucky to still be walking properly."

Peter adds, "Audu likes them old but fresh, women of their late thirties and early forties who are either divorcees or single mothers. He takes them young only in his territory."

The three men laugh but to be abruptly stopped by Audu's revelation, "I've slept with Latifat and Liliat also. As you know now, I like them young but not only in my territory."

The place is silent for about ten seconds as shock waves run through the environment. Sule asks in aggression, "Which Latifat and which Liliat, if I may ask?"

"Of course, the ones you know."

The president turns towards his direction, "You slept with his only daughters? Are you mad?"

"I couldn't help it Presido. They were coming at me for so long, I couldn't resist."

Sule gets up and slaps him, punches from both ends then begin to fly as empty bottles fall off and shatter, creating so much chaos in the vicinity. Peter and the president do their best to separate them and after putting a lot of effort, the two get separated.

"I'm disappointed in you, so disappointed. No one has the right to cross that boundary. No one! We are blessed with a lot of beautiful women in this town. Look at how men from other cities rush in to come and get some for themselves, why should we be misbehaving like this? Audu, Sule is your friend and colleague. We should be having each other's back, not stabbing it. What you did was…" Sule gets up again and begins another round of punches. The president takes him out of the scene to a solitary place which is about thirty meters from the bar to talk to him, leaving Audu and Peter in the bar. The bar woman comes out to meet them but Peter assures her, "Don't worry madam. We will pay for everything. It is just a minor issue that will be resolved in no time."

"Okay sir," she replies and returns to the inner rooms.

"Oga Audu, you fuck up o! You fuck up big time! Why would you do that?"

"He thinks he has an authority as a philanderer, I needed to show him that he knows nothing."

"No Audu, that's where you're wrong. You have no excuse whatsoever to say that. I can see that you take this your so-called territory seriously, for you to get so mad about your nurses being swindled."

"At least, he'll mellow down now. Sule's mouth is an automatic rifle that needs to be deprived of bullets. I love women too but we need to respect them as well."

"So what would you say about the presido then?"

"I respect him just because of his age and position but his time is also coming." Peter looks at him, comes close and whispers, "but did you actually sleep with his two daughters?"

Audu smiles, "yes, but at different times. I've slept with Latifat thrice and with Liliat once. I will soon have another time with Liliat again. She is a sweet girl."

Peter laughs, "let me tell you a secret. I've also slept with Liliat twice now. That girl is something else."

"What!" Audu exclaims and screams, "What is wrong with you guys?"

Peter laughs. "What is the problem? Why do you like making the women you sleep with exclusive to you? Or you think you're the only one who likes sweet things? Even our presido was with Latifat last night and she promised to bring Liliat the next time they meet. You know, our presido likes them multiple."

"Father in heaven!" Audu exclaims but is quickly interrupted; "don't just start that now. Don't blaspheme against God because He has nothing to do with this issue. Leave this matter to men and men alone." Audu looks in surprise, still in shock of what he just heard, but peter shows indifference to his reaction as he suggests, "as soon as they're back, apologize and tell him you were just joking. Emphasize that you wanted to get back at him for meddling into your affairs."

On the other side, the president speaks to Sule, "we are friends. I'm sure he didn't do it. He just wants to get back at you, so please, calm down, Sule. Now is not the time to fight. We need to stick together and get stronger. See how we just embarrassed ourselves in public."

"Okay presido, but if he really did it, I'll never forgive him and our friendship ends here."

"We will work things out, don't worry. Sometimes these things do happen against our will. Do you know that I've slept with his ex-wife?"

"Supaninlah!" Sule exclaims, moving backwards in reflex.

"Come on Sule! That's life and by the way, she is his ex. It just happened and nobody's leg is missing. My head is still on my neck and I'm still alive. We are supposed doctors here and the ladies both young and old, keep coming at us, so let's just enjoy the moment since we have only one life to live."

"Sir, how would you feel if I slept with any of your wives?" The president laughs out loud, bending his waist to lean forward before speaking, "I'll not have an issue with you. On a normal day, I know you'll never be the one to lure them to your bed so I'll assume, she was the one who lured you."

"Is that all you will say? You'll act normal just like that?"

"Of course, Sule, so let's go back and resolve this issue as friends." The two get back to the table and apologize to each other as Audu takes back his statement to the relief of his aggrieved friend. But interestingly, they resume their lewd jokes as the fun gradually comes back to its initial intensity.

"There's this yellow pawpaw in that new doctor's hospital," the president informs.

"Yes boss, that girl is definitely not from here. My God! If you see her eh! The other day when she was walking across the road, the vicinity stood still. Every activity stopped as everyone watched, admired and even hated, from the women's angle. God used the services of a hundred professionals in creating that girl. Front o, back o, sideways o, all is perfect." Audu adds, and Peter continues. "I swear, that girl will be on my CV if I can take her for a night. My two hands had to be in my pockets to maintain good behaviour when I met her for the very first time."

Sule then reveals, "She is a friend to one of my nurses. She's always in my place in the evenings after her morning shift. We speak a lot. The girl is almost perfect and incredibly decent o. I don't think she'll be easy to get."

"Get away! Almost every woman is like that until you get close." The president ascertains and continues. "I'll find out more about that yellow pawpaw. I wonder how the new doctor, as young as he is, will gather such jewels in his hospital and yet no rumours of scandals springing up from his nest. That guy is really good all round o."

While they converse, a car zooms in and parks. Immediately, Mr. Bassey comes out aggressively, banging his car door and approaching the men in a fierce countenance. Just as the four men are standing up, he approaches the president and pushes him to the ground, immediately throwing blows at him. The mauling produces chaos to a degree equivalent to volcanic eruptions and even against four men, Mr. Bassey handles the contest with ease. The other three men resurrect from their different knocks to grab him from behind but the huge and strong Mr. Bassey isn't an easy individual to lift. He struggles with them while at the same time giving the president more lessons he will never forget in a long time. The affray gets messier and this time, passers-by gather to watch the incident, some of whom put their phones on video recording. Mr. Bassey is gradually lifted up but not without more accompanying kicks towards the president.

"See this mad man! What is your problem?" The president furiously asks. "You almost made my son become less of a man today. You didn't even know what was wrong with him, yet you gave fake treatments and collected thirty five thousand naira from me." He rushes towards the president again but the other men, who are now more alert, stop him.

"Leave me alone, you men-whore!" He screams on top of his lungs with saliva flying out of his mouth like missiles. "Stop killing people! You hear me? Stop killing people. You almost took away the future of my son today. You almost killed his manhood. Can you imagine? You were even praising him for becoming a man so quickly. You are not a doctor! Stop this wickedness!" Audu tries approaching him but ends up receiving a devastating slap, and almost immediately, Sule rushes to retaliate for his friend but gets thrown to the ground with a swift move, much to the enjoyment of onlookers. Mr. Bassey faces the four men, "listen and listen good, I will write a petition against the four of you. If you don't know, don't treat. How many people have you killed? Tell me! You go about molesting and sleeping with women, basking in the glory of what you're not. I may not be from here, but I have lived here long enough to know my rights and what is bad for me and I will say you four are canker worms to this society." He then turns around talking to the spectators, "a real doctor is in town now, forget these animals or put your lives and that of your families at risk." He returns to the four men, still manifesting in his fury, he spits on the floor. "Fools!" He walks away, enters his car and zooms off.

The bar woman immediately comes out. "Oga Presido, your money is twenty five thousand naira. I've already included all the damages." The president exclaims, "Twenty five thousand!" But he is quickly interrupted by the woman in a much furious, red-faced looking countenance. "Yes, twenty five thousand naira! Or do you want to see my own madness too? Pay my money o! Pay and get out of here. I don't want to ever see the four of you come here again before you ruin my business. So you go about killing people and yet you come here and talk about sleeping with bread sellers and wives of mechanics?"

Peter cuts in, begging, "Please calm down mama Chidinma, we will pay you…." The woman interrupts in an even angrier tone, "Thunder fire you there! From your ancestors to your descendants, na thunder go kill una. Give me my money and go. Useless men, I just bought a dog last week and it is already pregnant. I am sure one of you is responsible, foolish men! Doctors my ass!"
The men quickly sort themselves out by contributing everything they've got and, luckily for them, the money is complete. They pay and walk out in shame.

CHAPTER 2

"Why are you nurses so slow? Don't you know your work?" Madam Cecelia, one of the waiting patients in the reception scolds. "Haba Madam! Calm down, there are still about ten patients in the queue before you, and they are not complaining."

"That is not my problem. You are measuring height and weight; do you want to sew clothes for us?" The three nurses laugh when immediately another responds, "no madam, but you in particular need all these measurements and when you meet the doctor, you'll understand what I am saying." Madam Cecelia stands up angrily, trying to daunt the nurse, "are you insulting me? You people just want to collect more money abi? Which hospital here is doing all these nonsense you are doing? So you collect money for card and still collect money for measurements, what nonsense!"

Refusing to be intimidated, the nurse responds, "madam, it is called vital signs, don't worry. As I said, you will know its importance when you meet the doctor". An old man intervenes; encouraging the woman to be patient and reserve her questions for the doctor. But she hisses in response.

Another woman from the rear joins Madam Cecelia in the attack, prompting more outbursts; but all through the next fifteen minutes of ranting, no one gives her the attention she wants, making her feel greatly piqued but eventually calm. The nurses seem resigned, acting excellently well when dealing with her.

"Good morning, doctor."

"Good morning, Cecelia Johnson. How are you madam?"

"Doctor, I am not fine o," answering in protest. "Why all these measurements? Since when did clinics start measuring patients? Now that there is no money in the country, and businesses are folding up, instead of you people to understand, you are finding more ways to exploit patients. It is not fair o." The doctor laughs and asks, "how much did you pay for the vital signs?"

"Extra two hundred naira. Two hundred naira, Doctor! It is not fair." He laughs again and replies, "so let me get this straight, your blood pressure, temperature, respiratory rate, pulse rate, weight, height and waist circumference were measured while your body mass index calculated, all for two hundred naira? Madam, you should be grateful, very grateful. If you really value your health, you will see the great service we are rendering to you here because you should be paying nothing less than 2000, and in places like Abuja, up to 5000 naira for all this checkup. You don't even pay consultation fees in this place and I had to blend to that custom to satisfy you in this community. Notwithstanding, I will not consult anyone if these vital signs are not checked."

"Ehen Doctor! So now, it is us you are helping abi?"

"Yes madam and funny enough, you in particular need this checkup. Your BMI is not good, neither is your respiratory rate. Your BP is in borderline and your waist circumference is a time bomb, and you are just 34."

"What! Doctor, I hope I will be fine."

"Tell me what brings you here first."

"My breath sounds are becoming something else o. Also at night, when I sleep, my breathing usually seizes. My husband has threatened to leave me if it continues; that I will not die in his house. But worst of it all is my severe joint pain, especially in both knees, elbows and ankle joints. Sometimes, the joints around my fingers too hurt severely".

"Do you sometimes feel chest pain?"

"Yes doctor, it occurs more often now, as if my heart beat is closer to my ear."

"What about the feeling of weakness or coldness or stiffness in one side of your body?"

"No doctor, I don't feel those?"

"Any changes in the way you urinate?"

"No doctor."

"How many times do you urinate in the day time and also at night on an average?"

"Like five times during the day and about twice at night."

"Is there any change in colour of your urine?"

"No, doctor, only when I wash my system."

"Wash your system?"

"Yes, doctor."

"How?"

"There is this other doctor just before the college of education. We usually go and meet him every two months. In fact some people visit him every month to wash their systems to avoid sicknesses."

"Interesting! How does he do that?"

"We will lie down for him to give us some bags of drip. While still there, our urine colour will change. Some red and others pink, which is the positive sign to show that our systems are being washed."

"And that's all?"

"Yes doctor."

"What if the urine colour doesn't change?"

"I've never heard of anyone whose urine colour did not change o. But I think if there is no change, then the person's system is clean already."

"How much does he charge you?"

"Thirty thousand naira sir."

"My God! Well, that's by the way..."

She interrupts him. "Doctor, he is very good o. We see instant result with our urine. Anytime you go there eh, you will see a long queue of patients waiting."

"That is interesting but let's stick to your case now. Any headaches, generalized body pains, increased sweating?"

"Yes doctor and the frequency is increasing these days."

"What about your menstruation?"

"There is a huge difference doctor. It is not like before."

"How? Explain please"

"It flows for up to six days now, unlike before that it used to be four days. Also, it skips. I can stay for two months without seeing it."

"Okay madam, what about your last child birth?"

"Five years ago, doctor."

"Didn't you attempt giving birth again?"

"Hmm. It is a long story but to summarize it, we have been trying o, doctor. The doctor in the hospital we usually visit always says we are normal."

"How many children do you have?"

"Two, sir."

"Well, I think you are suffering from the complications of obesity."

"What is Obesity doctor?"

"It is when you have so much weight to the point that you start having different body problems. Your BMI is $38.8Kg/m^2$, hence you are grade II obese.

"Doctor, please is it serious?"

"Yes and not really at the same time. Madam, you see, this kind of weight or fat accumulation can lead to some of the symptoms you've complained of. Obesity can lead to hypertension and heart disease. Fats can also accumulate on your heart and put it under much stress."

"Jesus!"

"Calm down madam. Obesity also can lead to some joint diseases such as osteoarthritis or gouty arthritis. It can even affect your hair dispersion, cause urinary incontinence and menstrual abnormalities. Obesity is also another risk factor for infertility. And going by your complaints, you have some of these symptoms." The doctor starts filling out some laboratory request forms.

"But doctor, can it be cured? I have been to several hospitals for the past three years now. I have spent more than one hundred and fifty thousand naira on treatment o! I am tired."

"Oh! You are tired right? I see! What if you have to spend another one hundred and fifty thousand naira to be completely fine, would you take the chance?"

"Ah! Doctor, I don't have money, but for the sake of my husband, I will try."

The doctor laughs "for the sake of your husband? You aren't even considering yourself? So if not for your husband, you will leave your body like this? Anyway, that is good but focus on you and your health first."

"Ok doctor."

He hands over the forms he just filled. "Take these forms to the laboratory for different analyses, then this particular one is for scan. Ensure you do them all and come back with the results. For now, you will have to start a serious exercise regimen," he recommends. "Ah Doctor! No gym here o! I cannot start jogging round the streets for people to laugh at me."

"Okay, Madam Cecelia, buy a skipping rope and ensure you skip just before your bath each time. So you can start from any number but ensure you increase the frequency over time. I tell others to skip until they sweat, so try doing same. Eat lots of vegetables, reduce the quantity of your calories by at least 50% and replace with vegetables. If you can afford fruits too, please I encourage you to eat lots of them and in this case, you can reduce your normal food intake to 25%. That is to say, you should divide the usual quantity of food you eat into four portions and eat only one. The remaining three portions should be replaced with fruits and vegetables. Do these for now, while you ensure you come back here with the results of your investigations."

"Thank you doctor. I will start today."

"Good. Every four weeks you will be coming here for your BMI to be checked. I will not be happy with you if you do not improve."

She kneels down and raises her hands up "I swear doctor, I will not joke with this."

"O Madam Cecelia! Please get up. I hope you now appreciate our vital signs."

"Ah doctor, next time, you can measure my tongue, ear and fingers." He laughs while she leaves his office.

The doctor continues his outpatient sessions as a severely distressed woman is brought to the hospital with a crowd of twenty nine people. He suspends his ongoing consultation to attend to them.

"Okay, Nurse Fatimat, dress a bed for her. Angela, open a folder and card for them," he instructs and faces the crowd. "I am sorry people; you all will have to be outside. I will need only one person or two people max to help begin the admission process." A man steps up to follow the instructions of the receptionist and nurse while a woman with a lachrymose look comes to the doctor to help in giving valuable information. The doctor walks into the admission bay with the woman. "So what exactly is the problem?" He asks.

"Oga doctor! She never pollute since two days now. Her belle just dey swell and she no dey comfortable," she replies in pidgin English.

Two nurses enter with the patient's folder as the history taking continues. After taking her history, he orders them to take her to a nearby diagnostic centre for a contrast X-ray examination. When they come back with the result, he collects it and enters into a smaller room with his nurses while three women and a middle-aged looking man holding a big Bible walk into the admission bay.

The man with the Bible opens it, reads some passages and begins to pray aggressively with the other women. The nurses come around to bring them to order but immediately they leave, the noise gradually comes back up again. The pastor prays,

"Father, she is your creation, your image and whichever devil, force and weapon against her today, we cancel in Jesus name! We decree and declare that at the mention of your name, we command right now pollute! Pollute! Pollute! You must pollute!"

The other women move around also screaming, "pollute" several times, then the doctor walks in. The patient is helpless but still manages to cadge some water from the man of God. "Calm down everyone. I know this is a private ward but we have other patients in the other wards. Pleas sir, " referring to the Man of God, "can you go outside?" He then continues his conversation with the others, "after careful analysis of her symptoms and the investigations we carried out, I do not think her case is as serious as first feared. If it was an obstruction in her intestine as I thought, there would have been a possibility for surgery. But I think what she has is irritable bowel syndrome, it's just my initial diagnosis and we will still carry out further investigations. Has she also been depressed in anyway?"

"Yes, doctor. Her two sons died last year, and since then, she has not been herself."

"Oh dear, I am sorry for your loss, and her husband?"

"He is a farmer in Akure. We have informed him, and he is on his way. Ehen! Another thing doctor is, for the past four months now, this problem starts or gets worse during her menstruation."

"Thank you for that information." The doctor walks out alongside his nurses, collects the folder and writes on it then comes out and meets them. "Follow my plan effectively. Do not let them pressurize you because I see no forbearance in them. They will definitely worry you for quick results. Start with the paraffin oil, 20mls before you commence the intravenous antibiotics and oral tablets. She should not start taking the pregabalin now until later this evening, and please, vital signs check must be done every two hours. You have been assiduous ladies. Do not relent, okay?" The Man of God sneaks in, from time to time to attend to the patient and consequently chased out until he is finally banned from entering the ward.

Later in the evening, the doctor comes around in his usual intrepid countenance to see some of the patients. While he is in the general ward, a sudden shout of joy and several screams emanate from the private ward prompting a rush from him and the nurses towards it.

"Hallelujah! Hallelujah! She has polluted! No devil, no demon or no idiot is capable," the pastor also rushes in from the hospital compound and joins in the screams of joy. By the time the doctor gets into the ward, the surrounding is messed up with foul smelling flatulence. They wear nose masks and enter, spraying air freshener in the room.

"Calm down everybody. Please I need you all outside," the doctor pleads, as he turns to face the nurses. "How did you allow so many of them in here?"

"Sir, they are very troublesome. They keep sneaking in against instructions," one of the nurses cravenly replies. They attend to the patient who continuously farts, changing the room's air chemistry with pungent smell.

Meanwhile, outside, in the hospital compound, a crowd sings, exclaiming holy indignations, some chant in unknown languages while some others exclaim, "she has polluted! You will never stop polluting in Jesus name!" Despite pleas from the nurses, they refuse to stop.

XXXXXXXXXXXXXXXXXXXXXXXXXXX

Two days later, the doctor attends Sunday service and after the praise and worship sessions, the service leader walks up to the pulpit to announce the testimony session. Mrs. Comfort Emmanuel is called on stage to the joy of everyone including the doctor. She wears typical Nigerian attire with a diaphanous top which reveals an inner wear but adequately covers the top part of her body.

"Praise the Lord!"

"Hallelujah!" Everyone responds.

"I say praise, praise, praise, praise the Lord!" She waves her right hand, shaking her hips in joy.

"Ha-ha-hallelujah!" The congregation replies.

"I am here because of God's mercy in my life. He has deemed it fit for me to be alive, despite all the arrows from the enemy's camp. No demon, no devil, not even the doctor's report can change God's plans for me."

The doctor's eyes widen in astonishment as he focuses all of his attention on her.

"I couldn't pass out gas for three days. I was in the hospital and the doctor said it was something about my intestine. He called it 'immitable bowen' something like that. I said no. Not my intestine. The pastor said no! I must pollute. They said there is no cure, but I can adjust my life to reduce its re-occurrence in my life but I said no! Jesus is my perfect adjustment. Pastor said by His stripes I am healed. They said I should be coming to the hospital at least once in three months, but from the moment I released the first gas, it went straight to hell and scattered the planners and agents of darkness over my life. Even the doctor was surprised; from the hospital to hell fire, everyone was shamed." The congregation jumps up in excitement, almost every worshipper, shouting on top of their voices, then she continues. "I am a winner, I am a fighter, no more immitable bowen problem, no more intestinal problem. No more gas traffic jam in my stomach. When they stopped, the heavens shouted, 'be released!' and everything came out. If you hear the smell eeh, it can dig a borehole." The congregation laughs in excitement as she continues, "now I can pollute ten times a day and even more. I dey use mess do modeling." They laugh again as she continues, "no more hospital for me in Jesus name." The congregation yet again, rises up and the worshippers scream on top of their voices while some go into prayers, making the arena a disorganized gathering. But all along, the doctor sits, shaking his head in amazement as he ironically smiles to the show.

XXXXXXXXXXXXXXXXXXXXXXXXXXXXX

The four men and officials of the clinic association sit in the shade attached to Mr. Correct bar, a new drinking place they have found and, as usual, they crack jokes on every lady who passes by. Mr. Correct bar is the first building along the street which leads to the doctor's hospital. Then comes Nurse Onyinye, walking along the street to get to work and resume her afternoon shift. She's on long braids, a pair of tight blue jean trousers which showcases her voluptuous curves and moving gluteal muscles as their planes change axis on every step she takes, elucidating her perfect thickness. The body-hug blue and red T-shirt exposes the "body-scape" of her mammary glands, so well expressed like street broadcasters to both the interested and uninterested. The down lines of the anterior side of her neck which communicates with her down-slanting shoulders, emit sheer glamour, all charmed by her endless smiling outlook, water-shedding an evolving and electrifying captivation to the admirers on one side and the envious on another side. Men long to be owners of her will, boys want to lick the ground she walks on. The stingy instantly gets generous to bankruptcy and the lazy wouldn't mind emptying the Nile River, just to meet the demand of her expensive companionship. Tongues fidget on the imaginative taste of her private sanctuary. The heart of men wrestle in her ring and what lingers in their thoughts is the absolution of precious stones and ornaments finding their colours from her 'feminity'. If beauty has hands, she is its fingers, which will most likely always find it easy to buy their attraction at a giveaway. Mechanics hold their tools still, tailors hang their legs above the machine's wheels, commuters stand from walking, drunks take loans from sanity's stores and house dwellers replace windows and doors as gazes are dragged by an imaginary web to this being who walks, greets and draws all energies towards herself like a cosmic wave.

The four men look in keen interest, using their heads to follow her direction, while their souls sink in pink foamy fantasies. Despite the ground breaking site, the knowledge of how unreachable this sweet scenting flower is, peels the ego of men like the onion for their engine of confidence to get knocked. Each of her road-walk harnesses the raw materials of good excitement, but to have an end product of unrealistic wishes and self-humiliating hopes.

"Forget it guys, I've heard so much about her. She is unreachable." Abdul laments.

"How does the doctor do it? I cannot cope or concentrate with such a beauty around me o," Sule confesses.

"Doctor is very lucky to have this rare being working with him." Peter comments as all three are still lost in the euphoria.

"Okay guys, come back to reality," the president urges and continues. "There's no way that young man isn't sleeping with the girl, but that is by the way."

Peter speaks, "speaking of the doctor, that young man is getting increasingly popular by the day. The guy is really good but is putting us at risk."

Sule agrees, "that's true. I've been treating one of my patients for an eye problem for three years now. I even thought it was glaucoma, just for her to try the new doctor and he said she's suffering from the complication of hypertension. Somehow his treatment has worked and her entire family has now shifted base."

The president speaks, "everyone talks about the vital signs that his nurses do. That is not a problem. I can copy that as well, but the measurement of weight, height and stomach is what I don't understand."

Audu interrupts, "I heard that too."

The president continues, "I thought it was initially a tactic to get the people's attention but a lot of my patients have said he uses those values to calculate something and then uses it for counseling and treatment."

"Does it actually work?" Peter asks.

"Yes of course. If not, what explains the shift in allegiance of almost all my patients he has consulted using that calculation to solve their problems?"

Peter adds, "Mrs. Abiodun, my popular patient with throat problem…."

Audu interrupts, "Is it that woman with swallowing problems for years?"

"Exactly Audu! He sent her to Akure to do some X-ray with Barium. She came back for a six-week treatment with some injections. Can you believe, she now eats all kinds of swallow comfortably? What scares me is that she has spent up to four hundred thousand naira over my treatment, but the doctor charged her only twenty five thousand naira."

The president screams, "Exactly! That guy charges so low. He beats us in everything, giving him all the advantages over us. This doesn't look good at all. I smell disaster in our business." The president leans on the table with his bowed head rested anteriorly on both vertically placed hands, reacting as though the issue is knackering.

Mr. Sule urges, "please don't exaggerate things. You guys talk as if he has an out-of-this-world clinical dexterity. He is good, that is correct, but not that good."

"You are just jealous," Audu retorts. "He trained abroad and his experience is vast with a good level of exposure. That guy is good."

The president adds, "even the almighty Dr. Hasi is scared of him, so you live in a fool's paradise if you think, that guy is not good. We learnt modalities in solving joint issues from Dr. Hasi but when this new guy came to town, he came with his own methods. There's this acid he checks in the blood, I've forgotten the name, before he gives Allupurinol tablets. He doesn't just give it like that as we all do, until the test is done. And you know what? He has had a lot of cases where the test shows to him it isn't a case needing Allupurinol, so he prescribes something else and it works! This formula, none of us knows. I've discussed with Dr. Hasi who reluctantly accepted that the doctor is doing the right thing. To worsen the situation now, the test is done only in his lab at the moment. Dr. Hasi's patients have been comparing his methods to that of the doctor's. It is frustrating, annoying and demeaning. You can imagine a stranger coming to challenge your skills with his own skills even to the notice of the people who are in your own backyard."

Audu adds, "I heard he uses new sets of antibiotics for typhoid fever, toilet infection and pelvic inflammatory disease."

Sule speaks, "yes, that guy is gradually degrading our skills to mere Jacobean protocols. I was with the boss of Princehood Pharmacy and he said they've added some more drugs, about 13 of them because of the doctor. He treats toilet infection with some nitro-something tablets like that, alongside the antibiotics sensitive to the organisms causing the infection."

Sule chips in, "I've had this middle-aged woman who has been suffering from this skin disease for three years. We've done everything possible for her, sent her to more than three big health centres to no avail. She has spent over 3.5 million naira on treatment. She met this doctor and he recommended one cream for her in addition to some injections. I've been following her up for a while now and her recovery is remarkable. Here is the cream, I took a picture." He clicks on his phone several times to show them.

"Ah! This cream! That is what he's also using to treat my patients with some serious skin diseases. All of them have shifted base to him now." Peter laments and continues. "I've searched heaven and earth for this cream to no avail. My contacts in Lagos and Kano said the cream does not exist. My Abuja people don't even know it. When I finally talked to a friend in the UK, he said the Diavobet cream is available and he will send it to me. The mystery now is, for me to sell it here with profit, I will need to do so for a minimum of sixty two thousand naira but the doctor currently sells each for forty five thousand naira."

The four men give a long sigh to ease out some tension. "Who is this guy?" The president asks and continues, "what kind of wahala is he bringing to us like this? Why didn't he stay in his Abuja or Lagos or abroad and leave us alone? He's really packing all the patients and they are happily changing base."

Audu suggests, "Mr. Presido, you need to meet with Dr. Hasi as soon as possible. This guy isn't good for business at all. See how that man embarrassed us the other day. We need not only make money, but keep our reputation intact. We may not be doctors, but the four of us are graduates, our minds are highly developed, whatever it is that we lack, we are capable of learning and even getting better at it. We shouldn't allow that small boy come and ridicule us o. We need to do something immediately. This new doctor is bad market for us o. He's already exposing us too much in just the short time he has stayed here. Imagine if he remains here for years."

"God forbid! I totally understand you Mr. Audu," the president replies and continues, "Dr. Hasi is very worried also. Do you know that just last week, he was battling with a case of a nine-month old baby who was vomiting and purging for five days? Dr. Hasi did all he could but the problem persisted. Is it the ORS, antibiotics, intravenous fluids? All, he administered to no avail. The patient's parents took him to the doctor, he admitted them and travelled all the way to the capital city to get the drug he needed. He administered it and, two days later, the boy was discharged with no issue."

"Seriously!" The three other men exclaim.

"I swear to the God who made me! This doctor is really taking over and to worsen this situation, he charged seven thousand naira less, despite his journey to the capital for the drug. Dr. Hasi has tried to know what the remedy was and how the treatment modalities were but he couldn't get it."

"Didn't he ask the doctor?" Sule asks.

"No, of course! Dr. Hasi is a proud man and he sees the doctor as his son's age mate. He will never do such a thing. He involved some of his nurses, told them to check the patient's folder but the stupid nurses are so loyal to a fault. I just don't know how this new guy does it. The greatest mistake Dr. Hasi made was to involve that pretty yellow pawpaw nurse. Even with ten thousand naira, she refused. That nurse is loyal, so loyal and in fact, because of his persistence, she went ahead to hide the folder so that, even when one of the other nurses finally agreed, the folder was nowhere to be found, despite her thorough search."

The president looks at them all in a single, long gaze, "this is serious. He also told me of the three migraine patients he has been treating for years but they seem very okay with the new treatment modality from this new doctor. One of the thirteen drugs he has introduced into our pharmacies is what he uses for the migraine treatment. So if you say this guy is not a threat, you're only deceiving yourself. Even our very own doctors are scared of him now."

The doctor, meanwhile, attends to the last outpatient and goes to the reception. "I'll go and freshen up. Keep things stable and good." He instructs and Onyinye answers. He enters his car, but it does not start. After about five failed attempts, he comes out and walks home, returning compliments to neighbours and passers-by.

"Talk of the devil," Mr. Sule alerts as they adjust their sitting position to give him an obvious long stare. As soon as he passes them, he greets and the four men reply with fake welcoming countenances. He reaches the edge of the road and waits a while for it to be clear for crossing. He crosses but at exactly the middle of the road, his right leg gets stiff with a sharp pain, causing him to scream and remain immobilized. Meanwhile, two trucks — one on each opposing side of the road — approach in high speed. A retail meat seller and traditional wear dealer scream his name, take the risk to jump on the road and quickly pull him out. Just when they cross the other end of the road, the two opposing trucks pass each other adjacent to the same spot he felt immobilized.

"Doctor, wetin happen na?"

"Wetin do your leg doctor?" The meat seller and dress dealer ask respectively. A few women gather around to know what's happening and to the amazement of everyone, he is fine. He makes quick assessments of his movements and discovers that there is no problem at all. He looks at everyone, thanks them and continues his walk to the house.

"Why didn't you die, young man?" The president laments as the four men watch from the bar, all hoping for the same outcome.

"It's not his time. This town is definitely not his to take. The sooner he realizes that, the better for him." Sule adds.

"This is just the beginning. He either dines with us or joins his other colleague who also came here to show us he's a champion in removing fibroids. This town is ours and ours alone," Audu comments.

The four men continue their drinking, switching their discussion to another issue.

CHAPTER 3

It is yet another day with the usual activities going on. The doctor is running his antenatal and postnatal clinics while patients troop in and out into a very busy reception. By 2pm, just, after the clinic session, some officials wearing a green T-shirt and cap with bags and folders enter into the reception, after a brief conversation with the receptionist. They sit and wait for a while until the last mother and child are attended to. They enter the doctor's office with an obvious impression of dramatized seriousness, flashing their legal documents, government stamped cover letters and badges serving as the pith of their authenticity and authority. They exchange pleasantries with the doctor and he offers them seats.

"We are members of the clinics association of this region. I am Abdulfatai Mohammed, the president and here with me are the Vice President, Lookman Suleiman, the secretary, Innocent Peter, and the treasurer, Audu Paul."

"Oh, you are highly welcome," the doctor replies in a welcoming countenance and continues. "So, how may I help you?"

"Good question. We have heard so much about you and your hospital which is becoming the talk of town already. Your methods are new and very effective, so it will be our pleasure if you will be a part of us".

The treasurer continues, "we know you are not aware of this association. We have lots of benefits we share among ourselves and you will never regret it if you join us."

"So, what are the benefits?" The doctor asks. The Vice president tries answering but stammers for a while before composing himself to properly talk, "sharing of similar interest, end of year get-together, protecting ourselves and many more."

The doctor smiles sarcastically. "End of year parties are nothing close to an advantage for me and what are you protecting yourselves from?"

The secretary replies as a form of picking up the challenge, staying cool, and exhibiting some sort of a picaresque flare. "Sir, we understand you are new here. We cannot start telling you everything. Why don't you attend our next meeting slated for next Saturday? We will have time to rub minds and get to know each other better."

"Yes sir, but it is still not out of place if I have a basic knowledge of who I am dealing with and the association I am about to join?"

"Oh yes! Oh yes!" Innocent agrees.

"So, are you all doctors?" The doctor asks.

"Does that matter sir?" The President replies.

"Yes sir, it does. Not that I condemn you for helping a community lacking healthcare and personnel, especially because this community in particular really needs healthcare and if extra hands can be equipped to at least meet basic health needs, then that is not an anachronism in the 21st century, especially in our reality. I, myself, am grooming auxiliary nurses but I cannot see myself paying homage and giving undue reverence to someone in my field who has no license to practice in it. No! It undermines my pride as a doctor and my relevance as a skilled worker. Six years in medical school, one year internship, one year service and another five years of experience as a medical officer should not be compared to a product of informal training, no matter how experienced the person is. Being a doctor is no child's play. So, it is wrong in so many ways and completely immoral."

The secretary looks at the others. "Let's go! I say let's go!"

The doctor gets surprised, "Already? Was I contentious to you? I don't think so. By the way, I am with the Nigerian Medical Association and registered under the medical and dental council of Nigeria which as well regulates the running of clinics and hospitals. What do I need this association for? Parties? Protection? No sirs. No!"

The vice president stands up. "You think you know it all abi? Yes, it is your field, but remember that this is our land..."

The doctor cuts in. "Yes, it is your land, but that does not mandate you to kill your people. A quack still remains a quack. Also remember that I am Nigerian and have full rights to practice or run my business anywhere in the country. So, I am not a stranger here. Your land or not, I see that threat as cheap. I am a doctor who's saving lives and you have acknowledged that. I do not have to be in your association to get your support. If you are scared of patient traffic, please don't be. The patients are enough to go round, trust me. I can deduce from our brief conversation that three out of the four of you are educated, but it is not enough. If you are not a Doctor, you aren't one."

The president stands up at this point. "You've vituperated us in so many ways because we came to your office, right? Guys, let's go!"

They walk out on him, banging the door behind them. The doctor laughs out loud. "At least, his English is good. Let me give him the benefit of doubt of actually being a graduate." He leaves the office as well.

The doctor does some paper work as nurse Onyinye comes in. "Sir, the line is very difficult to set. We've tried over and over again and the patient is getting frustrated," she said.

"Okay, Onyinye. I am coming, just give me a second." She leaves the office as he finalizes his writing.

"Hello, Miss   Khadijat," the doctor greets.

"Hello doctor," she smiles at him and continues. "This has always been my problem anytime I am admitted in the hospital. It is always difficult to get my veins and I hate it. You see why I don't like coming here?"

He laughs, "no one likes the hospital, not even me.

She looks at him in shock, "even you, the doctor?" She questions.

"Yes my dear. If not for the fact that we are here to save lives, I am not interested in seeing people suffer, seeing so much blood and cutting through people's skins for radical procedures. But Alas! I'm here and though the circumstances are gross because I'm human, I'm loving it as a professional."

She sighs in relief, "that sounds much better doctor." He navigates her upper limbs while talking to her and after a while of careful assessment, he gets a spot, ties a tourniquet and begins his venepuncture. "Are the items ready?" He asks, but no one answers while the nurses get busy with immediate alacrity to make available all that he needs. An intravenous fluid is set and then he secures the line with bandages. "Well, the almighty line has been conquered." He taunts jokingly and she laughs, "who else is the conqueror if not the great doctor himself?" She replies as both laugh while he stands up and leaves the ward to another.

One of the nurses directs him and his team to a particular patient. "Sir, there is an issue here."

"What is it?"

"This particular patient is refusing blood transfusion sir."

He looks at the very pale woman and asks, "Madam, what is the problem? Why are you refusing blood?"

"Oga doctor, we don't take blood in my family o."

"So what should we do? You need blood seriously. You are very pale and no matter the treatment we will give to you, blood is most important."

"I will drink tortoise blood."

"What!" He looks around as he exclaims, "Tortoise blood! Where did you get that idea from?"

One of the nurses informs, "it is a common practice here sir. A good number of our people here prefer to drink tortoise blood to taking blood transfusion and, unfortunately, the other clinic owners encourage it."

"So where do they get the tortoise blood from?"

"Sir, it's a booming business here o. We have a particular market where a lot of individuals sample and sell the blood and the tortoise."

"Jehovah! What am I not seeing in this place?" He exclaims yet again as he faces the patient. "Please madam, you will need blood. I will not accept tortoise blood here. If you insist on taking tortoise blood, we will discharge you to go and do so, then continue your treatment in another hospital."

"Haba doctor! You are very good, we all know it, but why can't you just respect my wishes and allow me take my tortoise blood. I will be fine. Please, continue with your treatment and allow me take it."

"Thank you for believing in me and acknowledging that I am good, if you believe that, allow me do what I know how to do best. Please take blood transfusion or we discharge you. That is simple. I won't negotiate this with you any further, madam."

"Okay, discharge me. I will go elsewhere. This is not the only hospital in town, Dr. know-it-all." He smiles while giving instructions on her discharge, emphasizing on the need of the nurses to ensure she signs the 'leave against medical advice' on her folder, then he leaves the ward.

On reaching the reception, he meets the landlord who stands at the front door. "Oga landlord, good morning."

"Good morning, oga doctor. How are you sir?"

"I'm fine and you? How's family?"

"We are fine. Thank you for asking."

"Let's go to my office. As you can see, we are not that busy, so we have some time to discuss. Right this way sir."

"Thank you."

Both men walk into the doctor's office and continue.

"I have juice and water in my fridge."

"Oh no, I am fine. Thank you."

"Okay then. Let's get to business right away. I have been in touch with the ministry of health to get my hospital registration certificate but, funny enough, they keep bringing new protocols to make the already annoying bureaucracy more frustrating."

"Hmm… I see. I understand your situation. This is Nigeria, you know. So how may I help you now, my doctor?"

"They came up with this crazy thing of providing the architectural plan of the hospital. They said I will need to provide the plan of the building then re-label it to show where the various segments of the hospital would be located. As ridiculous as this sounds, they are very serious about it."

The landlord laughs. "Oh doctor! I cannot help you with that. No one has the right to ask for my building plan. It is infringement of my right and the violation of my privacy. I know the ministry comes for inspection of health facilities and, if not satisfied, they make recommendations until standard is met. But to give out my plan and then you re-label it! I cannot do that doctor. I just can't."

The doctor leans back on his seat as he looks up in distress then he looks at the landlord. "Then what should I do now? You won't give me a plan and they, on the other hand, won't give me the registration without this plan. I am so angry right now. They should have mentioned it at the start of processing this registration."

"Good! That should tell you it is just another money-making loophole for them. Once you get to the end of this situation, you will realize that it boils down to giving them money."

"Well, oga landlord, since you are already here, let me call them and put our conversation on speaker."

"Please doctor, go ahead."

The doctor takes his phone and makes the call. The recipient picks, on the second attempt of calling.

"Good morning, Mr. Momoh."

"Good morning, doctor" the voice from the phone responds audibly, via the speaker for the two of them to hear.

"Sir, I've been talking to my landlord and he has refused to give me the plan for the building. He claims that it is an infringement on his right and violation of his privacy to even ask for that. So what should I do now?"

"Doctor, you are not the first person to register a hospital in our state and you won't be the last. Others are doing it, so you will not be an exception. Please find a way to do it. It is a normal thing and we are not infringing on anyone's right here just by asking for the building's plan. So please, tell your landlord to comply or else we cannot inspect your facility and as such we cannot issue a certificate of registration to you."

The landlord gets furious and responds, "You listen to me. I am the landlord and I am here. It is very wrong of you to do so. Come and inspect his facility and stop looking for ways to harass this man who, as a matter of fact, is helping this community immensely. This protocol is wrong, very wrong."

Mr. Momoh from the phone responds. "Doctor, why didn't you tell me your landlord is there with you?"

"What difference would it have made Mr. Momoh?"

"Oh! Are you trying to show me you are smart?"

"No, Mr. Momoh. I just want to show you with evidence, the dilemma I'm in, so you know that I'm not being smart as you already suspect."

"Okay Doctor! Come to the capital city so that we talk about it."

"But Mr. Momoh, what's the need? Just tell me what to do so that I don't waste time, money and efforts going to the capital city just to return with nothing achieved."

Mr. Momoh laughs. "Okay, draw your own plan, come here and submit it to us together with thirteen thousand five hundred naira so we get an actual professional architect to draw it. Please ensure you label very well."

"Thirteen thousand five hundred naira!" The doctor exclaims and to his amazement Mr. Momoh hisses and cuts the call. The doctor looks at the landlord with eyes wide open, who gives an "I told you so" gesture while laughing. "So oga doctor, you can see clearly that money is actually what they want."

"This is unbelievable. All this ministry of health wahala is supposed to be a maximum of thirty five thousand naira in expenses. I'm already spending eighty five thousand and, as it stands right now, the milking is not stopping anytime soon. This is very unfortunate. What a country!"

"You know, doctor, our state is the worst hit in the country presently in terms of salary payment. Some of the civil servants have not been paid for two years. This is what a lot of them have resorted to doing to make ends meet."

"You are right sir, but it's still not an excuse to make others suffer just because you are suffering. I was surprised the other day when I went to the ministry for the first time and observed a lot of pot-bellied workers which made me wonder if these are the same people who are not being paid for years. The problem with this is, even when they are eventually paid, they will not stop the corrupt practices they have adopted."

"Well doctor, either you stay here and preach to yourself; which will yield nothing, or stand up and do the needful. You cannot do anything. If you fight, you fight alone. I'm sorry, I suggest you start drawing your plan now or just go there, negotiate and pay whatever they want."

"No way sir! If I go there without a plan, then expect them to suck away a minimum of thirty thousand naira from me. I won't let that happen. I will draw the plan and go with the money being asked for."

The landlord laughs, "Mr. Due process, Mr. Legality, Mr. Protocol. Don't allow this country kill you o. I suggest you do and go back to where you came from because with the way you are handling things here, get ready for more shockers. Trust me, you haven't seen anything yet." The landlord stands up and the doctor does same. "I'm equal to the task, oga landlord."

"Well, I believe you, doctor. Just be careful, sometimes these situations are beyond us and the only thing we can do is to conform. You are powerless and I mean, so powerless. I wish you the best of luck in adapting to our system here. Please do not hesitate to let me know whenever you need anything."

"Thank you very much, landlord. You've always supported me and I know I can count on you." They shake hands and the landlord leaves.

The doctor calls out for nurse Onyinye and requests she sends the ward attendant to get some stationery and, minutes later, the items are brought for him to begin sketching a rough plan. After several minutes, he comes out of his office, seeks the attention of the attendant as she assists him to measure the lengths and breadth of every segment of the hospital. He gets back to his office as soon as they are done to continue with his plan. Nurse Onyinye becomes very curious as she stays on the attendant's neck almost choking her with questions to know what the doctor is up to. Interestingly, the attendant has no idea, which frustrates Onyinye the more. About thirty minutes later, she bashes into his office unannounced to his disdain. "What effrontery! Are you insane?"

"Sorry sir, it is unusual to see you make an order for stationery and then lock yourself up in your office for hours. We are here if you need something sir."

"Jesus! Is this why you bashed into my office like that? Get out!"

She rushes out in fear but comes back about an hour later, knocks on the door and enters on his approval, "I came to apologize sir. I allowed my curiosity consume me."

"Then it'll kill you like the cat someday. You're very diligent and hardworking but sometimes you can be distracted. When your madness starts, you become someone else. You do not take note of instructions or our rules in this place anymore. I'm beginning to get tired and I really do not know what to do with you anymore."

"I'm so sorry sir. It won't repeat itself again. You're a wonderful boss, very calm, intelligent and different from other doctors that I know, so understand with me if I sometimes get confused sir."

He gets shocked on her persistence. "Haven't I warned you against flattery and unnecessary compliments?"

She scratches her head with her left fingers. "Oh my God! I'm sorry sir, so sorry sir."

"I will be polite this time, please leave before I get mad again." She leaves with her head bowed.

The doctor drives home and after about ten minutes on the road, his phone rings. By the time he parks aside to pick up, he had already missed five calls from his nurses. The phone rings again and he picks up. "What is the problem? Eclampsia? Okay, I am on my way". He makes a U-turn and heads back to the hospital.

Upon arrival, he is welcomed with a welter of complaints and explanations by relatives. He calms everyone down and goes straight to a new patient's bed. "What's her name?"

"Alaba," one of the nurses replies.

"What's her BP?"

"120/80 sir."

"Are you sure of that?"

"Yes, sir."

He touches her body. "Ahhh! Her body is hot."

"Yes sir, she's 39.9^{0}C."

"And her respiratory rate?"

"33 cycles per minute, sir."

While he asks these questions, an episode of a burgeoning convulsion begins.

"Have you given her PCM?"

"Yes sir, we have."

"Good, Nurse Blessing and Mary, get me the ropes immediately."

They tie her four limbs with silk-woven ropes.

"So what else have you done?"

"Just that sir."

"Okay, set up an intravenous access, get normal saline, diazepam or paraldehyde, Artesunate, ceftriazone and metronidazole. Mary, ensure that you take blood samples for immediate PCV, full blood count, serum electrolytes and creatinine, grouping and cross matching and serum parasite. Nurse Aisha, you should place her on urethral catheter and collect urine samples for a quick urinalysis and MCS. As we can see, she is pregnant, so I need the foetal echo sounder now to know if the baby is still alive. Oya! Quick, quick, quick! No time," clicking the fingers of both hands as he instructs.

Everyone moves around, creating so much activity, an intravenous assess is passed to a stolid reaction. He checks her blood pressure yet again, checks the foetal activity and supervises the other instructions he gave. Two intravenous accesses are eventually passed while her covering, soaked with a squalid fluid, is changed. He walks up to the relatives.

"Who will follow me to the office to tell me what happened?"

The patient's mother volunteers and after about twenty minutes of discussion with the doctor, both come out of his office. He asks, "Who was also with her within the last one week?"

Her sister responds and walks into his office with him. After about another fifteen minutes, the doctor comes out and walks to the father of the patient. He politely asks the father to follow him to his office.

"Pa Alaba, good afternoon sir."

"Good afternoon doctor. What is happening doctor?"

"Nothing papa. All I want is sincerity, that's all. All the signs in Alaba show that this sickness did not just start this week or three days ago as her mother and sister are saying. If the cost of treatment is what you are all scared of, trust me papa, you will spend more if you don't tell me the truth. We will treat her based on what you tell me and if treatment is not adequate, you will definitely come back here again. Is that what you want?"

"No doctor."

"Good! If you had come earlier when the symptoms were mild, you would have spent less, and more importantly, Alaba wouldn't have been in this state."

"You are absolutely right, doctor. You see, we are farmers. That is why we are very careful. We are scared of going to limits we will not be able to recover from."

"If you were careful, you should have brought Alaba much earlier. If you want to correct that, now is the time, else you will eventually reach those limits you fear."

"Okay doctor. What do you want to know?"

"Everything."

"It actually started three weeks ago. She started shaking uncontrollably and my neighbours said she was possessed. We took her to a traditionalist and she was there for seven days, lying near the fire and taking only herbs and warm salty water. When the fever was getting unbearable, we then took her to a prophet. She was getting better and even walking, before she was brought back home, but the fever never left her. This morning she started shaking uncontrollably again until she hit her head on the sewing machine. Despite the fall, she was still shaking. Three clinics and the general hospital here rejected us, telling us to go to the federal medical centre which is very far. That is why we came here."

"How much did you give the herbalist?"

"Twenty five thousand naira and one goat."

"And how much did you give the prophet?"

"Fifteen thousand naira, doctor."

"So you had this much money and yet were scared of coming to the hospital? Is it not an irony that you spend so much for nothing just because you do not want to spend for something?"

"Oh doctor, we are sorry. Please help us."

"No problem, Papa. We will do our best and she will live. Just make sure you are financially ready. We cannot even start our antibiotics therapy properly because she will need at least four pints of blood. So we are going to start from there. Meet the nurses. They will calculate your initial expenses. As soon as you pay sixty percent upfront, we will begin."

"Doctor, please help us. No money in the country."

"Yes papa, I know that, but remember that the hospital is in the country as well. We do not get the drugs through begging. I don't pay salaries through begging and I do not feed my family through begging, so please understand with us, papa. As soon as some money is deposited, we will continue from where we stopped in our treatment plan."

"What about the baby, doctor?"

"Let us concentrate on getting your daughter back to life, then we will talk about her baby."

Alaba's father thanks him and walks out of the office while he writes on the folder.

XXXXXXXXXXXXXXXXXXXXXXXXXXXX

It is evening. The doctor is at home, playing with his one-year old son while his wife cooks in the kitchen. She speaks as she goes about her cooking, as he converses with her from the living room, keeping his son good company.

"My sweetheart, you doctors are trying o. I just breezed in and out of the clinic today when I saw the nurses handling two impassive patients, one as young as our boy." The doctor's wife observes.

He laughs. "Was that all you saw?"

"No, I saw another, but this time, a man who was lying flat with a turgid body and breathing as if a tank of water is inside of him."

"You saw that too?"

"Yes, my love, would he make it?"

"Sure! Why not? He is yet another victim of quackery. You know, here they believe if you are a candidate for admission, the algorithm must begin with a bag of drip or intravenous fluids. This man has congestive heart failure and the clinic didn't know, so they bombarded him with about four to five litres of intravenous fluid for the two days he has been on admission. Can you imagine? How he survived that is what I can't fathom."

"My God!" She exclaims.

"The quackery here is just out of this world. Do you know that the person in charge of that Power International Clinic is a fourth-generation quack?"

"What!"

"Yes, my love. My nurses were gossiping when I eavesdropped. They said he stopped at secondary school level of education and learnt his clinical trade from another quack who learnt from a two-generation apprentice."

"Hmmm! No wonder almost ninety percent of the diagnoses here are malaria and typhoid. My husband, you need to be very careful o. If they get too envious of you, we will be in trouble o."

"My dear, I am not against them. The system needs more hands and if doctors are not available, some can be trained with clear restrictions. But trained as health officers under doctors or approved skilled personnel to manage the common health challenges and referring complicated ones to appropriate facilities and not mismanaging congestive heart failure and even carrying out surgeries."

"You don't say! Some even do surgeries?"

"You say some? Virtually all of them do herniotomies, appendecectomies and caesarean sections. It is wrong, totally wrong. But I blame the system anyway. You work with the government, you get frustrated. You do four or five people's jobs on a little salary scale which does not even come on a regular basis, then you are subjected to work in a hostile environment with limited or no facility to work with. You then leave the government and open your own, face a people who believe more in herbalists, some having no value for their own lives and I particularly detest their bargaining system in this locality. I have never seen where patients bargain for hospital fees and clinical services as if we are in the market square. It's really appalling here. We have experienced four patients who ran away during treatment. I am getting tired and cannot continue like this o! Look at the tax system, multiple taxation, left, right and centre with some rogues proving to you that you are a stranger in their locality as if I am not a fellow compatriot."

"Oh my husband, don't worry, everything will be fine."

"I hope so sweetheart. If by the end of this year, nothing happens, we are relocating to the UK."

She dances from the kitchen to the living room where he is and then kisses him.

"I don't mind if we go now," she responds. "You have no idea how ineffable the joy in me is. My dear, your concern is veritable and, God helping us, we will do our best, but we've got one life to live and children to secure their futures. If you are not a politician in this country, you will be standing on one leg to survive. Who would have thought even doctors will be suffering this way? If you've tried all means to give your contributions to a country that doesn't give a shit about you, then leave. UK here I come! UK here I come." She dances in joy as she goes back to the kitchen.

He laughs in response. "Women! You love enjoyment eh! Anyway, you deserve it and I will make sure you have it."

CHAPTER 4

The doctor is in his house playing with his baby boy while his wife who is in the kitchen, prepares some fried rice and pepper-spiced beef. After a while, the boy is put to sleep, he joins her to prepare some fruit salad. When the fruits are gathered, he spanks her buttocks to much of her excitement before holding her warmly from behind to cause a great sensual excitement. "Oh boy! You're so sweet, my darling." She praises and he replies, "thank you, darling. Today has been quite busy. I miss you so much my love."

"You get better each day, sweetheart. I hope you do not rehearse these things with those nurses of yours?"

He laughs, "oh come on! You just ruined the mood. The smushy feeling is dead."

"Don't change the subject my love. Are you rehearsing with any of them? Tell me the truth now."

He laughs louder and asks, "where is this coming from? How do you women do these things? Just look at how you have turned a romantic moment upside down."

"I am just being concerned, that's all. My territory seems intact but I want to be sure I am in charge and not actually in a fool's paradise."

The doctor peels the pineapple after rinsing it under the tap. "My love, you're the commander-in-chief of this territory. You have nothing to be afraid of."

"Thanks for that, honey, but as the commander-in-chief, should I not be worried if there are generals, lieutenants, majors and even order ranked officers around my command?"

He laughs out loud, "is there any of my nurses in particular that you are scared of?"

"Of course, yes! What's that her name again? Onyinye! The way she looks at us whenever I'm with you in the hospital scares me. I see destruction in her eyes. She smells asunder and the envy I sense coming from her diffuses with bitter stings."

"Wow! Negativity well expressed in poetry." He shakes his head in disbelief while starring at her.

"I'm serious, honey. This is not a joke."

"I know, my love. I do not blame you, if you think this way. God has given you women these instincts to sense danger in your space. I'm really impressed."

"Stop the unnecessary speech, Mr. Man!"

"Okay, don't be mad at me because there's no reason to be, but you're absolutely right. I sense danger from that young lady too."

"You see! I said it. I knew it and I hope she isn't trying anything funny."

"No, my love, but she's definitely up to something."

"Why do you say so?"

"Some months ago, I was busy typing when I overheard her through my window, talking to someone, seemingly a friend through the phone. She was talking about how cute, full of life, energetic, kind and caring I am. In fact, she told the person how attracted she is to me and she wouldn't mind working twenty four hours every day, provided I'm always around her."

"Holy ghost fire!" She exclaims! "And what did you do about it?"

"What should I do, my love? Go out and talk to her? I cannot do anything for now, sweetheart. Overhearing a phone conversation is not enough reason to reprimand her, no matter how terrible that conversation was."

"Do you want her to be a Lese-majesty criminal before you do what you need to do?"

He laughs, "I guess you are the ruler here. You are taking this too personal and you have every right to, but that's not even all. Nurse Fatimat has reported her to me on two occasions when she acted unprofessionally with some young female patients. The first time was a patient on admission who never hides her admiration of me, even to me. One of the days, during ward rounds, she insisted I do a physical assessment on her abdomen, though it wasn't necessary. So I checked her abdominal region and auscultated her chest but Onyinye got furious and, later that same day, attacked the poor lady, calling her all sorts of bad names. The girl is quite attractive, but in my opinion, in a gamine way and I suspected that also intimidates Onyinye to great repugnance of the lady."

"That is so wrong and unprofessional of her and you still allow such a beast work with you?"

"Oh dear, can you tell me any nurse around who is better? Yes, she has her flaws but she isn't that bad. She lets her emotions sometimes get the best of her, but overall she is good and dedicated. Great motivational skill is needed in this hospital and I think I am not doing badly. I need to give them some encouragement to be better while at the same time tame their excesses, before this place explodes someday. Nurse Onyinye epitomizes what's going on in this part of the country when it comes to running public health facilities and established private clinics and only a very few are actually very nice and highly professional. Since you cannot read a person's qualities on their forehead, I guess I should continue with her until the last straw is chewed."

She pauses for some seconds and thinks with a static gaze at the wall opposite her "Hmmm... I think you are right, but I will still emphasize that, that nurse is dangerous and a time bomb waiting to explode. Mrs. Peters, the woman I usually buy food items from, once told me when I was in her shop that the same nurse was arguing with the others about your fidelity and discipline. While the others spoke well of you and showed how impressed they were about your personality and skill, she was busy telling them there's no possibility a man like you exists. 'The imperfection of a man showcases in any of these: women, alcohol or money. A man falls in any or some or even all of these categories, and so, it is not possible for a man to be generous, not a womanizer and at the same time not friendly to alcohol.' She went further to say that any man who is not into any of these is a dangerous person."

"What!" He snaps and asks, "she said that? When did this happen?"

"Yes, honey. The woman came to the hospital last week with her child to complete his anti-malaria dose when she heard them discussing."

"That is to say, if what the woman said of Miss Onyinye is true, this nurse considers me dangerous. And as much as I do not know what she actually means by that, I am shocked."

"Yes, my love. That's her thought of you and I believe it completely."

He prepares the fruit salad, drops it on a table, folds his arms and leans on one of the ground cupboards as he continues the conversation, "this is getting interesting." He comments as his wife continues the conversation. "Not only that. She argued that you seem perfect now because you've still not gotten used to the local girls here. You were abroad for a while then were in Lagos for two years where there are lots of beautiful and sexually appealing young women, and then you worked in Abuja for another two years where there are equally appealing and attractive women. So she believes you're yet to adapt to the local girls here, and all you need is time for that to happen."

"This lady is unbelievable. Really unbelievable! Do you know that some days ago, she came into my office offering me food?"

"Really? Which food? Did she prepare it herself?"

"Yes, my love. She made it herself. It was beans porridge. I politely refused but she insisted and kept insisting until I yelled at her and later warned her never to try such again."

"Honey, can't you see she's gradually getting out of hand?"

"Yeah, I can see that and I've been warning her to no avail. At the right time, I will do what I have to do if she refuses to change."

"Honey, have you observed she has even changed her fashion style?"

He laughs before responding, "oh, I thought it was only me who observed that. She no more wears frumpy clothes. She's now a regular on tight jeans, T-shirts, fitted knee-level skirts and cool makeup. And you know what? She doesn't wear her uniform from home anymore. She comes around in mufti, ensures I see her wonderful looks before she changes."

His wife comes close to him, kisses him and warns, "I trust you so much my love. Whatever we do at home, please, don't try it at work."

He laughs, "thank you sweetheart for your trust, but what about the hotel?" He jokes.

She frowns, "not the hotel, not even another house or apartment."

"Not even outside the city?" He jokes again, smiling with his teeth exposed.

She gets furious, "I am not joking, man. I am serious. That young lady is setting a trap for you, just be careful. But put it at the back of your mind that if she tries anything funny, I will be her short cut to meeting her creator."

He gets surprised, "oh no, you are not a murderer and you will not start now."

"Just as you cannot be foolish enough to get intimate with a lunatic like her."

After a few minutes, the atmosphere in the kitchen cools down. They stare at each other and smile as she pats his left shoulder. "Food is ready, my love. Let's eat."

"Absolutely!" He replies, as they walk to the dining room, carrying the different trays with plates and bowls of food.

XXXXXXXXXXXXXXXXXXXXXXXXXXXX

It is a Monday morning and, as usual, the hospital is full of activity. The doctor stays in his office as he gives his consultations, while outpatients walk in and out of the reception and his office. He just finished consulting with an old man, asking him to call the next patient by name Dorothy Samuel, on his way out.

The young girl enters the doctor's office with her parents.

"Good morning doctor," her parents greet.

"Good morning. What are you feeding her with?"

"It is God o!" Her mother answers and challenges the little girl, "oya greet doctor nah, say something."

"Good morning doctor," the girl greets in diffidence.

"Good morning, my princess. Come, let me see you very well."

She gets close to him but is shy as he does a quick physical examination round her body, all to the excitement of her parents. "She is getting taller, but thinner. I hope this is not some sort of human spaghettification." All laughs as he continues, "please o! Be coming every week before she snaps around her waist." They laugh again.

"So how is school?" The doctor asks.

"Fine, sir," Dorothy answers.

He faces her parents. "Any improvement?"

"Yes, sir. I must say she is improving very well. You know she refused leaving boarding school, so we had to engage her teachers, hostel potters and officials to ensure she always takes her carbamazepine and, truly speaking, she has had only three episodes of seizures in the last four months."

"Excellent! I am happy, but she is definitely not eating the way she is supposed to……" the door opens and the consultation is cut short.

"Sir, the ministry of health officials are here," Nurse Fatimat notifies.

"For what? They did not even give me a notice of their coming."

"I don't know, sir."

"Okay, tell them I will be with them shortly."

"Okay, sir." The nurse responds, leaving the office.

He excuses himself and leaves. He walks to the reception where three officially dressed men stand.

"Oh, Dr. Hasi, you are here. Good morning Sirs, I am not aware you would be coming."

"Do we have to inform you?" The leader, Dr. Hasi, replies.

"Is anything the matter? You've already inspected the hospital and I have paid my dues. What is left is my certificate of registration."

"You do not have to tell us that. We know already. It has come to our notice that you are training auxiliary nurses."

"Yes sir. Is it a crime? I was not told the first time you came for inspection."

"You are too confident, young man."

"No, sir, that is not the case. I know my right. If you are doing this in response to a complaint against me, then such remonstrance is definitely with an ulterior motive. You, Dr. Hasi, run a clinic not far from me here and you also run an auxiliary training program. You and I are two of the very few doctors in this place that should actually take it upon ourselves to teach the right practices and protocols here because whether we like it or not, there will be quacks."

"Now, you put yourself in a position to lecture me?"

"No, sir, I just want us to be pragmatic. I hate quackery too, but let's face it; this community is in dire need of medical services. If we are not sufficient in number to deliver, half-baked hands are everywhere to carry on the baton."

"That sermon is not for you to preach. When you take part in the regulation of these services, then you can have your say. As for now, just do what I say. I am warning you to stop, and if we ever hear that you still run such a program, we will embarrass you in ways you have never imagined".

"It's okay, Dr. Hasi. I will stop, but the food for thought here is: there are nineteen clinics and hospitals in this community. Only four of these are run by doctors. Who then is giving the remaining fifteen the registration to run, considering they are quacks? Is there another ministry of health doing this?"

Dr. Hasi gets furious. "Watch it, doctor!"

The doctor interrupts as well. "No, you should be the one to watch it, Sir. It is unfortunate that you, a doctor, will allow yourself to be used by some bloody amateurs to intimidate me, another doctor. I am sure the so-called clinic association is behind this. They have steered you against another colleague, yet you accept to be a useful backstabber. Just look at you, sir. You and the other two doctors are over sixty years of age. I am not up to forty. I should be seen as the future of this place. I should be encouraged and not intimidated, be guided not insulted. Let me be very clear to you Sir. I know my worth and I will not let anyone look down on me. If you use your powers to stop me from training auxiliary nurses, so be it. I will stop but the sufferers are these people in the community and not me."

Dr. Hasi comes really close to the doctor. "You really have guts, don't you?"

The doctor looks at him eye ball to eye ball. "You think you will walk up to my yard to embarrass me in front of my patients? Even my registration which is supposed to be thirty five thousand naira, at most, you frustrated me for months, collecting about four times that amount in the process, while I am yet to get it. I will be laconic with you, Mr. ministry of health. I will walk away if you think I am not needed here. But know that you are not upholding the tenets of your profession. You are ready to fight a colleague over crumbs from quacks. It is a big shame on you. Registration or not, I still remain a licensed doctor to practice anywhere in Nigeria. Choosing killers over healers leaves you with no pride, Dr. Hasi. I cannot continue to say 'yes sir' while I am ridiculed and cheated, enough is enough. You are a disgrace to this profession."

They stare at each other, breathing on each other's noses for about forty seconds in a quiescent reception full of patients who watch in awe.

Meanwhile, in his office, Dorothy dances around while troubling her father whose attempts to make her stay calm prove abortive as her freedom grows to much of her enjoyment. The doctor walks in to an abrupt change of her dramatized mood as she dissembled in composure. He rounds up his consultation with them and they leave for the next patient.

After his outpatient session, he summons his nurses. He specifically speaks to the auxiliary nurses who are about six in number, and explains to them why the program will have to be stopped. Suddenly, a convulsing child is brought to the hospital, accompanied by about thirty people. Everyone gets busy, some putting the place in order, while others set up proceedings to save the baby's life. About three minutes later, the baby stays calm beyond any form of lassitude. She seems lifeless with salient features of malnutrition and Anaemia.

The women put themselves into groups just outside the facility as they begin to mourn. The father tries his best to be brave and insouciant but later breaks down in tears. The gloomy atmosphere creates a great deal of discomfort that the doctor has to come out and talk to them, emphasizing that the child isn't dead yet. Samples are taken for investigations and an intravenous fluid is set. After about ten minutes, 160mls of blood is made available, then the doctor and one of the nurses sit down at the bedside to carefully transfuse the blood, using a 5ml syringe repeatedly, lasting for two and half hours. Halfway through their transfusion, the baby starts responding, first with the lower limbs, then her hands and then her head. After the transfusion, the doctor makes some calculations, writes in the folder and instructs the nurses to carefully follow his plan. He walks to the baby's mother and asks for her husband who has left; so both walk into his office.

"Mama Nuratu, we will do a lot for your baby."

"I know that, sir."

"Good. So you should meet the nurses for more explanations."

"Why, doctor? You are here already. Let's talk. Don't you know we are from the same state? I am your sister."

"So far as you are Nigerian, you are my sister. Everything will be forty five thousand naira. If I say everything, I mean everything."

"Oh doctor, where can I get that kind of money?"

"Mama Nuratu, this hospital remains the cheapest place in town. I hope you know your baby's case will cost a minimum of a hundred thousand naira in other places."

"Yes, I know doctor. That is why I came to you."

"Good! So you should deposit twenty five thousand naira for now and try to bring the remaining before she is discharged."

"Doctor, I only have five thousand naira with me now."

He laughs, "that is not even up to the cost of blood we just transfused."

"Please, doctor, help us."

"No, madam, I have been a victim of Mr. Good guy. You see, if I should go by my resolve, I shouldn't have touched your baby until you have deposited the amount I told you."

"Please, doctor, help us. I will come with my husband tomorrow but I would like to look for another ten thousand naira and add."

"When?"

"Hopefully, tomorrow, sir."

"As deposit right?"

"Yes doctor, as deposit."

"But still bring your husband here let me talk to him, because fifteen thousand naira out of forty five thousand naira is not good enough."

"Okay, doctor."

"Please, I have had terrible experiences here. Patients will be helpless mercy seekers before treatment, but after, they put me in a pillory. I am giving you the benefit of the doubt for the sake of your daughter."

"Thank you, doctor. I will keep to my word."

Later that evening, the father of the girl comes around, deliberates with the doctor and accepts to bring fifteen thousand naira in two days' time, but as a deposit fee.

On a very hot afternoon in the hospital, the nurses are busy, some taking vital signs, others giving injections to returning outpatients, one dresses a wound and another is engaged in the procedure room. An unkempt looking girl comes in aggressively, holding her chronically-ill looking child as she yells in pidgin English, "who dey here? I say who dey here?" she asks, but no one answers. She screams on top of her voice, dropping her child to the ground from a height of about a meter from her hands and immediately, the seventeen months old child starts giving a high-pitched cry. The scene prompts the receptionist and ward attendant to rush, coming to the place of event.

"What's the matter, young girl? Why would you drop your child like that?" The attendant confronts.

"My only child is sick. She is very sick."

"Is that why you threw her to the ground like that?" The cleaner asks, but the lady isn't paying attention as she starts moving about, yelling, "where is doctor? I say where is doctor? I must see doctor o. Doctor must come out o."

Nurse Onyinye rushes to the scene. "Madam, calm down, just calm down." She tries to comfort the homeless girl who responds in aggression, "don't touch me! Where is doctor?"

Miss Onyinye gets pissed, "and what if the doctor is not around?"

"I will turn this clinic upside down without hesitation," she threatens.

Meanwhile, her baby is carried by a patient's relative and pampered to keep quiet but to no avail as the high-pitched cry continues. Nurse Onyinye assesses the baby and takes her to the admission bay. She calls the doctor on the phone to inform him of the latest development and ask for what to do, after which she sets up an intravenous fluid on his instruction. The homeless girl quickly goes to the pharmacy as Nurse Medinat pursues. The girl grabs a sachet of painkillers and begins popping out the tablets to swallow. Medinat grabs her hand and a tussle begins. She throws Medinat to the floor and deliberately steps on her as she walks to search for drinking water. The sanitary office and ward attendants, seeing what just transpired, rush to immobilize the homeless girl. Another patient's relative quickly gets to the scene and, together, the homeless girl is overpowered and the stolen tablets retrieved from her. She is rushed to the amenity ward and tied down to the bed. Though, now no longer a threat to anyone, she still screams on top of her lungs.

After a few minutes, the doctor comes in. He attends to Medinat and gives her the day off, but she refuses and insists on staying behind. He goes to the baby who is severely malnourished, gets a folder, writes down the history from the information received from witnesses and as well writes down his plan of treatment. He goes to the amenity ward to meet the screaming mother. "Ah! Doctor, thank God you are finally here. Help me, please. Help me, doctor."

"If you don't stop shouting, I will call the police and some soldiers for you." She instantly keeps quiet but wails, "I hate police o! I hate police! I no like soldier. Please doctor, your people are wicked. They are wicked o! They want to kill me."

"What did they do to you?"

"That nurse tied me up, beat me, flogged me, even spat on me o, doctor."

He acts accordingly as he dramatizes, looking around with eyes wide open, then comes close towards her, bending on flexed knees and speaking slowly and faintly, "are you serious? My nurse did this to you?"

"Yes doctor. They want to take my baby away o. They threw her to the ground, pushed her, kicked her, flung her, carried her to the toilet, and then ran away with her again." She sobs with tears as he replies.

"Oh my God! I will deal with the nurse who did all these to you and I promise you that she will be carried to the police. Did they do any other thing to you?"

"Yes doctor. See my hand and leg. See how I am bundled like a she-goat that ate ten tubers of yam?"

He laughs, "sorry my dear, do you promise to be a good girl if I untie you?"

"Oh my doctor, you are so sweet like daybreak moi-moi, I swear. Please remove these ropes I beg you."

He laughs and gently unties her. He calls out for Medinat who comes in to take the ropes away. On seeing her, the homeless girl chuckles, "see fine girl. Why were you fighting me? Sorry, you hear? I didn't mean any harm."

Medinat ignores her and is about leaving the ward when the doctor calls.

"Medinat."

"Sir."

"Didn't you hear her? She said she's sorry." He faces the homeless girl.

"Can you apologize once more? I want to know if you meant it."

"Yes doctor. Oh, fine girl, you are just too fine, my sister. Please, no vex. I am naturally a bad person. Sorry, my sister. I beg you. Sorry, you hear?"

Medinat smiles, "no problem, Sikirat. You're not a bad girl."

She leaves as the homeless girl acts proud and happy with herself.

"Ehen, doctor. I wan chop food o. I need fufu and draw soup. I want two meat on top and Fanta. I no like coke."

He smiles and warns her to be calm as the only condition for the food to be served. She stays calm and happy while he steps out.

He orders the ward attendant to get her request while he goes to see the baby. Pap is made available as nurse Onyinye feeds him carefully, much to the doctor's delight, as if the baby is hers. He goes round to see the other patients as each narrates their version of the events that transpired, concerning Sikirat, the homeless girl. He goes back to his office and locks himself there.

After about twenty minutes, Nurse Medinat rushes in. "Sir, it is Sikirat again. She's disturbing the whole place and saying she must see you."

"Where is she now?"

"She's still in the amenity ward, restricted by the ward attendant and two patient relatives."

"Okay, bring her to me."

In a short while, she is brought to his office. "I thought we agreed you'll be calm if I give you food."

"Yes, doctor. I just want to say thank you but they are denying me access to you.

They don't want me to see you. You be God?"

"No, I am not God, Sikirat….."

She interrupts. "Good! If God allows me to see him, you are a nobody that I cannot see."

He smiles, "that is correct. Who am I? So you see God?"

"Yes nah, doctor, I see Him always."

"Wow! You must be a very lucky girl then."

"Yes, doctor. God loves me very well."

"That's good. I am happy you are feeling better now. Don't you want to see your baby?"

She looks at him in a static gaze for a moment, drawing up confusion from him, then lets out a hysteric laugh. "Doctor, doctor! I know my baby is fine with you so I am not worried. Let him remain there as he eats good food and drinks clean water. I will be here with you doctor because I want to tell you something very important."

He looks at her in curiosity as he remembers the cases similar to hers that he treated, prompting a sense of nostalgia. "What is it, Sikirat?"

"These nurses of yours like you a lot o. You know I am popular here, and as a celebrity, I go around to see my fans."

He nods his head in agreement. "Who doesn't know the chairlady, Sikirat, in this town? As for my nurses, I think it is normal to like someone. Don't you like me?"

She laughs sarcastically. "Ah ah, doctor! You know what I am talking about."

"So how do you know that?"

"I have been here three times already. I see how this your yellow pawpaw nurse looks at you. She even protects you like her beloved husband."

"Interesting! You know this?"

"Yes nah! One day like that, when I brought my baby to pass stool in the next compound, I heard one of your young nurses talking on phone, presumably to a friend, about you. This your yellow pawpaw nurse just appeared from nowhere, shouted at her, warned her to leave you alone and then gave her plenty tasks to do."

He draws back to lean on his chair as he shows keen interest. "Ehen!" He responds, making the conversation more engaging as she continues with so much passion.

"Trust me, doctor, she does not joke with any issue concerning you o. She can carry an entire stadium and block the road that gives access to you from other ladies."

He laughs, "You don't mean it!"

"I swear, doctor, she is your protector here o."

"Wow! This is serious."

"Another time, I was in your compound…"

He interrupts. "I hope not to bring your child to defecate?"

She laughs, "no nah, doctor! Life is turn by turn. After one compound is the next. My child will not stop shitting. That is the law of nature, doctor, but your nurses caught me and chased me out."

"So you mean to say, you were not allowed, right?"

"Yes, doctor. Are you happy now?"

"Yes, I am relieved to know that."

"But your toilet here is very good. I will be bringing my child to be using it often."

"No way! You were telling me something, Sikirat."

"Yes, doctor, but before they caught me, your yellow pawpaw nurse collected the phone of one of your auxiliaries and wanted to operate on it, so she asked for the password and the young nurse gave her as 'felixlove'. Your yellow pawpaw nurse got very angry and almost threw the phone away but that prompted me to shout from my hiding and that was in fact the reason I was caught and sent out of your compound."

He laughs out loud, "you've observed a lot going on already, in this place Sikirat."

"Yes doctor. I go school o! Forget my madness and roaming about, I go better school."

"Thank you, my dear. Go and be with your baby, but no more trouble, or else, police and the army will come and carry you." She stands up, "I swear, I will not cause trouble again, doctor. I respect you very much. You are my one and only doctor."

"Thank you, Sikirat. You can go now."

She leaves his office.

XXXXXXXXXXXXXXXXXXXXXXXXXXXXXX

At home, his wife showers, while he watches a news station; he notices some anomalous sounds from the gate. He peeps through the window to realize about three sets of hands on the fence, like people trying to jump over it. He quickly switches off the television set and in a swift move, switches off every light source in the house to leave the vicinity completely dark. He goes to the bathroom and alerts his wife who is just concluding her bath. He takes her to the bedroom, comes back to the living room, and then picks up his phone to dial the divisional police officer's number. It rings without response and after five attempts he stops. It is 11pm and he is not sure if some of the neighbours are awake.

Two of the intruders scale the fence to get inside the compound and burgle the gate's lock for three others to come in. All his windows and doors have Iron protectors, making it an impossible task to breech through. They walk into the compound where his poultry is. All the birds were sold the previous day, leaving about five hundred day-old chicks and three dozens of rabbits.

The intruders try making him come out, even involving threats, but he refuses to. The house remains silent, not even his baby boy is awake to make some noise. After three attempts, they go another round, trying even harder to burgle any of the house entrance but to no avail as a growing antipathy towards their clear inabilities ensures. In great repugnance, they go back to the bird house and kill all of them with their clubs, stealing the entire rabbits and bashing the windscreens of both cars present in the compound to much of their satisfaction and they leave. Three minutes after they had left, the police chief returns his call but he refuses to pick. He gives him two more missed calls and the event of the night ends.

CHAPTER 5

It is about 10am on a Monday morning and the day has been relatively uneventful, which is an unusual situation in the OMC. A car drives into the compound and a boy is brought out by two men. Blood gushes out from his mouth, while he wails. His mother reluctantly follows with her hands on her head as she cries in so much pain. They are immediately directed to the procedure room as Nurse Fatimat begins to set things in place for an emergency suturing.

"What happened?" The doctor asks.

"He fell from the stair and hit his mouth," one of the men replies.

"Oh yes! I can see how blunt and deep the wound on his Tongue is. This is definitely a cut from his teeth. Oya! Fatimat, Vitamin K immediately. Also bring one ampoule of diazepam."

"Okay sir!" she replies.

Administering the parenteral injections becomes a thug of war as the boy resists sternly, despite the pain he passes through and sedatives given. His stercoraceous short is removed by one of his aunts who immediately goes back to his mother who is acting crazy and uncontrollable, to calm her down. The doctor collects and cajoles him to open his mouth and after some minutes, the doctor observes a stop in bleeding and the extent of injury. From his reaction and facial expression, it is obvious the boy isn't so hapless and the situation is within the reach of a solution.

As soon as the boy begins to get dizzy, the doctor wears an Apron, a mask and places the boy on one of the men, positioning him at a sixty-degree angle along the man's trunk all through his body to his thighs, while he is clamped inferiorly by the man's two legs and superiorly by the man's hands. A molt mouth prop is expertly placed in the boy's mouth, which opens it to a good degree for the allowance of a good vision. Some local anaesthesia is administered around the edges of the deep cut against a weak resistance from the boy and the stitching commences five minutes after. He and his assistant are gloved and in about ten minutes, they are done. Despite the sedative given, the boy remains active, even when he is presented to his mother. The doctor takes nurse Fatimat to his office, writes on a folder and gives it to her.

"Tell them to take the syrups seriously. He should strictly be on drinks for now. No chin-chin, groundnut cake, biscuits or crackers, especially. No hot or spicy food."

"Okay sir".

Ten minutes after Nurse Fatimat leaves, a young lady in her late teens, wearing a long, loose black gown and a veil covering her head, walks in.

"Are you Salamatu?"

"Yes sir. Good morning, doctor."

"Good morning. Please have a sit."

"What's the problem?" She narrates her ordeal gracefully, answering all his questions in candour, but with a touch of weirdness, making him observe in suspicion. Her emotion already well expressed through her eyes and bodily gestures, makes her heart a complete sycophant to his. Their session is still in progress, but hanging on a thread because of the increase in uneasiness.

"Well, Salamatu, your symptoms are still quite vague to me, but we can start by undergoing an abdominopelvic scan."

"Okay, sir. I thought you would check me."

He immediately stops writing and looks straight at her, both gazes engaging in a psychological communication, sending their hidden but clear messages.

"Well, well... I seriously think there is no... I think there is no need for that, Salamatu." He stammers a little, while clearing his throat twice.

"This is the fourth hospital I am visiting and the others physically examined me, you know."

She speaks with so much confidence, tenderness and volubility.

"Okay, climb the examination bed over there and expose just your abdomen. I will be with you shortly."

The patient stands up gently and pulls down her gown in its entirety. She's now stark naked, no underwear nor extra coverings, just flesh covered by bare youthful skin. Her ripeness pops out its full fleshy intimidating powers, expressing some sort of a mental sight of vibrating springs and elastic ribbons seemingly beneath every muscle she possesses. She does not move an inch but stares at him to the face as her heart races in a lightning speed. Her very firm and perfectly rounded mammary glands dance to the rhythm of his inevitable surrender, resonating in appealing firmness like tender thugs begging for a fight. So inviting are these cute brown rounded timers at no O'clock as their central pinpoints, horizontally extended teats stand as the accusers of his gradual fall.

Her hips are well spread to create an out-facing, horizontal valley on both sides of her waist and the long tailed "Y" sign craftily designed by her closed legs, starting from the side borders of her 'teenage-plated' vaginal beats the best of freshness' invitation. The inverted tip of her hairless and seemingly untouched genital ignites his curiosity with an accompanying pharyngeal heat which burns his buccal cord and causes lingua spasms to prevent any sound from emanating. Electro-erotic waves now beam from his stare as his control station behind the zip loses touch of its entire buttons. He sits and looks with running compromising thoughts like a battered casualty in a hopeless sexual accident, then her hands gradually go up to cup both breasts in a raffish manoeuvre, exposing the nipples from in between her fingers as her eyes never stop looking at his. The present reality pounds and grinds and then his threshold of resistance gets crushed, defined by senses so alive in a mind so dead, suffocating in air so fresh but extremely hot.

"Do you like what you see? I am so surprised you still don't remember me, despite coming here on three occasions. It is said, a 'woman's beauty embraces a man's memory more than the aroma of food and the sight of wealth combined.'" She speaks with a very faint voice, almost whispering, but he does not reply as he is engrossed in this magical seduction from a sophisticated daughter of Jezebel.

Still holding his pen, his right hand exhibits tremors as his suffering gets obvious from his fast and heavy breathing. From her nails to long hair, up to her shoulders and every single detail on this raw anatomy, he sinks in the sea of her erotic wand having a hypnotizing effect beyond any form of diabolic impact. Suddenly, the door opens as Nurse Blessing enters.

"Oh sorry sir!" Blessing tries jetting out in reverse, but he objects.

"No, no, no, Blessing. Please come in, I need you inside my office right now."

He sighs in great relief while she obeys and simultaneously, Salamatu takes her clothes in shame and covers up.

"No, Salamatu, you will dress up here and now, and leave."

"But sir…."

"Don't sir me. You have an angel's countenance but a devil's personality. I will not give you another opportunity to showcase your arrant stupidity."

He forces the words out of his mouth in borrowed boldness. As soon as she gets dressed up, he gives her a filled laboratory request form. She refuses to accept and leaves, not even taking her hospital card along, after which, as an overcomer, he relishes on the clogged wheels of his morality from the over-secreting testosterone that oils his mind.

The doctor arrives home and tries removing his footwear when his phone rings.

"Aunty Tabitha, how is family? How are you feeling now? Have you completed your medications?" He speaks on the phone with one hand, removes his clothes with the other, while communicating with his wife in sign language, also making hilarious gestures to his son, and as well giving the ongoing program on the TV screen some attention.

"Look, aunty, your desultory wander from clinic to clinic does not make you experienced or more knowledgeable than I am. I have already told you. Leave a special place to hang your underwear and it should be for you alone".

He goes to the backyard to briefly supervise the ongoing construction of his new bird house.

"Ah! Aunty, who told you that?" He walks back inside the house as he rejects the sweet scents of sophistry coming from the person he converses with, through the phone.

"Listen to me. This is not an ambiguous situation. The standard is the same, and our methods are empirical. Stop trying so hard to convince me, you will have to burn all of your underwear and buy new ones. You want to soak them in jik for hours? Fine! But I will prefer you completely change them and burn the old ones so that another person will not pick them and get infected. Bye bye."

He turns to his wife, "why don't people believe in the doctor any longer? Hear-says, neighbours, grandmothers, traditionalists and friends have taken prominence over the doctors when it comes to health counseling."

His wife just gives a graceful stare without saying a word as he continues, "I mean, family members especially, are taking us for granted. They now call us not for help but to compare our recommendations with other alternatives. I am so appalled." His wife smiles and looks at him in a short gaze of gilt.

A neighbour quickly comes into his compound and the doctor goes out to meet him.

"Oga doctor, my daughter has been menstruating for the past 11 days now. Today's own just got worse o." The troubled man complains.

"Okay, Papa Kunle. Take her to the hospital. She will be attended to, there."

"Haba, oga doctor! Is there nothing you can do or give us now to make it stop?"

"No, Papa Kunle, unless you go to the hospital."

"No, oga doctor, help us now. I know what you are trying to do. Please help us. We are good neighbours now, why are you acting as if you do not know me?" He pleads with an increasingly morose face.

"Papa Kunle, I also know what you are trying to do. But understand that I am trying to help you and do the appropriate thing for your daughter. This is my house, not a hospital. The medical equipment needed to carry out our activities are all in the hospital and not my house. Moreover, I need to rest and if I am here, I should get the needed rest and as well spend some time with my family. I can only go back to the hospital if there is an emergency which must be confirmed by my nurses."

Mama Kunle comes in, "ha! Doctor, she is bleeding o! Two pads heavily soaked in the last fifteen minutes, doctor, please help us." She kneels down with her hands up, in serious supplication.

"Mama Kunle, make una go hospital o! Go hospital."

"What is it! You are not God o!" The man inveighs, "you be doctor, and so? Just give us some tablets, you don't want to. Must you always chop thousands in every ailment? You be doctor because God allow you o." The man rants on.

"Oh Papa Kunle, so you know the tablets to give nahim you still dey beg me? Go ahead and give her the tablets nah."

"Yes I will. The bleeding is no big deal you know. We will give her tortoise blood. Just give us the tablet that will stop this bleeding. God pass you, God will put you to shame."

The woman begs in great lament. "Doctor please! Doctor please. Don't mind my husband, just help us."

"Mama Kunle, the earlier you take her to the hospital, the better. If she's bleeding the way you say she is, she can lose a lot of blood and collapse, so hurry now. No amount of tortoise blood will save her, so please don't even try it."

"Please doctor, are you coming?" The woman asks agonizingly.

"Sure, don't worry about that. Mama Kunle. Just take her there; she will be taken good care of."

"I will not take my daughter to your place," the man warns. "We are going to Power International Clinic."

"Of course, Papa Kunle, the most important thing here is to go to a health facility where her problem can be arrested and if that is your choice, fine!"

A young boy enters the compound so agitated and in distress. "She has collapsed o! She has collapsed!"

All three run out of the compound, leaving the doctor who pulls out his mobile phone and dials the hospital.

"A young girl will be brought to the hospital. Do a PCV and grouping, and cross-matching immediately for her. Administer Tranexamic acid intravenously. One Ampoule for now and another ampoule of Primolut Depot intravenously. The lab man should get four pints of blood for a start. I will be there shortly."

"Are you coming or not sir?" The man returns to the compound, screaming on top of his lungs as he asks.

"I do not blame you people in this community. So it is me, the doctor you are shouting at like that? Well, just go to the hospital, adequate care is already waiting for her, the earlier, the better."

The man hurries out of the compound.

XXXXXXXXXXXXXXXXXXXXXXXXXXXX

It's the next day. The doctor sits in his office to relax his mind with the dulcet tones coming from the practicing bands of the neighbouring churches around. Nurse Mary rushes into his office.

"Sir, there is a problem outside."

"What is it, Mary?"

"Nuratu's mother tried escaping with the baby but we caught her in the process."

"What!" He jumps up and leaves with Mary.

Outside the hospital are the receptionist, cleaner, pharmacists and a nurse arguing with Nuratu's mother.

"Mama Nuratu, I least expected this from you. So with all the efforts we have put into reviving your baby, this is how you want to pay us?"

"I just want to bathe the baby at home." She tries to prevaricate the situation.

"But madam, we have a good toilet facility here, and besides, why going out without informing us, if you are so righteous with your dealings? The doctor asks while smiling.

"Everybody is busy sir. That is why."

"Just stop, madam. Please go back to your bed."

The doctor organizes a brief meeting, preparing his nurses for a serious upcoming case.

"The last time Aishat was here, Blessing recognized her and she knew it. I believe and I am sure you all must have known already that the popular Aishat 24 from Lamao FM will be admitted here for two weeks. It is a serious case and must stay confidential. If I hear anything outside, I will dismiss all of you. She was treated for depression with Ketamine in another facility. She has been addicted for the past three years and complains of hallucinations, increased salivation, sometimes memory loss, increased BP and reduced appetite. But the main reason she is actually coming here is the fact that she micturates in a high frequency with an accompanying pain. If you, Nurse Fatimat, can recall, she visited the Toilet seventeen times in a space of twenty minutes in my last session with her. So we are suspecting cystitis and irritative urinary tract symptoms secondary to ketamine intoxication. So, no one is working with torpor here, we have to give in our best. Finally, and most importantly, intravenous haloperidol is a part of our plan, which comes with its own side effects. I have drawn a chart here of the various side effects, horizontally, with the two-hourly time intervals, vertically. So, every two hours, it is expected of you to go and examine Aishat until 10pm. Is that clear?"

"Yes sir."

"Any questions?"

"Yes sir. Have you written your plan?"

"Yes blessing. Go through it and prepare. Get all we need, I/V Diclofenac, Ceftriaxone, Flagly, Nitrofurantoin and the haloperidol in the fridge in my office."

"Okay, sir."

Thirty minutes later, Aishat fecklessly walks into the reception like a misanthrope. She is directed to the amenity ward where she is well attended to. The doctor meets her there in a very low state. He tries encouraging her, but though she laughs on two occasions, her mood still does not change.

While in the amenity ward with Aishat, the receptionist draws the doctor's attention to what is happening in the reception. It is Mama Nuratu again and this time she fulminates while expressing herself. He rushes out to the scene.

"Mama Nuratu, you again? What is the problem?" He asks.

"If you people do not have truth in this hospital, then you will never see me here again."

"Okay, let's go inside my office." She agrees and walks into the office with him.

"So what's the problem?"

"I brought ten thousand naira. They collected but still do not want to discharge me."

He laughs, "mama Nuratu, did I tell you it's fifteen thousand you are paying? Your money is forty five thousand naira."

"Yes, doctor. My husband will come and pay the rest. I do not want to sleep here again."

"When you are home already, your husband will come and pay? Not possible!"

"Don't be wicked, doctor. This was what we agreed."

"No way! We agreed you would bring ten thousand naira as deposit. Then we went further to say your husband will come and pay, which he promised to add another fifteen thousand naira, also as deposit. Madam, so you mean to say you want to pay us fifteen thousand naira from a possible forty five thousand naira, despite all we have done for your daughter?"

"You don't have truth, doctor. You are all sick." She slams his table with her hands.

"You're going nowhere, woman, until the money is here."

She walks straight to the ward, takes her baby girl and walks toward the reception door. The nurses gang up and stop her to great resistance. The whole place becomes noisy and chaotic. She screams, fights, rants nonstop with a great degree of indefatigability, making calls and insulting the hospital right in front of its workers.

Gradually, the hospital premises begin to get filled with people. Some of the men try making attempts to reach the doctor to no avail. She calls the doctor all sorts of names — the devil who does not know the value of children, the hater of life, a money monger, an inconsiderate beast, a professional fool, a righteous bastard, a worthless animal — even going further to elaborate how he lets others go free with up to twenty thousand naira debt but refuses to let her go. Some people rally around and raise another fifteen thousand naira and one of the nurses notifies the doctor about it after which he lets them go.

The doctor locks his door, lies on his examination bed, faces the ceiling, deep in thoughts on yet another unfortunate drama which just happened.

At the reception, several people beg the nurses to see the doctor but are refused.

Some go ahead to his office against resistance but the door is locked. Some stay there to scream his name, even ascertain that they have the knowledge of his presence but all to no avail. Three patients arrive in an emergency state with severe chest pain, nausea and accompanying irritations of the nose and eyes, secondary to tear gas intoxication. The doctor only communicates through text messaging on their treatment plan but doesn't come out. When it's evening, he leaves the hospital through the back door to his car but to coincidentally meet the tax force from the ministry of commerce and industry.

"Oga doctor, good evening."

"Evening, sirs."

"We believe you remember us."

"Yes, I do."

"So let's go to your office and talk."

"No need, we can talk here. As you can see, I am not in a good mood. We can talk here so that I leave immediately."

"Calm down, oga doctor. Don't act all consequential with us. Just because we are here does not mean we are beggars. We are only doing our job."

"Sorry, if I said something bad."

"So how far, oga doctor?"

"Yes, I went to the bank and paid the money to the ministry's account. I have the receipt with me."

The three men look at each other, so flabbergasted, they stand still, then one of them speaks.

"Oga doctor! Oga doctor! In my place, dem talk say, if toad wan show say him fit jump pass frog, him go fall inside empty well meet hungry snake wey dey wait for am".

The doctor adjusts his posture to pay full attention. "So how does that relate to our conversation?"

"We specifically told you to pay thirty thousand naira to the ministry's account as a less preferred option to the ten thousand naira you would have given us with the same receipt issued in both circumstances. So you just want to be wicked and show that you are smart abi? You prefer to pay triple the amount we requested, to the government just to make sure we do not get anything from you, right?"

"Well gentlemen, just as you have rightly said, it is government's money," another interrupts "and we are the government. All these tax are meant to build roads, give us basic amenities and increase our standard of living; is the government doing all these for us?"

"Gentlemen, it is not my problem. They ask me to pay in order to establish a business and I did. As a matter of fact, I followed the due process to avoid exactly this confrontation I am facing right now."

"Oga doctor, nobody values your patriotism or penchant for doing the right thing in this country. You rub my back, I rub yours."

"Okay, gentlemen; next time I will give you the money instead."

"Hmm! Doctor, you cannot be a stranger and want to show us wisdom here o!"

"I am not a stranger, Mr. Man. I am a law-abiding and hardworking citizen of this country with the liberty to live anywhere and work anywhere within its boundaries. What the heck is wrong with all of you? What is with this 'stranger mentality'?"

The doctor raises his voice. "GOD! What exactly am I up against in this town? Can't you appreciate what I am doing here even for once? What the heck? Frustration from left, right and centre; are you people beasts? Even the direct beneficiaries of my skill also turn out to be agents of frustration, why, why, why?" "Oga doctor, leave all these English for Englishman. Shouting will not solve anything. One thing about life is that your tenacity will eventually pay off. You suppose to understand how we live our lives here, how we think and do things here. One doctor from the north came here and wanted to show us he knows it all just because he removes fibroids. Na just one woman! One woman! The woman was sent to him with a curse attached and directly, his life was also attached to hers, she was sent to him for a surgery, she died, and three months later, he followed."

"So, is this something to be proud of? Why the example? Are you threatening me?"

"Oga doctor, it is not a threat, just some advice. If you want to live here successfully and do your business in peace, follow us jeje o. Do as you dey see us do. Life is not by big English o!"

Another contributes, "we dey see you dey carry big Bible go church. Your Bible talk say give Caesar own to Caesar. Oga doctor! Oga doctor! Oga doctor! How many times I call you so?" The man drags his right ear with his right fingers as he cautions. "This money wey you pay for account na Caesar money you carry give John the Baptist o! We don talk our own." They leave him to their motor cycles and zoom off. He stays static in deep thoughts and wonders for a while before entering his car and then he leaves as well.

XXXXXXXXXXXXXXXXXXXXXXXXXXXX

At home in the late evening of the same day, the doctor lies on the bed under the sitting kneel of his wife while she massages his body from shoulders to buttocks. He is in a pair of boxers while she wears a bra and bum shorts.

"I am tired, so tired of this God-forsaken place," he laments.

"Oh dear, it is the country in general. Things are really bad right now and worse off, the future is blank. Hope seems to be lost and uncertainties on the increase. Just see how the declaration of our clueless leader to run for a second term caused a tsunami on our stock market. It is the country, my dear."

"I understand but we, in our own little ways, are not helping matters. You are seen as terribly bad if you do the right thing. Just see how I got the bashing of my life just because I paid my tax straight to the government."

She laughs loud. "But I warned you, sweetheart. This country is not worth it. Don't sweat it. Nobody acknowledges goodness now. Everybody is trying to survive by all means. So our survival instincts have grown so high to suppress the sense of humanity in us. No sympathy, nor empathy, just dog-eat-dog struggles. There is no brother in the jungle, as it is commonly said, so if you do not join them, you get eliminated on the way. And if you are too strong for them, you die of frustration because, one way or the other, frustration must come, if not vertically, horizontally. That is the country for you my dear."

"I wonder why I came back to this place."

"Oh dear, I understand your frustration but don't take it too far. Here still remains your home no matter what and secondly, having a family is enough reason to stand against any form of regret."

He smiles, "yes darling. That still remains the best decision I have made."

She smiles back but retorts, "by the way, if I catch that Salamatu eh!"

He laughs loud, "at least, she is the first cunny girl in about four months now, unlike when we first came here, when I usually meet three to four of her type every week."

"Was she that attractive?"

"Very attractive, my dear, but thank God it did not get far."

"So you would have done something eh?"

"Come on darling! I cannot say, but I would have tried resisting."

"Holy ghost fire!" She screams as she slaps his back with both hands.

"Yeeeeeeeeh! Do you want to kill me? I am just being honest now!"

"Sometimes, a woman does not need honesty. What she needs is to be told exactly what she wants to hear. That also speaks volume of her man's loyalty."

"Ehen! Don't worry love, nothing would have happened. By the way, Alaba, the febrile convulsive young lady is doing fine. As soon as we induce her to expel her dead foetus, she will be discharged tomorrow."

"Wow! What a miracle."

"Yes o! She has indeed been a miracle."

"So you see, even in the heat of the moment, we still have opportunities to smile. Do not let the thorn stings blur your vision to the roses' beauty."

"Yes ma."

"Well, honey, I have a surprise for you. I hired someone to develop our hospital website. It will soon be ready. It is well sophisticated and you will love it."

"Wow! But why? I am already giving up on this place and thinking of relocating and you are here developing a website?"

"Yes, honey. You shouldn't give up on helping these people, no matter what. The website will be of great benefit later. I don't know how but I am sure it will."

He turns around and grabs her to himself to much excitement and kisses her to show how impressed and grateful he is. They play romantically until the baby wakes up from sleep.

CHAPTER 6

The doctor watches a football match on TV when a call comes in. He lowers the volume of the television with the remote control in his hand before picking up the phone. After a while of talking, the call ends, and he increases the volume back to its initial intensity to continue the game.

"Who was that?" His wife asks, coming out of the toilet.

"It was Nurse Onyinye. A little girl was brought to the hospital with a case of a foreign body in her left ear."

"My God! Children with their troubles! So, are you going to the hospital now?"

"No, my love. She has already removed it. It was a little piece of bone."

"Jesus Christ! How come? That child must be very crazy."

"Calm down, sweetheart. They are just children."

"How old is she?"

"She is seven."

"A girl of seven being this careless? I'd flog her very well if I was her mother so she'd learn her lesson properly."

He laughs, "don't be mean, my love. It's all good now. I told her the antibiotics and pain reliever to give. That was why she called."

"But won't you go and check the situation later?"

"The child will be discharged immediately. If I will be going to the hospital, it will not be because of her case. There are other serious cases in there and I will check them but not now."

"What about the severe asthma case?"

"The boy is stable now, after nebulizing him, but his parents insisted he stay for the night. I will check on him as well."

His wife comes and sit-kneel on his laps. "You're my exceptional man. You know that, right?"

He smiles and nods his head in agreement as she continues, "I love you so much. Please continue the good work, despite all the challenges we are facing right now."

"Thank you, my love," he responds as she kisses him while getting off his body.

Later in the night, at about 2am, while asleep, his phone rings. He uses a great deal of effort to pick it, on the ninth attempt.

"Hello, Onyinye, what's the problem?" He listens, then speaks again. "Even after giving her metoclopramide?" He listens again, then responds, "okay, I will be on my way now."

He turns to the other side of the bed to notice his fully awaken wife, "What's the problem, my love?" She queries.

"One of the patients is profusely vomiting and it seems not to stop."

"Oh my goodness! Please hurry," she encourages him as he quickly dresses up and leaves for the hospital.

He hurries into the reception and into the wards on arrival to meet a very calm atmosphere with everyone fast asleep. He gets a little confused while going round to ensure everything is actually fine. Then he comes back to the reception and meets the three nurses on duty.

"Good morning, sir." They genuflect while greeting.

"Good morning, ladies. Onyinye, you called me about a serious issue."

"Yes, sir. It is just amazing how quickly the woman recovered. She's now asleep."

"Hmm... This is interesting but there's no sign of vomitus around her. I didn't even notice a recently mopped floor."

"Sir, we did all that and as you can see, she's on intravenous normal saline right now for rehydration."

"Okay then. I'll assess her again, while you, Onyinye, can drop your report on my table in the office. It is open."

"Okay, sir." The three nurses simultaneously respond.

He enters the ward, and after a while, comes out and goes straight to his office. He reads through their reports, writes his, and signs. As soon as he lifts the folder to call out one of the nurses, a neatly folded piece of paper with the tag, 'My dear Doctor,' drops. He gets curious as he picks it up and opens. After reading, he wears a face of obvious fury and calls out for Nurse Onyinye. She enters his office with an immediate observation of his mood. She slowly sits down on the chair directly opposite him, across the office table, while fixing her gaze at him.

"Nurse Onyinye!"

"Sir."

"Why are you this stubborn? Why are you like this? Why do you want to ruin your hard work and dedication to this hospital?"

She stands up but he snaps, "sit down, you schmuck! Don't provoke me the more. Do you think I will stoop that low to allow myself get entangled with you romantically? So this is the reason you disturbed my sleep right? I have assessed the patient of concern and I did not notice any form of dehydration or severe symptoms. Get this straight; even if I am a chronic womanizer, I would not jeopardize my business to follow any of you. So now tell me, am I too soft for you to have the guts to do this? I have tried to be a very understanding, down-to-earth and approachable boss so that we move together and make this place a very functional facility of healing, but I don't get it. Am I too soft?"

She gets on her knees and begins to beg with prayer arms. "I'm sorry, sir. I'm very sorry sir. I wanted to let it out of my chest." He snaps again, "You have no right! You have no right to do so. As long as this hospital is concerned, that is far beyond your limit. This audacity you exhibit is not healthy here, so save all the crocodile tears. I am very sure you do not regret your action."

She weeps, "I'm so sorry, sir. Please, sir, give me one more chance. I will not do this again."

He laughs, "one more chance? So that you perfect your next strategy? Is this how clinics and hospitals are run in this place?"

"I don't normally go for men, sir, not even doctors, but you've made me lose control of myself, sir."

"Imagine you! You cry and still spill nonsense. Work romance is a serious anathema to me and since you do not mind getting burnt or crushed, as written in your letter, that's exactly what I'll do now."

She weeps more, "I'll not stop crying sir until you forgive me. I am sorry sir. I am very sorry."

She's lies on the floor, pleading. He stands up, looks at her in disgust, "you're fired, Onyinye. Leave after this shift and never come back here again. And let me warn you, no matter how you beg afterwards, you are never coming back here again. NEVER!"

She gets back on her knees and holds his right leg, still weeping, but he shakes her off. "Don't touch me! Don't touch me, you fool! You're poison to this place and I will not let you continue working here. Even the homeless girl, Sikirat, has noticed your antics in this place. So leave!"

"But I've been hardworking, sir. I've been diligent and committed to making this place a standard hospital, sir. And what I feel for you contributes to making me committed. I give my all and I show so much passion. It is not my fault, sir. Things of the heart cannot be controlled. Please, sir, please forgive me."

"Thank you for your dedication and passion. You are hardworking, but diligent and committed? I seriously doubt that. Do you think I am not aware of how you charged patients extra money on three occasions last week? Or is it the Insulin syringes you stole from this place during night shifts? You now do home services, but instead of getting your own stuff, you use the hospital's items, and you think I'm now aware, right?"

 Abruptly, she stops crying, looking at him in surprise.

"Oh, no more crying? What can you say about these two incidences? I can only imagine the damage you are planning to cause to this place as soon as I fall for your trap."

She places both hands on her head, "oh! I'm finished, I'm finished o! Please sir, hear me out sir….."

He interrupts, "I am happy you couldn't deny. That does not stop me from seeing how despicable you are. Another thing, despite warning you about having visitors during working hours, you still have the guts to invite your Yoruba teacher during your last night-shift and he was in my reception for over four hours, doing your thing, shouting and disturbing the patients as they slept."

She looks at him in surprise again and he laughs and continues, "oh, you think I am not aware of the recent happenings here? I was just waiting for the right time to expel you out of this place and, alas! You presented the perfect opportunity to do so. I will not let my hard earned sweat go to the mud by involving myself with you, Onyinye. If other doctors or hospital owners are doing it with their nurses, then know now that I am not like them. So, get out! Get out now!" He shouts as he points the fore finger of his outstretched arm towards the door. She stands up quietly, reaches to the door, turns back and apologizes one last time before leaving. He calls the other two nurses on duty, gives them a set of clear instructions and asks them to leave his office in a show of transferred aggression. Before leaving the hospital premises, while standing at the main entrance of the hospital, he reminds her to leave immediately after running the night shift and never to return.

XXXXXXXXXXXXXXXXXXXXXXXXXXXX

It is dawn and this time, his wife's phone rings. They are expecting her younger sister to come and spend some time with them, so she updates them on her journey so far, which is getting closer to the final bus stop. Both brush their teeth and get into the car. They arrive the motor park which is just an open space, and they remain in the car.

"Honey, how was last night? So, what happened? Is the woman fine now?"

He laughs before responding, "I think the woman was never in a serious problem. Onyinye was at it again."

She adjusts herself in rapt attention. "What happened, sweetheart? What did she do this time?"

He looks at her and smiles, "You know I love you darling."

"Stop this suspense! Tell me what happened."

"Don't worry, sweetheart. I'll rush the story if I say it here, and trust me it is not one to rush. Let's get Sandra and take her home first. While I'm eating and ready for work, I will download everything to you, okay?"

"Oh...... Sweetheart, I hate this. Okay, give me some hint, please, my love."

"If you insist, then I will. A love letter is involved this time."

"Blood of Jesus!" She exclaims, prompting his laughter, "that devil is mad!"

"Calm down, my love. Here comes the 'God's will motors' vehicle. That should be the bus."

They step down, go to where the bus is parked and meet Sandra as she alights with the other passengers. A lot of people in the park recognize the doctor as floods of compliments and greetings distract their welcome of Sandra. He takes her luggage, they all enter the car and zoom off.

In the house now, the two sisters get engaged in an interesting, one-sided conversation full of body gestures and energetic dramatization from Sandra, while the doctor showers. He finishes and comes to the dining table for breakfast. Sandra goes in as his wife brings a tray of covered plates, jugs, cups and beverages to the table. She sits on the nearest chair by his left as she watches him eat.

"You have something to tell me, sweetheart."

He laughs gently and narrates everything while eating. She gets furious mid-way but becomes calm when he tells her the nurse has been fired.

"What insolence! What stupidity! If other doctors do this, my husband is not the same. Why would a woman want to be the problem of another woman? We compete with ourselves, downgrade ourselves, see nothing in snatching the love of another, look down on each other and easily victimize each other. Why? Why?" She rants.

"Calm down, my love. That is how the world is presently. Tell your feminists in Nigeria to also look into these issues concerning women, and not take it harshly on us to think we are the alpha and omega of all women's problems."

She smiles at him and softly pats his left shoulder, prompting his response. "Aha! Someone feels better now. I had wanted to read the love letter to you but I think I'll leave it for later when you're hundred percent calm."

"No way! You cannot drag my attention to it and leave me hanging like this. I want to hear, please read it to me."

He takes the paper from his pocket which showcases its bold inscription "My dear Doctor," and begins reading it.

"Good morning, sir. I know this will be a shocker to you but I cannot help it anymore. Right from the first week of my nursing training days in college, I've known so many doctors and I must say that you stand out sir. You are completely different, a complete boss who motivates, and not intimidate, correct, not mock our mistakes, humble, not arrogant, highly intelligent, so young, kind, soft-hearted, greatly understanding and, most strikingly, always punctual, despite being the boss. You are just so from another planet and it's no surprise you are a product of the European medical training system. I thought I was learned, an excellent orator and a sort-after professional until I met you. I just cannot stop thinking about you sir. I touch myself a lot because of you. My body has a high resistance to perspiration even when the sun is directly above us, but you make me sweat a pool even under an air condition and during the harmattan season. I just cannot do without you sir. I love you so much. I need you, sir. I want you, please. Pity my condition and touch me sir…"

"Idiot! Big fool!" His wife snaps, interrupting her husband's read. "She's a moron. Another person's husband fah! What kind of evil is this?"

"Oh sweetheart, calm down now. This read will not be interesting if you continue to interrupt like this. Let me finish reading before you make any comments, okay?"

"Okay my, love. Please continue."

"Even if your hand is a metal sponge, please sir, just touch me, look at me, hold me, and do anything you want to do with me, sir. I'm not interested in becoming your wife, even though I do not mind to be a second, third or even the tenth wife. I will never be a threat to her because I know how much you love her. All I want is for you to smile at me, touch me and make me happy. Let me be your spare part, sir. Let my body be your second hand shop. Let me be the waiting stew as you chew the rice at home and give me the opportunity to give you the variety in erotic pleasures and adventures of intimacy you may never know. I am aware you are a poet and so, I have taken my time to make this letter a little poetic. I

submit my pride, beauty, intelligence, wealth and, above all, my body to you, sir. I pleasurably mourn from the underground nightly activities of my fingers stimulated by imaginations of you, even when on my period. My heart races faster each time I know you're next door in your office, especially during a quiet and lonely night shift. Loving you is so powerful and inflammable and I am ready to get crushed because of it. I love you so much sir and there's nothing that can stop me from loving you. Please, sir, do not be angry with me. I know I just broke one of your rules, but seriously, I just cannot help it sir. I love you, love you, love you and love you so much. Please, sir, even if it is just by two percent, reciprocate this feeling. That amount is enough for me to bring another spark and corner of paradise to your world.

Signed, Nurse Onyinye Chukwudi Evarest."

"She's a big fool!" His wife continues with the insults while he comments, "I think she's really good and a wonderful poet also."
"Don't even dare!" She strongly warns.

He laughs and gesticulates a surrender. "Alright, fine. The issue is how to get another registered nurse. There were two registered nurses with seven auxiliaries. I've axed one and the other is pregnant, and will soon go on maternity leave."

"That's true, my love, but I thought you said your auxiliaries are good."

"Yes. Practically, they are, but are just good robots because they do not know the theoretical aspects of all the clinical manoeuvres they've learnt. The registered nurses are always better."

"So, what should we do now?" She asks in a little distress.

"I don't know, honey. Maybe we will request for more applications. The first registered nurse was the only one out of 91 applications. Nurse Onyinye came all the way from Owerri to work here. She's lucky to have a friend in whose house she has been staying."

"Don't worry, my love. Everything will be fine. I will start working on that now."

"Thank you, sweetheart. I give this letter to you as a wonderful token from the bottom of my heart." He jokes and hands over the letter to her, she collects, squeezes it and throws it at him to much of his pleasure and then he leaves for work.

XXXXXXXXXXXXXXXXXXXXXXXXXXXXX

The next day, at home, he wears his tie while his phone rings. He picks it up and after a while drops it.

"Everyone thinks a doctor plucks money from the tree."

His wife smiles as she assists him. "Responsibilities come with a lot of expectations in this part of the world," she replies.

"But, honey, it's getting too much. In ten days, I've received requests from three cousins, five uncles and four distant relatives. Where would I get all these monies from?"

"Oh sweetheart, that's life. You cannot kill yourself, my love. Do what you have to do and leave the rest. No matter your efforts and sacrifices, you cannot please everyone. Always remember that you are not the last option of whoever seeks for money from you, so don't kill yourself trying to please anyone."

"Thanks, honey. Is this what you are wearing?"

"Sure, my love, anything the problem?"

"Yes. The décolletage is too revealing. It's a naming ceremony. I don't think the people will like this."

"So, what should I wear?"

"Another fitting traditional wear, but let the upper part of your top go a little bit higher."

She murmurs in protest while going back to the wardrobe. Meanwhile, two ladies knock at the gate and Sandra goes out to meet them. After a brief introduction, they are let into the house. The ladies look around as they marvel at the pristine condition of the house. They sit in the living room while Sandra serves them drinks and notifies the doctor. He comes out of the bedroom into the living room. "Helen! What are you doing here?"

"Good morning, sir. I had to leave from Abuja today to see you."

"And why didn't you call?"

"Uncle, I wanted you to know how important the need is."

"Interesting! Gladys, how're you?"

"I'm fine, brother. It was my idea."

"So, what has made you two come all the way from Abuja?"

Gladys answers, "Brother, my wedding is in three months' time and I would love you to get a new set of sofas for me and a deep freezer."

"Imagine! Is this so urgent that you had to risk your life to be on the road for four hours?"

"Brother, I just have to. I know I can call you but I suspect you're getting a lot of those calls as well. I want mine to be a priority in your list."

"What about you, Helen, what do you want?" He turns to the second lady.

"Sir, I want to start a business. I think I will need three hundred thousand naira," Helen replies.

"Three hundred thousand naira!" He shouts. "Am I a money making machine? Just hear how you talk as if you gave me some money to keep for you."

"Please, sir, you're my last hope."

"And which business are we talking about here?"

"Just any business. I'm still thinking."

He laughs out loud, "so how did you come about three hundred thousand naira when you do not even have any business in mind? Okay, Gladys and Helen, first of all, you came to my house unannounced, travelling 250kms without informing me. That's your number one offense, and trust me, you're going back home today, both of you. Secondly, Gladys, give me time to think over it but in the meantime you'll have to choose between a set of chairs or a deep freezer. I cannot and will not give you both, and that's if I make the decision to help you. As for you, Helen, go back home, think of a business you can do, make sure you know everything about it, do your research, take surveys, then do a detailed business plan which should also outline your estimated capital and expenditure, you must project how you will make your profit and at which rate. Come back here and convince me adequately, then we will start from there."

The two girls grumble and then Gladys begs. "Sir, life is not easy o. We really need your help. We are your family o. Please help us."

He shakes his head, "did I say I'll not help? Thank God you just said it. A lot of relatives are on my neck and so you played smart by coming yourselves. If I meet every need thrown at me, I and my family will end up wretched. This is my final decision. Sandra will get you both something to eat."

He goes inside while, immediately, his wife comes out to exchange greetings with them. He comes back to meet them, and he hands over some money to them. "This is your transportation fare back home. Greet your parents for me."

The girls receive the cash with frowned faces. The doctor is indifferent to their reaction as he and his wife leaves Sandra with some instructions concerning their child before leaving for the naming ceremony.

XXXXXXXXXXXXXXXXXXXXXXXXXXXXX

They arrive the venue when the longueurs of the ceremony just ended — the speeches, testimonies and sermons. On arrival, the father of the baby rushes to meet the couple to everyone's notice and admiration, but stained with envy from a majority of the people present. The elegant couple walks in the midst of the people as they show and reciprocate respects. Their matching traditional wear threatens the occasion as the attention of all is diverted to them with a swift production of side comments, gossips and local headlines. The people reverence him much to his notice as his composure speaks volume of his reputation in the environment. But the talking point is his wife, who is almost never seen in public. She's a difficult sight to behold as her presence is only made possible by unlocking the abstract codes of her special preservation. The story of her beauty has enveloped the land which in reality is like a sweet scenting aroma coming from nowhere. Those lucky enough to see, hardly get the chance until the sun revolves round mars. She's tall and exquisite, humble with so much authority; a nemesis to the two sides of love, drawing the hormones of men to boil like melting magma, shattering to pieces their mere wishes. This one-woman government puts desires to a reschedule, smacking every ungodly thought, even from its conception to never notarize their transition to actions. She's gorgeous, putting the sight of men under mockery for their women to gather ammunitions in the backyard of their hearts. Her dress which sparkles, accentuating high class taste in modern fashion, gives beauty its completeness. Her makeup is less compartmentalized in her radiance, contributing immensely to the rich emanating feminine flare while staying truly African. No man resists the temptation of looking at her at least twice as her glamour bounces from heart to heart without end. She is glad to have listened to her husband because the full covering of her traditional attire is de rigueur at the event from her keen observation. The couple stands at a corner to join others in full concentration of the ongoing event. After some singing, food is served, giving the opportunity for people to move about and socialize. The father comes up and greets them again, and while interacting with them, three men come along to join.

"Good evening, gentlemen. I'm sure you know who this big man is." The father speaks to the men, praising the doctor who is obviously the big wig in the occasion. They exchange pleasantries and the man continues, "God saved my baby's life but most importantly, the life of my wife. Help me thank doctor too, for being the hand of God in my family's case. If not for him, I don't know what would have happened."

The doctor feels embarrassed and smiles. "All thanks to God."

One of the three men speaks, "we heard all about the situation. The woman was in a nursing home and after about twelve hours of labour, she was sent to one of these clinics, and again, she was there for another eight hours."

"God of thunder and lightening!" The second of the men screams while the first continues, "it was when they came to the doctor that he quickly did an emergency CS."

The father continues, "my wife bled o. She was bleeding seriously so that we had to get six pints of blood and later added two more. If not for doctor, I wonder how the story would have been by now."

The doctor smiles in modesty, "thank God for everything sir."

"Your wife is very beautiful, doctor. You know good things o."

The doctor and his wife smile as she appreciates, genuflecting as well.

One of the men becomes opportunistic. "Ehen doctor, for the past three days now, I cannot sleep properly. I swear to God, I sleep a maximum of three hours every day. I've spoken to some of my neighbours and they said it is a sign of madness. What should I do, doctor?"

He smiles. "Just come to the hospital tomorrow and see me. I'll give you some recommendations."

"But doctor, is there anything I can do or some advice or tips you can give me?"

"Yes, but only when you come to the hospital."

The man immediately gives a facial expression of strong disappointment as he speaks in his local dialect to the other two who immediately leave with him. The father takes the doctor away from his wife to a room of men, so austere, as they interact and eat. After a wave of pleasantries and immense flattery towards him, one of them speaks. "You see, doctor, I am Mr. Bello, his elder brother. And his son is named after me. His family is my family." The man beats his chest in pride. "That boy is my godson and he will do better than all of us, his parents."

"Ameen!" The others answer while he continues, "he will be richer than we will ever be."

"Ameen!"

"So, doctor, I want to specially thank you on behalf of everyone seated here. We are all aware of what you've done. We are very grateful."

The doctor smiles, "thank you too. I am very happy to be here as well."

"Please, sit down." The man encourages, but the doctor insists, "I'm fine here sir, I'm not staying too long."

The man continues, "If you say so, doctor, I have a complain o. You know, anytime we see a doctor, we always remember our problems, even the ones that haven't manifested but we anticipate." Everyone laughs as he continues, "it is not me actually. It's my son. But whatever affects my son affects me. He has been having series of hiccups for the past five days now. I've never experienced this kind of a situation o! I initially thought it was a spiritual attack but after I visited my spiritual father, he told me it is not, and gave me some herbs which did not work. So, what should I do now?"

The doctor smiles while looking at everyone, "well, it's a simple case, sir. Let him come to the hospital. We will attend to him."

The man passively protests, "haba, doctor! Must he come to the hospital?"

"Yes, sir, that is why the hospital exists. Let him come. Don't worry, it is not a case requiring admission. We will handle the situation very well."

Everyone in the room gets displeased with the doctor's response and a subsequent two minutes of absolute silence is cut short by the entrance of an old woman being brought in by two men. "Doctor, this is our mama. She has been having joint pain for more than eighteen years now. But since last year, we've noticed that she also complains of chest pain. Can you help us? Just tell us what to do."

The doctor sighs off the building tension from within as he scratches the region of his face just above his right eyelid with his right thumbnail. "So, for 18 years, mama has been having this problem?"

"Yes doctor."

"And what did you do about it?"

"We have been using some traditionally prepared water and other local herbs."

"Was there any improvements?"

"Initially there was, but it later became worse."

"And what did you do?" The two men stammer. "Sir, sir, sir, we emm, emm, we were managing her at home."

"And has that helped her?"

"No, sir."

"Why didn't you then bring her to the hospital?"

"No money, sir."

"So, for over eighteen years now, you had no money to bring mama to the hospital?"

The men keep quiet as silence takes over the room again, while the other men watch with keen interest.

One of the boys speaks, "but doctor, we did not exactly avoid the hospital o. There is this doctor that washes the inner system of the body. We always take mama there for her system to be washed. It's just that nothing changed after washing her system for more than four times."

"So, you've taken mama to the hospital not for treatment, but to wash her system. What did you plan to achieve by doing that?"

"Sir, maybe if we wash her system, the disease will also go. And every time that doctor washes her system, we will see how the urine colour changes. Mama's system is very bad o. It has been bad for so long."

"Please stop saying nonsense! Mama needs proper treatment. You had to go there for that number of time and spending all that money before thinking about the hospital. Why not take her to a hospital? Why?"

"Sorry, doctor. Now we know how foolish we have been. Please help us doctor."

"Well, mama's case would be best treated in a hospital. It mustn't necessarily be mine, just take her to a place you trust. They should be able to handle her case."

Mr. Bello rants, "no, doctor, this is not good, even this mama? Have some human feelings for heaven's sake! They just need some advice. Is that one also too hard for you to give? Please, doctor, be a human being for once."

The doctor feels very offended but stays calm, swallows hard thrice then speaks. "You want me to do the right thing for mama?"

"Yes, but for now, just do what they wish for. That is the best way you can help them."

The doctor smiles, "I swore an oath to do the right thing, Mr. Bello. If we prioritize the wishes of patients before our expertise, most would be avoidably dead. The right thing for mama still remains going to a hospital."

Some grumbling emanates, as the men now see him as a dead loss while he speaks. Mr. Bello tries interrupting, "but doctor…"

The doctor stays his ground to continue his talk, "no, no, no, Mr. Bello. Let me finish. It offends me for you to say I should be humane for once. After acknowledging my contributions in making this naming ceremony a reality, you forget so soon to make such a vicious statement. It is not fair to me as a person and it isn't fair to the medical profession. I have a life outside the hospital. I'm here to rejoice with one of us and have fun but yet you want to cajole me to work. Don't we have the life of our own anymore? We go to the market, place of worship and in fact any other public place; and all people see us as, is doctor and not just that, go a step further to try and take advantage."

One of the men encourages, "It's a blessing doctor, but the blessing is also a cross you doctors must carry."

"Not true! That's not true at all. A blessing should never be a cross to carry.

It's no longer a blessing if that be the case. We are first humans, before doctors. I am here to celebrate. Why can't we talk about politics, football, our challenges as men, women and other exciting issues? I know you were discussing these things before I came in and now, you want to turn this place to a consulting room. I am a man, asides being a doctor and this place is an excellent opportunity to interact with me as a fellow man like you."

One of the old woman's sons pleads. "Okay, doctor. Please, I beg you in the name of God, just help us."

He looks at him, "what do you do?"

"I'm a mechanic sir."

"Okay, just before I came here, I was driving and smoke started coming out from my bonnet. Despite refilling the radiator with water three times, it still goes empty after driving for ten minutes. Please mechanic, tell me what to do. Give me hints, suggestions, clues and advice."

Everyone looks at each other in surprise before they stare at the doctor while he continues.

"I guess you're already getting irritated when I was asking you for an advice right? You don't give people their needed solutions for free, be you a mechanic, carpenter, painter, Tailor or what have you. Lawyers ask for consultation fees even before they hear what their clients have to say. Travel agents do likewise and you all adapt to that system with them, so why is our case as doctors different? You call it 'just some advice' but you all have forgotten that we spent six years in medical school, one year internship, another year of national assignment, then more years of clinical practice, either as medical officers or as specialists, all to acquire the knowledge to give quality services that will sustain the human life, a part of which is giving 'just some advice.'" He looks round at everyone. "I'm sorry to disappoint you all but please meet me in the hospital for any case."

One man who squats all through, tries standing and screams. "Ah! My leg, Doctor, my leg." Some men alert.

"Doctor, help him. This is not a hospital case o! It is a now-now case."

He smiles, "just hold him well. He has pins and needles. The blood that was initially blocked will flow back now. He will be fine."

The man walks normally after a minute as the doctor politely walks out of the room.

Meanwhile, his wife's attention is taken by some women who come around, encouraging her to join numerous associations. A set initially takes her to a room which is too frowsy for her to stay. They come out to convince her after which another set comes with their sermon on the need to join a cooperative. He comes and joins her.

"How is the occasion going so far, my dear?" He asks keenly.

"It is quite eventful. The women here are hardworking and highly productive. I love it."

One of the women takes the opportunity, after greeting the doctor. "Oga doctor, I always feel something moving all over my body, especially in the evening. This has been happening for the past two weeks now."

"Okay, madam, just come to the hospital."

"Okay doctor. Is there nothing I can take?"

"There is, madam, but come to the hospital first."

"So it is only when I come to the hospital that you can find a remedy for me?"

"Yes, madam, only when you come to the hospital."

Immediately, she leaves, another woman with a young girl between the ages of six and eight comes to the doctor. "Please, doctor, my daughter is having serious stomach pain. Sometimes, she will roll on the floor, crying and sweating because of this pain."

"And you still left her at home? Why are you people in this town so careless with your health? You take life for granted here, not knowing you only have one life to live."

"But doctor, your hospital is too far from my house."

"Is there no other hospital near you?"

"No, sir. I swear."

"Is the distance of my hospital to your house more worrisome than the life of your daughter which is at stake?"

The woman keeps quiet.

"Please madam, visit a hospital." The doctor says, and the woman leaves.

"Sweetheart, we need to leave this place right away before the entire guests line up for free consultations. I thought I came here to relax, not knowing I'd still be at work."

She laughs, "three men approached me while you were away," she quickly announces.

"What! I didn't get that," he reacts in shock.

"Yes, you heard me right, honey. Three men came at me. I was in one of the rooms with the women and there was this well fed Alhaji who perambulated the arena. His frequent smiles and stare at me were a cue for his approach. He eventually did and left this with me."

She hands over an open cheque, signed by a strange name, with a one hundred and fifty thousand naira sum and a note with nothing more than a phone number.

The doctor smiles, "we are now one hundred and fifty thousand naira richer. What about the other two men?"

"They just came as random men, engaged me in a nice conversation and asked for my number which I politely declined."

The doctor shakes his head, "my God! Is there no more respect for marriage in our generation? Please let's get out of here before I collapse with work and then someone will take you to his house."

She laughs as they walk away.

XXXXXXXXXXXXXXXXXXXXXXXXXXXXX

He drives into his compound with his wife in the car. Gladys and Helen come out to welcome them. Sandra is inside, playing with the baby.

"Brother, we want to go tomorrow, please. Your baby is cute." Gladys requests.

"No way, Gladys. You came here unannounced. You have to go back today. It's not yet afternoon, so I do not want you still in this house by 1pm today."

Helen protests, "Ah! Are you chasing us out, uncle?"

"No, I'm not, but this is the 21st century. The world is a busy one, moving faster after each revolution. You two don't realize this because you've been living on relatives' generosity. But, thank God, one of you will soon be married, and the other, independent. You'll understand how the world works."

His phone rings and after a short while, he goes inside to alert his wife of an emergency in the hospital. He goes out, takes the car and with the help of his niece and cousin, leaves the compound to the hospital. He arrives to meet so much chaos as fifteen people, including the elderly, accompany the patient. He goes inside the reception to meet two men arguing with his nurses, while a chronically ill-looking helpless boy collapses on one of the chairs. His body feels very hot, his bulging eyes are so yellow with obvious signs of extreme weight loss. Everybody fears, Samson is already on his way to the other side. One of the nurses rushes to the doctor. "Sir, he's 40.7^{0}C in temperature."

"So, what are you waiting for? Administer 600mg of intramuscular paracetamol immediately and then tepid sponge. Why must you wait for me to tell you this?"

"Sir, he's one of our debtors. They still owe us seven thousand five hundred naira from the last case.

"Give me the ledger, please." She does and he reads through. "Okay, go ahead with tepid sponging and the paracetamol. I'll see you."

The doctor approaches the relatives. "Where are his parents?"

His father comes out. "I am here, doctor."

"Please, follow me to the office."

They walk into his office and both sit at opposite sides of the table.

"You see, you owed us five thousand naira the first time you came to this hospital and left without paying until the second time you came. After much argument with you, you paid your debt before treatment, just to end up as a debtor again with an even higher amount of seven thousand five hundred naira. Now, your son is suffering from a serious case here. I suspect thyroid crisis to rule out an acute case of liver disease. We need to run some tests and start rigorous treatment. You'll need seventy five thousand naira for this. So, I suggest you take your son elsewhere, because we cannot afford to spend money on treating him, just for you to run away. Together with your debt, you are to give us eighty two thousand, five hundred naira. Once you deposit sixty thousand naira, we will commence treatment, or take your son elsewhere."

The man falls to the ground, "please, doctor, don't do this to me."

"Please sir, stand up. You embarrass me. You're a man like me, so please don't do this. No matter how you beg, there's nothing I can do, where do you want me to get that kind of money, since obviously, you want free services? Just take your son elsewhere."

The man begs for the next ten minutes to no avail. He stands up and leaves the doctor's office. The doctor does some paperwork and leaves also. As he is about leaving the reception to the compound, ten elders and seven women start begging, some genuflect severally as they beg, while others, completely on their knees, keeping his nerves jangling.

"Please, stand up. I'm begging you people to stand up. You beg me as if I'm the giver of life. Please understand me. We use money to treat you, so why won't you pay? If everybody came here and paid only fifty percent, we would not be standing here right now. Please, I'm begging you, go to another hospital."

Some on their knees already, cling unto his legs, not letting go as they prevent him from moving. "I can't help, I'm very sorry."

A middle aged virago bosses them around to leave the hospital even as she insults him to his face, but suddenly some men come in with fifty five thousand naira which the doctor rejects.

He manoeuvres himself to finally get loose from the begging relatives but they rush and surround his car door to even frustrate him more. He decides to walk on foot but the gate entrance is quickly blocked by some relatives. After about thirty minutes of drama and a better financial contribution to seventy thousand naira, he agrees and goes back in with some urgency.

"Take the folder and bring the boy to the amenity ward. As you're coming, bring the oxygen tank, lugol's solution, hydrocortisone and the others as written in my plan."

The boy is placed on oxygen mask and the windows of the room widely opened for ventilation while also being placed on intravenous fluids.

The same day, Alaba's family and friends are in the hospital to give her a triumphant exit. Some women stay around the hospital vicinity to sing songs, while the young boys and men move around in eye-catchy dance moves. After finalizing payments, the doctor walks up to them in the ward as everyone there thanks him. Teary Alaba embraces him in sincere gratitude as the older ones around proclaim blessing after blessing on him. The scene becomes an emotional one for the doctor as he rejoices with them. Immediately after they leave, the boy who had tongue trauma comes for check up with his mother and aunts. The tongue is back to normal and he is passed fit to start eating solid foods. His mother kneels down to thank him, while the other relatives bless him in great appreciation for what he has done. He goes inside his office, sits and crosses his leg over the table in an ecstatic mood, thinking out loud, "do not let the thorn stings blur your vision to the roses' beauty indeed! My wife is right, so right", he ponders in great joy.

CHAPTER 7

It is a relatively quiet day. The hospital reception is just bear with only the wall television giving the place some life as the nurses sit in their station to watch and wait for the next round of vital signs monitoring. A police van rushes into the hospital compound and a huge obese man in uniform comes out with another officer, but smaller in stature, who clearly is an aide-de-camp. They walk into the reception, leaving two other officers in the car. The nurses adjust their positions, welcome the officer and execute the necessary protocols to prepare him for the doctor. The doctor, on the other hand, is busy with an evacuation procedure in the procedure room, after which he cleans up and meets with the police chief in his office.

"Is this the doctor? I've heard so much about you. I thought I would meet a very old man here. You're so young, doctor." The police chief speaks in a deep and cracked voice.

"Thank you, sir. So you're inspector Adams?"

"That's correct, my doctor."

"Before I hear your complaints, I must comment on your weight, sir. You are almost morbidly obese and this is dangerous for you, sir."

"What does that even mean, doctor?"

"What it means is that your weight itself is a disease to you. Your weight is a sickness. You need to reduce it. We will talk more about this later. May I hear your complaints now?"

"Ah! Doctor, three days ago, I urinated with so much pain. It is so unbearable o! I can't stand it. The pain comes with a hot sensation. My regular doctor is my church member and that is why I did not go to him. Besides, the man talks too much. That is why I decided to try you out."

"You're in the right place, sir. So, why didn't you come since the onset of this symptom?"

"I thought it was just a small issue. I took herbs, stopped my sugar intake and drank a lot of water only for fever and headache to surface the next day. I took panadol and a chemist gave me ampiclox and flagyl, only for the fever to worsen today. The pain too has doubled. You can imagine that my priced asset now scares me. I cannot even touch Mr. President who sits between my legs."

The doctor laughs, "okay sir, don't worry. It's a minor issue."

"Minor issue you say! Really!" The police chief screams.

"Yes, sir. We will take care of it, but I'll ask you some more questions."

"Please doctor, ride on. I'll not hide anything, I swear. I'll tell you all you need to know. I just want this pain to go."

"Good! I like that, sir. I'll appreciate your sincerity, and be rest assured, nothing will leave this room. It'll be between you and me."

"Thank you, doctor. I'll really appreciate it."

The doctor asks further questions for about twenty minutes. He writes down the history on the patient's folder, calls out Nurse Fatimat to administer intramuscular injection of paracetamol. After writing for a long time, the doctor speaks, "We are going to admit you, sir, and run some tests. I think you have gonorrhoea infection. I'm most certain it is what you're suffering from, considering the symptoms you present with and your history. Don't worry, we will take care of it, but please sir, you will have to reduce or even stop your sexual contact with women for now. Sleeping with twenty seven women in four different cities just in one month is terrible, really terrible Sir. At least, always use a condom."

"Doctor, I know. This has been preached to me in the church, community, even in the office and now you. I will try, doctor. E no easy o, but I will try. My wife sometimes sneaks in some packets of condoms in my bag anytime I am travelling out of the city for national assignments, but you know say banana no sweet together with him back nah."

"Your wife does that? Unbelievable!"

The police chief laughs out loud, "oh, my doctor, are you in this world at all? We the men cannot help it and our women have come to terms with it. Any mature woman will accept this. If she leaves me now, what is the assurance the next man she jumps to will not be worse? Or she wan stay lonely? My wife is just awesome and her understanding and maturity is out of this world. Oga doctor, we only have one life to live o! Just when you think you've seen the beauties of the beauties, you will see queens of queens the following day. God has punished man with so many women."

"You call it a punishment, sir?"

"Yes nah! With all these women everywhere, He asks us to choose only one? I just cannot help it, doctor."

"But it's bad, sir, very bad. You must find a way to stop it. Seek professional help, sir."

"Where can I get one, doctor? This is not America or Europe where you came from o. We don't have all those specialized psychologists and psycho-therapists like the West does. What we have are pastors, Imams, babalawos, prophets, healers, elders and friends, shikena."

The doctor laughs out loud, "okay, sir, if you say so. For now, first things first, which is giving you treatment. We are going to admit you, take samples for laboratory investigations and then begin to execute our treatment plan immediately. Don't worry, sir. My nurses are very capable. They will follow my treatment plan judiciously and always let them know of whatever thing you need okay?"

"I like that. Thank you, doctor. I am counting on you."

"You have nothing to worry about, sir." They shake hands and he leaves for the nurse's station.

"Sir, would you prefer the amenity ward or we should take you to the general men's ward?" one of the nurses politely asks the police chief who is now in the nurses' station in the reception.

"Haba, nurse! As you fine like this, you suppose get sense. Use your brain nah. So you think a whole me, big man like me will want to be in the general ward?"

"Sorry, Sir. It's just protocol, sir. We don't assume in this place."

"Anyway, that's good."

"So sir, a three-day intensive antibiotic treatment with analgesics will amount to nineteen thousand five hundred naira, sir."

"That's too much na!"

"No, sir. Our treatment in this region is the most reasonable. Even as a big man, we still did not inflate the price."

"Anyway, it is good. So, what should I do, beautiful?"

"Deposit ten thousand naira so that we can start, sir."

The police chief speaks to his aide-de-camp who goes to the car, comes back and pays the money in cash. The police officer is taken to the amenity ward where Nurse Fatimat and two other auxiliaries attend to him.

"What's your name, sweetness?" The police chief asks.

"Fatimat, sir."

"You're so beautiful."

"Thank you, sir."

"Anytime I'm bored, I will need your company. I hope you'll be available."

"I'm working, sir, and my shift will soon elapse."

"That's good. Then you will have time for me after your shift. I am a big man o! Make me happy and I will turn your life around, sweet Fatimat."

"I have to be at home to cook and do other domestic engagements, sir."

"Won't you come later to see me?"

"No, sir. That's the doctor's work. Nurses will always be here to attend to you and monitor your vitals, sir."

"Oh Fatimat, beauty with brains, you're very smart."

"Thank you, sir."

He catches her unawares by the right hand and kisses it, "see you soon, Fatimat."

She gets uncomfortable but remains polite, "thank you, sir."
The nurse leaves, while he lies down to rest as the drip gradually flows into his vein.

In the evening of the next day, the doctor comes around for a quick evening round, assessing everyone, then he gets to the amenity ward, where the police chief is.
"Good evening, sir," he greets.
"Good evening, my doctor. You are a magician o! The pain just disappeared like that."
"Really?"
"Yes o, my doctor."
"I'm happy, sir, but please ensure you stay and complete your medication. You don't treat any infection halfway. It's very dangerous."
"I know, my doctor. I am just so happy."
"I'm happy too, sir, only that you did not allow the nurses place a urethral catheter on you yesterday, even after I came back and insisted. I specifically instructed

them to do so, so that you can bypass the painful urination you experience."

The police chief laughs in guilt, "you see, my doctor, I did not feel comfortable with that. Since you're sure of your treatment, all I want now is to get well."

"If it is because they are females, I would have done it myself."

"Ah! Worse! I would prefer them to do it."

The doctor laughs, "worse? This is a hospital o. We do not care about what we see, which we do see almost on a daily basis. What we care about is the health of the people who own what we see. So, how about the painful urination now?"

"It has reduced drastically, my doctor."

"That's good. Okay then, I'll see you tomorrow."

"Okay, doctor. Thank you very much."

Just when the doctor and his evening round team are leaving, the police chief winks at Nurse Miriam.

It's 1:30am in the night and the time for yet another four-hourly vital signs check.

Nurse Miriam goes round the wards with the other nurses before she finally comes to the amenity ward alone. Interestingly, she finds the police chief fully awake.

"Oh my beautiful Nurse Miriam, how're you?"

"I'm fine, sir. Why aren't you asleep sir?"

"I'm just thinking about you and the next time you'll come and see me. The last two vital signs that were checked were done by others, not you."

"Yes, sir. We take turns, but I'm here now, sir."

Nurse Miriam begins to place her thermometer under his right armpit, while trying to check his blood pressure on his left arm.

The police chief speaks mischievously. "You know I am a big police officer, right? I am the chief in the capital city and I am not from around here, are you aware?"

"I know sir."

"That means, I am a very big man and with great influence."

"Absolutely, sir," she replies while concentrating on her work without giving him a stare.

"So, roll with me, sweet girl. I will spoil you and treat you well."

He gropes her behind and, immediately, she slaps his hand off, controlling herself to hide her disdain.

"Please sir, don't do that again. I am not interested."

"Haba, sweet Miriam, you are a mature girl nah. Why are you behaving like a newly admitted secondary school student? I cannot even sleep because you're around me. Make me happy now! I'll maintain you and keep you happy as well. I don't care if you have a boyfriend elsewhere."

"Thank you for the offer Sir, but unfortunately, I am not interested."

He grabs her waist and she resists. "Please sir, stop it! I am begging you, just stop it. Allow me do my work."

"Why are you shouting, Miriam? Is it because I just touched you?"

"You're harassing, me sir."

"Oh, my Miriam, I will not be offended by your theatrics. I am not your enemy. I am your friend, and I want to be more of a friend. Is that wrong?"

"Yes, sir. It is wrong when harassment is involved. Besides, I am not your friend." She packs her things and leaves.

Minutes later, he comes out and goes to the Nurse's station.

"Where's Miriam?" He asks and the other nurses reply.

"She's fast asleep in the other room."

"Tell her to come and put that rubber you wanted to put in my penis yesterday."

"But sir, you said the pain has drastically reduced."

"Yes, but the pain is back again. I need it now and only Miriam is allowed to fix it for me. No one, and I mean no one else will fix it for me."

"But sir...." He quickly interrupts the nurse.

"If you do not want me to be mad at this hospital, better go and wake her up now."

He walks back to his ward without giving ears to their mild protests. One of them calls the doctor, he gives them a clear instruction and then they go to Miriam's place of sleep and wake her up. They explain things to her and give the doctor's instructions. They put together the necessary items for the procedure and head to the police chief's ward.

"Oh, my Miriam, you're welcome, but why are you three?" He complains as they enter his ward.

"The doctor clearly insists we all come here to assist Miriam as she performs the procedure after we complained about your behaviour. Besides, it is also not a one-person's work, so we will assist her in doing that."

"No, I want only Miriam!"

"It is not possible, Sir. You cannot stop us from doing our job, Sir. If you do not want it, we will put it in writing and fully document it, but we advise that you cooperate with us to make this simple procedure an easy one."

After a back-and-forth exchange of words, he finally agrees. They do the procedure on a gradually and eventually very erect penis to much of his pleasure and their discomfort. He stares right into her eyes the whole time she is fixing the catheter and when they finish and about leaving, he grabs her left arm.

"Why are you angry with me, Miriam?"

She stands still, mute and looking elsewhere.

"Am I not talking to you, sweet girl? I really like you, Miriam."

She does not give an answer as she stands with the other ladies. He opens her right palm and drops two thousand naira on it. As soon as he releases her, she drops the money on his bed and leaves, refusing to respond to his numerous calls.

XXXXXXXXXXXXXXXXXXXXXXXXXXXX

Two days later, during the day, the doctor takes two labourers to the backyard of the hospital compound.

"This is where I want the incinerator to be. You will dig up to ten meters before we build a room around it," he directs them while they nod in agreement. When they finish and walk back to the front of the hospital, Nurse Onyinye and two elderly women approach them.

"Good afternoon sir," she greets, rushing toward him and kneeling down, right in front of him. He gets confused as he tries processing the current event.

"What's going on, Onyinye? What's happening here?"

"Sir, I came with my mother and my aunt…" One of the women cuts in.

"My son, my son, biko, please forgive her."

The woman joins Onyinye in kneeling down, but the doctor quickly holds her and begs her to stand up. The other woman also tries doing same, but he leaves the first and rushes to her, stopping her from doing it. The first woman speaks.

"I am her mother, and this is my elder sister." She points at the other woman and continues, "We came all the way from Owerri to this place. My daughter is very brilliant, she knows her work, but five years, I mean five years now, no work. Men have promised her heaven and earth, some even molested her, leaving her with nothing. She has told us so much about you and how you accepted her without any unholy request. Biko, please my son, in the name of our Lord and saviour, Jesus Christ, please forgive her, whatever wrong she has committed."

Her aunt takes over, "for us to come from Owerri, all the way to this place, you should see that we really want this. Please, my son, she told us everything. Some of us women can be foolish at times and what she did was very stupid, but please, biko, you are her father here, her elder brother and her uncle, because she doesn't know anyone in this place. Please, help us. Help us, doctor."

"But mama, if she has actually told you what she did, don't you think it will be a mistake bringing her back?"

"What is it that cannot be forgiven, my son? Maybe she did not tell us the truth or the complete truth, but we are here now."

"Interesting, mama, this is very interesting. I am a married man and she wants me to compromise my marital commitment for her, are you aware of this?"

Her mother reacts in shock, "I am not aware, my son. But now that I know, I will talk to her. She will behave from now on."

The doctor laughs, "Mama, whatever it is that she feels for me can only be temporarily suppressed. She sees me every day. I will be flirting with disaster if I re-hire her."

Her mother comes close and holds his hand, "my son! My son, biko, which tribe are you?"

He smiles, "it doesn't matter, mama. We are all humans and Nigerians at the same time and that makes you my mama as well."

"Okay, my son, look at Onyinye my daughter, just look at her. Isn't she looking remorseful enough for you to forgive her? She has been worse than this ever since she came back home. Onyinye was almost killing herself because of the frustration of staying at home and not going to work."

He looks at the three women still smiling, "Please, don't get me wrong, mama. I have forgiven her completely. I have nothing against her. But are you sure you know the actual reason for her frustration? She's dying of obsession, mama, and bringing her back is playing with fire. So, tell me, what about my wife? She is aware of everything that transpired. How do you think she will take it when she knows I am taking Onyinye back? Don't you think it is gross disrespect to her?"

Her aunt responds, "we can talk to your wife…"

He immediately snaps, "enough! I say enough! You now want to go and talk to my wife? Haba! Don't you have shame?

Don't you even have a little dignity? Put yourselves in her shoes, would you have accepted? Mama and aunty, I respect elderly ones, but I must tell you the truth. This will not happen. Onyinye has crossed the line over and over again and she has even shown some red flags indicating disaster if I had behaved foolishly to be sexually attached to her. She's smart, hardworking, kind and respectful but deadly, an opportunist and a crook. I am so sorry, mama, I cannot do this. I just can't."

He tries leaving but the three grab his legs and fall on their knees as they give an outpour of supplications. Meanwhile, Nurse Blessing rushes to the scene. "Sir, the Ogbologbo boys are here." The women release him as he attends to Blessing. "Who are the Ogbologbo boys?"

"Sir, they are thugs o. They terrorize the neighbourhood, especially those who are hardworking and making ends meet on a daily basis."

Onyinye adds, "they are dangerous boys, sir. Please take it easy with them."

He rushes into the reception with the nurse as he confronts them, "can I help you?"

One of them comes to the front, "let's go to your office, oga doctor."

"No way! You do not have that luxury. Speak now, I am listening."

They look at each other before the gang leader speaks, "You have guts o. We have heard so much about you. We can speak English too. You dare tell us no? Why haven't you paid your tithe?"

The doctor gets confused, "Tithe? Are you a pastor? Do we pay tithe under duress?"

The thugs look at each other and laugh as the leader points at the doctor, "look here, you this fool, today you must wake up from being an idiot. So you think you can come to a strange land and dominate it like that? How dare you display such arrogance at me? I can finish you right now within a second."

"I understand, you have some powers here, but let me remind you that I'm

Nigerian with every right to establish anywhere within the borders of the land."

"Really? Can you try this nonsense in the south-south?"

"How do you mean?"

"You will pay for matching ground and security money every month to boys if you establish there. Ordinary barbing saloon that I established there, they disturbed me until I finally packed up. If you are a Nigerian as you say, then do as we say because you are in our land."

"Oh dear! I'm sorry for the harassment. But I'm neither an indigene of that place nor one of the people who harassed you. So don't put this on me. Please, if you have nothing doing here, just leave. You're disturbing my patients. Just leave."

The boys get angry and start pushing down tables, chairs and anything they come across.

The police chief inside the amenity ward, realizing what is happening, makes a crucial phone call and in no time a van of about ten policemen arrives. The officers get into the reception, chase after the boys and catch them one by one in a complete mayhem. The gang leader takes a retractor and tries hitting the doctor's head from behind, but Onyinye quickly places her own body to protect him, raising her right hand as it hits with great impact. The leader is eventually captured and all put to the ground and cuffed. The doctor and other nurses around quickly take Onyinye to the procedure room as the police inspector comes out of his ward.

"I've heard so much about this stupid gang," the police chief says. "So this is how you operate? You come to where hardworking Nigerians are and disturb them like this, right? I'll deal with you, I swear. You will regret this."

One of them screams. "Ah! Police chief, we are finished o. Ah! Doctor, you didn't tell us you know the police chief. Oga police, we are very sorry. We didn't know this is your territory. We didn't even know you are around sir. Please sir, forgive us."

"You're very stupid, you'll pay for this. Oya, officers, take them away. Take them straight to the headquarters in the capital."

The officers grab the boys and take them into the van, it zooms off. The doctor thanks the inspector, places Onyinye on admission while her mother and aunt stay back with her as he goes home.

Some hours later, the police chief goes to the female Amenity ward where Onyinye is.

"Good afternoon, my mummies," the officer greets, they reply, all smiling, "Good afternoon, sir."

"Yellow pawpaw, how are you feeling?" Referring to Onyinye, and she responds with a smile, "I'm fine sir. Mummy, this is the police inspector of the entire metropolis here o. Na big man him be o."

"Ehen! This doctor has connections o!" Her aunt comments.

"This doctor must really be good," the mother remarks.

The police chief interrupts by clearing his throat before speaking, "I just came to check on you. This one that you gave your body to save the doctor, it's obvious you like him more than like."

She smiles, "he's my oga. He has been very nice to me. I've never come across a man like him before, so don't blame me, sir."

"Is that so? See me here o. You'll never see a man like me either." All laugh while he continues, "so, will your mothers stay here with you?"

"Yes sir, but not for long, they'll soon be going to the capital so that they can get the evening bus back to the east."

"I'll tell my driver to take them if they don't mind." Everyone becomes shocked. "Oh no, Sir, that is not necessary," the mother objects, but he remains adamant,

"I insist mama, and there's nothing you will do that will change my mind, so when you're ready, just let me know."

"If that be the case, we will be ready in two hours' time. Our baby here will be fine."

"Okay then, I will let the driver know."
"Thank you very much, sir." Onyinye appreciates him.

"No problem, fine yellow pawpaw. Didn't I tell you, you'll not find another like me?" The three women laugh and she responds, "You're right, sir. You're a man of action." He nods, "That's correct. Okay, beautiful. Since you're fine now, I will go back to my ward. It's the Male amenity ward over there." He points at the direction and continues, "if you also need anything, just let me know, okay?"

"Okay, Sir," the three women reply simultaneously as Onyinye shows more gratitude.

Later that evening, some hours after the two elderly women left, Onyinye goes to the amenity ward to see the police chief. "Ah! My fine yellow pawpaw is here," he exclaims in joy.

"Thank you very much, Sir. So, you still gave them twenty thousand naira cash, even after paying for their travel fare? That's so nice of you, Sir."

"Oh no, my darling pawpaw, it's nothing. I appreciate beauty when I see one and I tell you, this is just a dust particle compared to the heaps of fine sand coming your way." She laughs at his awkward idiom.

"Really, sir?"

"Yes, my darling."

They keep each other company for hours, laughing and having fun and when it is some few minutes to 9pm, she tells him of the need to go back and prepare for the doctor's evening rounds.

Shortly after, the doctor arrives, goes to the wards for his rounds and reaches her bed as the last patient.

"How are you feeling now?" He asks.

"I'm fine, doctor," Onyinye replies with a helpless gaze and a body language sending a clear message of the need for warmth and comfort. He shakes his head in pity.

"I'll not fall for your schemes Onyinye. You think I didn't come prepared for you? All these drama will not work. Your hand seems to be doing well now."

She quickly steps down from her bed and holds his arm, not minding the other nurses around.

"Please, sir, I beg you in the name of God. As you can see, I don't even care if the other nurses are looking……" He cuts in.

"That's exactly the problem now. You've already acquired too much effrontery. Keeping you here would be disastrous. Look here, we will discharge you tomorrow and you should just leave. I do not want to see you anywhere near this vicinity."

She starts crying to the amazement of the other nurses present.

"Please sir, please accept me back. I prefer dying inside of me, knowing full well I cannot have you even though I see you every day than staying away from you. Don't do this to me sir," she pleads on.

"Okay, Onyinye, I've heard you. Wipe your tears." He turns to the other nurses, "go back to your stations; I want to talk with her privately."

They leave with an obvious stare of disgust towards her while she adjusts to an upright sitting position to get ready for their discussion. He examines her dearly to much of her pleasure.

"You are slightly pale," the doctor says.

"Yes sir, I have not been eating properly for the past few days now."

"Why is that?"

"I'm missing you, sir. I just cannot do without you around me." She gives sensual responses in their conversation.

"So, why didn't you drink tortoise blood?" He jokes as both laugh to it.

"Oooooh! I am very serious sir, you are the reason for my illness but if only you recommend it, sir, I will drink a lot of it, not minding if I want to or not."

"Okay, I will prescribe seven tortoise full of blood for you." Both laugh again as she gets more comfortable with him.

"I've never seen a stubborn person like you, Onyinye."

"I cannot help it, sir. No man has made me go this crazy too. I guess there is something about you that is unique but hidden."

"And I guess you are bent on finding out what that is, right?"

"No, sir. I'm just following my heart. It beats for you sir."

The doctor stares directly into her eyes for about two minutes, then makes a suggestion. "I am shy to express myself here, Onyinye. Somebody may see or hear us. I think it is better you go to my office and wait for me there. Once we are there, I can fully express myself too you. You are crazy but I am beginning to love it. Go and wait for me there, but mind you, the switch is bad, just lie down..." In a quick reflex, he hisses, squeezing his face and shaking his head in self-disapproval as though it is a slip of the tongue. "Sorry," he continues, "I mean, sit down. Sit on the examination bed and wait for me. My discussion with you is a passionate one and I will not risk letting it get into another ear."

She looks at him in shock, swallowing hard, her saliva, as tears slowly drop down her left eye. "Are you saying what I am thinking right now? Is this a dream, Sir?"

He smiles, "you are wasting time. Can you sit in the dark and wait for me? I will be with you in a few minutes, let me just brush up some things with the nurses."

"Yes, Sir. I prefer the suggestion from the slip of your tongue, which is lying on the examination bed. I can engage in any conversation with you in that position, Sir." She speaks overwhelmingly as the growing disbelief eats up her sanity.

He smiles, "okay then, I will see you there." He pats her left shoulder and leaves.

Onyinye sits still for two minutes in great disbelief, then jumps up in ecstasy, dancing round the bed before leaving for the doctor's office in her best mood ever. She gets into the dark room and whispers several times, "how would doctor want it?" She takes off her clothes, entirely naked, lies on the examination bed in a supine position, and with legs wide open for her nudity to be well expressed.

A minute later, the switch goes on, just for her to realize the doctor's wife is in the room. In reflex, she jumps out of bed as she wears her clothes at the same time.

"Hello, Onyinye. How are you?" The doctor's wife greets calmly.

"I'm I'm I'm fine ma," Onyinye stammers.

"Come on, dear pretty nurse! Don't feel shy. We are just two women talking, and what is making us talk right now is one man you and I should actually not be talking about. While one of us owns him, the other is trying to steal him away."

Onyinye gets sober, "oh ma, it's not like that. I do not want to steal him away from you."

"Oh yeah! You just want to play with him and that's it? How convenient for you."

"I'm so sorry ma, but I swear, I never wanted to take him away from you."

"Nonsense!" His wife snaps, but controls

herself by breathing in and out twice and then she gradually calms down.

"You never wanted to take him away, yet you wrote a love letter to him? How more desperate can a single lady be, other than persistently going after a married man? If that's not stealing, what is it then? Have you ever been in love?"

"Yes, ma."

"Are you sure?"

"Yes, ma."

"So, you know how it feels to love someone passionately and with your life right?"

"Yes, ma."

"Do you understand how crazy a person who's madly in love can be?"

Onyinye drops her head, "yes, ma."

"And you understand how far that person can go to protect her territory?"

Onyinye stares at her, drops down her head again and hesitates before answering, "yes, ma."

"Good! You are a very pretty lady, very smart, intelligent, humble and decent. I don't know the demon that is trying to ruin you like this and this demon did not think of any other iniquity than giving you a set of binoculars with my husband's inscription on it. Let me tell you, I will knock that demon off you, even if it results to a terrible eventuality."

Onyinye stares at her in great fear while she continues.

"Based on everything my husband has told me and from what I see from you, getting a man should not be difficult for you. Just look at how pretty and ripe you are. You possess every physical thing a man wants from a woman, so what is your problem? Why must it be my husband? I am begging you, from one woman to another, leave my husband alone. I've got my own man and, though I am not perfect, I know I'm doing a good job keeping him. Go get yours and learn how to keep him as well. Even if you snatch him away from me, he'll be liable to be snatched away from you too. We are women. We shouldn't be doing this to each other. You're not the first or even the twentieth woman I've encountered trying to do the same thing you are doing now. So, even if you have him to yourself, you will have to be ready for the uphill task of chasing away the flies coming around. I know my man, I trust him and I make sure I keep him happy. For that reason I am not stressed up. But let me tell you now. If you succeed in taking him away, another woman will do likewise, and trust me, Onyinye, the women are always there. They never stop flocking around."

Onyinye kneels down, "I am very sorry ma. Please forgive me. This is the last time I will go after your man again."

"Aren't you surprised I'm calm?"

"No, ma, you make me so scared. It is scary for a woman like you to be calm in this kind of situation."

"Exactly! That's where I am heading to. Better be scared and get lost. You see that man in the reception you're chasing after? He is mine and mine alone. I'm not leaving him for anyone, no matter what, and I'll do anything to let things stay this way, even if it means wasting some sorry, pathetic lives like yours."

Onyinye stares at her in fear while she continues her calm talk.

"Under that examination bed where you thought things would happen is a two-litre container of acid. That was for you, but I will let today pass."

Onyinye, still kneeling, opens her eyes wide as she looks up to stare at the doctor's wife.

"Better stare well, because even in prison, no one will touch my man and I'll make sure of that. He's one of a kind and very rare to find. I'll not let you spoil him for me or even take him away from me. Not even Kayan mata or Garuma has the power to give him to another woman. So, if you know what's best for you, pack your belongings and leave after your discharge tomorrow. I've activated the other side of me and, trust me, you won't like what is coming. I'll leave you to dress properly and go to sleep. You have been warned. Leave us alone!"

The doctor's wife stands up from her sitting position and walks to the door, as soon as she holds its handle, she turns back.

"That reminds me. My husband was thinking of discharging you without receiving a dime. Not in this hospital! I didn't ask you to protect him so I don't care if you suffer what you got yourself into. I don't give a damn and I'm not thankful. Find a way to sort yourself out. Your money is three thousand naira and you must pay before you leave. By the time I'm back here tomorrow by noon, I do not want to see you around this vicinity and you cannot leave without paying. Is that understood?"

"Yes, ma."

"Good night." She bangs the door after her.

The doctor waits in the car for his wife who walks through the reception and the main entrance to meet him. While walking, the police chief spots her.

"Hey madam! Hey madam!" The police chief calls, running towards her.

She stops and turns toward his direction.

"Lord of Abednego and Melchizedek! Where are all you fine women coming from? Goodness! Did you also come for treatment? I want more sickness to remain in this feminine-rich clinic."

The nurses in the reception laugh, but in a contained manner, as he amuses them and extends his hand for a shake.

"I'm inspector Adams, the police chief of the metropolis," he says.

She shows him a very clear facial expression of not being impressed but accepts his handshake.

"I'm the wife of the doctor who's treating you. Watch it, sir. He may get angry and mix your drip with diesel. Look at me very well." She moves closer to be on a face-to-face presentation with him. "Oga doctor doesn't joke when it comes to me, his wife, so be careful. When you leave here, you can go back to the capital city. I'm sure a lot of ladies will be dying to be with you. If you misbehave too much we will happily receive you back into the ward."

The nurses nearby laugh even more as he gets confused and quickly pulls out his hand.

"Who has provoked you this night, madam? Did any unknown insect bite you? Calm down, you are overreacting. No one is too married to get compliments," the police chief says.

"Good, let it be at the compliments level." He sighs, showing some indifference. "But let me get something clear, did the doctor tell you about my problem here?"

"No, sir. I have no clue what he's treating you for, but clearly, you cannot see a woman and look the other way and this is unfortunately a serious condition that even he, the doctor, cannot treat."

"Don't insult me, young woman. I am old enough to be your father."

"Great! Then act like it, Sir. Have a wonderful night rest, Mr. Inspector. It is nice knowing you. Get well soon." She walks away as he stares in amazement.

The next morning, two vehicles with the police insigma come to the compound to take their boss. He gets to the nurses' unit. "I've been calling the doctor but he's refusing to pick my calls. What's the problem?"

"Sir, he's currently in a meeting. So, he cannot pick," Nurse Medinat responds. "I'm going home, give me my take home drugs."

"No, sir. We can't. You still have about nine thousand naira to pay."

"After all I've done for this hospital? I used resources and money to call my people to save your fucking situation with thugs and I arrested the Ogbologbo boys and now you charge me?"

"Sorry, sir. The doctor said if you don't pay up we should not give you your drugs." Immediately, his phone rings and he picks, "Oga doctor, what nonsense is this? Are you still asking me to pay, despite what I did for this clinic?"

"Mr. Inspector, it is your duty to protect me and my hospital, for which I pay you through taxation. You won't intimidate me into waving nine thousand naira just because you performed your duty.

Besides, you also protected yourself, because, if anything would have happened, you stood the risk of being affected. I am Nigerian, I know my rights and I'm learned."

"Imbecile! You're a fool! You know your rights abi? This is the highest level of ingratitude. I do not bloody care about the drugs anymore. I am going. Nonsense!"

"Mr. Inspector, insult me all you want. You are the police and the law, so we do not have the power to stop you if you choose not to pay and leave but we will not give you your take home drugs, and by the way, Nurse Onyinye's bill, who is your friend, is three thousand naira. You can add that one as well, else she isn't leaving."

"I'll never come to this fucking useless place again. So local, so stupid and immature..."

The doctor hangs up. The police chief walks to Onyinye's ward.

"Hello, my beautiful yellow pawpaw. How are you? I can see you've packed already."

"Yes, chief. I am ready to leave."

"So, where are you going to?"

"To my house of course."

"Where is it?"

"It's just some blocks away."

"Follow me to the capital, spend some time with me, let me treat you like a queen and use you to build my ego around the city."

Both laugh and she replies, "hmm, all with me?"

"Yes, my yellow pawpaw. I've never seen a beautiful diamond like you. You're so gentle and soft, really so soft, and right now, just mention anything and I will do it."

Onyinye looks at him carefully and observes how serious he is as she sees a huge window of opportunity.

"You say anything?" she asks.

"Yes my dear, anything, my sweet yellow pawpaw."

"Then we will begin with paying your hospital bills and mine as well. Please, don't fight the doctor, he has tried for you."

The police chief immediately calls for one of his aides. The officer rushes into the ward.

"Oya, open the suitcase and pay this useless place their twelve thousand naira."

"Sir, it is nine thousand naira," the aide politely objects to the disdain of the police chief, prompting his boss to yell, "are you mad! Do as I say! Money is their problem here, not mine. Let me show them that I have more than enough to even throw away."

The officer fidgets, "okay sir." He quickly runs out of the ward to Onyinye's amazement.

"Oga chief! Take it easy with your boys nah," she pleads.

He laughs, "they are also your boys from now on. Anything you need, let them know."

"No, I will never do that. I will be dealing with you directly."

The officer comes back after a short while, "Sir, it is done. I'm with the receipt."

"Good, my sweet pawpaw. Let's go."

He turns to the officer, "oya, pack her things, call Yahaya to come and assist you."

The police chief faces Onyinye, "let's go, my dear." He takes her by the left hand and then they walk abreast of each other. When they get to the reception, he asks the officers to walk Onyinye to the car, leaving him alone with the nurses in their station. "Medinat, you have not given me your number," he says to one of the nurses.

"Is your yellow pawpaw not okay for you, Sir?"

"No, she is not. You are my brown pineapple."

Medinat laughs, "brown, you say?"

"Yes, my dear. Give me your number and anytime you are around town just give me a call to make sure the town stays red for you."

She laughs again. "I am so sorry, sir. I am not interested."

He gives her a note of five hundred naira, but she refuses. He doubles it, and yet again she refuses. He checks his other pocket and makes it four notes, still she refuses. He calls out for one of his officers.

"Yahaya, come here. Go and bring me five thousand naira from the car."

Yahaya rushes to the car and returns with five thousand naira and hands it over to the police chief. The police chief puts the money on Medinat's palm, and this time she smiles and collects it.

"Thank you, sir," she appreciates.

"Can I now have your number?"

"No, sir. You can have your money back, if you want."

The chief laughs, "okay then, you win. I will surely come to this hospital just because of you."

"Make sure you don't leave your yellow pawpaw behind, Sir."

Everyone laughs. He gives the other nurses a thousand naira each, then leaves.

CHAPTER 8

The country sinks more in its current demise as all negative indices shoot up. Unemployment rate has increased to 18%, an all-time high, leaving more than 20 million extra citizens jobless, and about 98 million citizens living below poverty level, setting an increase in theft, scam and insecurity. The health sector is not exempted as maternal mortality rate rises, people die on a daily basis due to preventable causes. Hypertension and stress induced ailments are becoming lords of destruction, making the affordability of medical care almost impossible. Everyone, except the politicians now feel the heat — academics, professors, engineers, lawyers, traders, and even doctors. No one is left out, which includes the Omega Medical Centre.

It's been five days without a patient and this is the second time in two weeks such a streak will occur; work is becoming something of a snooze fest. The doctor has been forced to lay off some of his workers, leaving just three nurses and a cleaner to run the hospital. Prices are shooting up, no salaries, prosperity is non-existent, yet some still believe the hospital has enough to carry out services for free. Despite the doctor's efforts to disabuse this notion, nobody cares to understand, resulting in numerous clashes between the nurses and patients; himself and patients.

XXXXXXXXXXXXXXXXXXXXXXXXXXXX

It has been four hours since the doctor arrived his office for work. He sits on his chair to console himself with the melodious sounds of music coming from the churches around his hospital vicinity. Nurse Fatimat comes in and drops a folder.

"Sir, we have a patient."

"Let him in." A man walks in, seemingly unhappy, but not in distress.

"Good morning, doctor."

"Good morning, sir. Your vitals look good, really good, so what's your complaint?"

"I am sick, doctor," he malingers.

"Okay, I can see that. How do you know you are sick?"

"Headache, body pains, my joints, my mouth is bitter and sometimes I cannot sleep. I even found it difficult to walk to this place."

"Oh... So many complaints, let's take them one at a time. How did your illness start?"

"I had headache yesterday. It was so serious, my eyes were almost coming out."

"Then?"

"Then fever. I took panadol but it didn't go."

"Any vomiting or feeling to vomit?"

"No, doctor."

"Okay, continue."

"Then my joints started paining me."

"Did you do anything about it?"

"Yes, doctor. I rubbed methylated jelly on it."

"It?"

"Yes, doctor."

"Is it only one joint?"

"Oh! Sorry, doctor. My knees, elbows, fingers and hip joints."

"Did you lose appetite?"

"No, doctor."

"Could you sleep at night?"

"Sometimes, doctor."

"So, what happened next?"

"My mouth started tasting bitter."

"And you could still eat with the bitter taste?"

"No, doctor, this illness is serious."

"I do not want to vomit again as I did the other time, that is why I cannot eat."

"But you said there was no vomiting among the symptoms you feel."

"Oh! Sorry doctor, I vomited like four days ago."

"So, are you saying this illness started four days ago instead of yesterday as you've previously said?"

The man laughs in guilt, "yes, doctor."

"How was the vomit?"

"Serious vomit o, with plenty blood."

"What about watery stooling?"

"I purge a lot doctor."

"How is the purging then? The colour, its consistency and contents?"

"It is water-water with blood too."

The doctor then writes on the man's folder, fills out some forms and gives to him.

"Do all these tests. Come with the results then we will know how to treat you."

"Ah! Doctor, all these tests?"

"Yes, sir, we must give you the appropriate treatment."

"Okay, doctor! Why not just give me a medical report to take to my place of work?"

"Oh! I see! Is this what all this is about?" The man tries to cajole him, "haba, doctor! You know now! Understand now! I actually want to travel to Ibadan and meet one very fine chick there. We met on Facebook and, unlike other girls, she said she will not come until I come first. Doctor, that bush meat na special one from Holland o! I cannot afford to miss it."

"I am sorry to disappoint you, sir. Such atrocities will not carry my hospital name."

"Ah'ah, doctor. You are a man now, I know you understand. Body no be wood o!"

"Mr. Man, do these investigations and come back here with the results."

"Ten thousand naira."

"No sir!"

"Fifteen thousand naira!"

"Mr. Man, I am not interested."

"Twenty thousand naira."

"Get out!"

The man carries a frustrated figure out of the doctor's office.

The doctor walks out of his office to stretch his legs when a woman in labour pains walks into the reception.

"Doctor! Doctor! My water don burst," she announces in severe pain while the nurses run to make preparations for her.

"Mrs. Ngozi, that is good, but where are your items for delivery?"

"Oga doctor! I no get, I no get o, I no get ooo…" She is rushed into the labour room while the doctor stands still in confusion. He eventually follows them into the labour room as the midwife checks her cervical dilatation.

"But Mrs. Ngozi," the doctor calls, "you are our regular antenatal patient and you were duly informed of the requirements for delivery. Why don't you have anything? No pad, no olive oil, no cord clamp, no mucous extractor, nothing?"

"Doctor! Doctor!" She cries in agony, then the midwife reports, "sir, she's already 6cm."

"Oh! That is very good."

He walks out of the ward unhappy when he meets a younger woman. Are you with Mrs. Ngozi?"

"Yes, doctor."

"Good, we need a pack of pads, olive oil, a bottle of jik, surgical gloves and razor blades. The rest, we have here."

"Okay, doctor."

The woman runs out immediately. The midwife walks up to the doctor.

"Sir! She is insisting we augment her labour. She said, she doesn't want to suffer this pain for long."

"Did you inform her it is an extra three thousand naira for that?"

"Yes, sir."

"Are you sure?"

"Yes, sir."

"For someone who came with absolutely nothing, we have to be very careful in rendering them services."

The doctor enters the labour ward.

"Mrs. Ngozi, you want drip?"

"Yes, doctor."

"Na another three thousand naira o."

"No wahala, doctor, please give me drip, please."

"Madam Ngozi, once again it is another three thousand naira you go pay o!"

"No wahala, doctor," she affirms, bathed completely in sweat.

The intravenous combination is set up for her and in fifteen minutes' time, she delivers. The doctor congratulates her and goes to his office. A few minutes later he returns to meet a middle-aged man who sits abreast her. He is fluent and mellifluous in speech.

"Thank you, doctor," the middle-aged man says.

"Oh! We thank God."

"But doctor, I am not aware of the drip o! You should have waited for me to come. The doctor laughs sarcastically.

"Whatever issues you have with your wife, you better resolve it, and by the way, she is our patient, not you, hence our priority. She was asked four times before we set the drip and she gave us her consent. I will not join issues with you; and you definitely cannot come here and appropriate for yourselves free services."

The doctor walks away.

Later at night, the man brings seven thousand five hundred naira, but the nurses reject it. He tries to get the doctor's number to no avail. A little bust up ensues but the nurses stand their ground. Other men come around, insisting they are neighbours with the clinic and always greet the doctor anytime he passes by, but the nurses stand their ground, more yelling and quarrelling erupt until the men retire back home.

The next day, as early as 7.30am, the doctor arrives the clinic and locks himself as he insensibly stays in his office. The men come around again, insisting on seeing the doctor but are denied access.

"Is this how he will treat us? We use to greet anytime he passes this street to come to work. So now because of money! Useless money! A thing of the world! Something that we will die and leave behind, he behaves like this to us. No wahala!" The men rant on.

"But sir," Nurse Fatimat calls, "where in this place will you take delivery for seven thousand five hundred naira?"

"There are a lot of places," one of the men replies.

"What! You even say a lot'?"

"Yes! There are a lot of places."

"Okay, sir. That said, she came with nothing and was given drip. What would you say about all that?"

"Let us see him first! Can't he reduce for us? The country now is hard."

The husband sneaks through, towards the office under a chase from the nurses, but unfortunately for him, the office is locked from the inside when he tries opening.

"Doctor! Doctor!" He calls, "I know you are inside. Don't treat us like this o! Thirteen thousand naira is not my problem. I just feel we can relate at this level. Doctor! Open the door. Please, open the door."

The other man approaches him already fuming in anger, "let's go!" Don't waste any fucking time here. Let's go! Money is not everything. This guy has proven to us that he is a fool. Let's go. Pay the money and let's go. We will stick to the other clinics that have been here before this idiot came." They pay up their fee; refuse to collect the baby's birth certificate and leave.

The hospital enjoys a period of calm when a black Ford SUV zooms inside its compound. The driver and another man on the front seat come out in a rush to the reception and speak of their predicament. A wheel chair is brought to the right back door of the car. An acutely ill-looking woman, distressed in pain and almost paper white in skin colour is carefully dropped down and adjusted into the wheelchair. She is wheeled into the hospital to meet the doctor who is already making calls for the lab man to be present.

"She is about five months pregnant, sir. She has been bleeding. She lost a lot of blood in the past four days now and, about twenty minutes ago, she collapsed." A man explains.

"Are you her husband?"

"Yes, doctor."

"You were careless, I must say, very careless. She has been bleeding all these while and you refused going to a hospital? Why the dilatory response? More dragging of feet would have attenuated her state to death. Is she on an antenatal program?"

"Yes, doctor"

The lab man enters. Blood samples are quickly taken while intravenous fluids are set up. Her scary breathing both in rate and sound is accompanied by a cold body from head to toe. A quick obstetric scan is carried out as the nurse returns and reports. "Sir, her PCV is 21%."

"Thank you."

The doctor turns to the new patient's husband. Her condition is not good at all and the baby's heart beat is 98 beats per minute, which is lower than normal. We will gamble now by giving her four pints of blood and some fluids while we monitor the foetal heart rate every thirty minutes. In larger facilities, there is an equipment used to monitor the child's heart beat but we do not have it here, so I will use this small device in my hand," he shows them the foetal echo-sounder, "to monitor the baby. Once there is stability, the frequency will reduce to a two-hourly check."

"Okay, doctor. How much are we talking about here?"

"A lot, sir. We have no time to calculate. Just deposit seventy thousand naira."

"What! That much?"

"Blood alone, at the initial phase of transfusion is already forty thousand naira out of a possible total of a hundred thousand! My lab man has already gone to get blood and he will be here any minute from now."

"Okay, thank you, doctor."

The lab man enters hurriedly with two pints of blood. The transfusion is started while he rushes out again. The doctor writes down his plan and delivers it to the nurses.

The patient's husband and the doctor walk into his office as the doctor begins to explain the situation.

"What your wife is having is what we call grade 2 placenta praevia. In this situation, the placenta covers the round hole beneath the womb where the child should pass during delivery. Grade 2 means the covering is partial and not much so we can manage her conservatively and watch diligently. No need for surgery or termination of the pregnancy just yet."

"Doctor! Leave all that language. How much is my bill?"

"She should be here for at least two weeks, but preferably a month so that she stays for days without bleeding to convince us she's fine. In total, your money will be two hundred and twenty five thousand naira. We will check her foetal heart rate fifty times at five hundred naira per check, bed space, blood and fluids are also included."

The man kneels down and pleads. "Doctor, please do something. No money in the country. This just came unexpectedly when I am still struggling to attend to other basic needs."

"It's okay, sir. I have treated your other two wives here and it is obvious you like our services. I have also known you for a while now so we can afford a compromise. I will reduce the bed fee from five hundred naira to three hundred naira and the foetal check from five hundred naira to two hundred naira but, I cannot change the fee for acquiring blood, screening and transfusion. Is it good?"

"Thank you, doctor," he appreciates with relief, while the doctor re-calculates.

"Your new fee is a hundred and eighty five thousand naira for a two-week stay. You have deposited forty thousand naira, so, a hundred and forty five thousand is left and please, you need to deposit more by tomorrow, at least another forty five thousand. Please and please, ensure you pay up so that we can render our services to your satisfaction."

"Thank you, doctor, I can get thirty thousand tomorrow and I swear, I will deposit it."

The doctor comes out of his office to meet some men who greet him in chorus, "Good afternoon, doctor."

"Good afternoon, sirs. How may I help you?"

"Can we go to your office, sir? We are from the local government secretariat," one of the men speaks.

"Sure," the doctor replies.

Now in his office, the doctor asks again, "so, how may I help you?"

One of them brings out a letter-headed form and gives to the doctor; he reads it and looks at them.

"So I'll pay forty five thousand naira for the two billboards I placed for advert and for the wealth I accumulate based on any income generating power as a doctor?"

"That's correct, sir."

"But forty five thousand naira is too much now."

"Good! That is why we are here. You can deliberate on how much you can give."

"Thank you for your understanding. As you can see, there's no work now."

"A clinic must always have work, sir. Let's cut the chase, bring thirty thousand naira."

The doctor laughs, "you've tried, but where can I get the money from?"

"You just got blood for forty thousand naira now!" One of them snaps.

"How did you know that?" The doctor asks in shock, while the others prick him for letting his guard down.

"Okay gentlemen, ten thousand naira is what I can give you."

"No, oga doctor! That won't do."

"Don't be dogmatic, sir. I don't have money and the hospital isn't generating any income at the moment. Whatever it is you know about the money I just got is not completely mine. So, if you want more, then give me another month to gather something."

"Well, doctor, make it fifteen thousand naira then."

"Deal!"

They open up some files, get a receipt ready, he pays up and they leave.

"What a country!" he sighs in disbelief.

At about 9.00pm, the doctor returns to the hospital to meet relatives of the patient around the hospital vicinity. They greet him in appreciation, some, in the local dialect, ignorant of the fact that he can't understand them. The gateman greets him but stays alert, acting irritated and bossy, especially to the female patients. Despite his boss telling him to lighten up, he isn't relenting. The latest pregnant patient with the issue of blood sits upright to exhibit her nascent strength and joy, as soon as the doctor enters.

"Thank you very much, doctor," she appreciates.

"Oh, no problem, how are you feeling now?"

"Very strong, doctor."

"Any vomiting, headache, dizziness or weakness?"

"Not at all, doctor."

"That is good."

He reads through the noted activities in her folder.

"I can see your baby is fine now. The last thirteen readings show a foetal heart rate of between 138 and 155 beats per minute. That is very good."

She smiles and responds, "thank you so much, doctor."

"Okay, madam. You need complete bed rest with no disturbance, no shouting, no arguing. All your visitors will stay outside. I have instructed my nurses not to allow anyone in."

"Thank you, doctor."

"If you need anything, do not hesitate to let any of them know."

"Thank you, doctor."

"If it is a situation needing my attention, I'll come immediately."

"Thank you, doctor".

He leaves to wild celebrations.

It is now the next day, he arrives work and meets a moody atmosphere. "Mary, what's happening?"

"I am so sorry, Sir."

"What are you sorry for? Where is everyone, why is the whole place quiet? Where is your other partner?"

"Sir, the patient escaped."

"Escaped? How?"

She kneels down. "I am so sorry sir, I'm very sorry."

"Where's the gateman?"

"He's nowhere to be found since the patient escaped."

The doctor's hands begin to tremble, eyes watery and red and his breath deepens. He walks around helplessly. Speaking in his own dialect, but the words coming out like a barrage of imprecations. He clenches both fists as he stares at both nurses who are on their knees in great lamentation, bowing their heads to the ground in shame.

"I don't just know what to do to you ladies. Obviously you were caught off guard on your duty posts. You are both fired. Leave Immediately!"

In fear and haste, they hover around to take their belongings and leave the hospital immediately. Nurse Fatimat comes in to resume her duty but is warned not to talk. He treats her with great contempt, and then walks back to his car and goes home.

XXXXXXXXXXXXXXXXXXXXXXXXXXXX

It is two days after the incident. The doctor only goes to work at night, refusing to be present in the day time, irrespective of events in his hospital. He searches through previous applications and hires two nurses to replace the recently sacked ones. He asks the new nurses to resume the same day he reverts to his normal working activity. One of the days, while at work, a couple meets him inside his office and, after a while of conversation, he comes out with them in a positive mood and announces, "Ladies and gentlemen, our seventh success story of infertility." Nurse Fatimat and Angela, the receptionist, being the old employees in the vicinity give a round of applause. The couple holds hands in all smiles as they showcase their happiness, flaunting their matched cerulean wear.

Meanwhile, at the beginning of the same street of the hospital road which starts from a highway is Mr. Correct bar. The bar is the first building on the street and located about fifty meters away from the highway. The popular bar has also dropped in business due to the economic situation of the country. The arena is a spacious room containing 28 chairs, 7 tables, a bar and a small office. The bar also has an open extension, outside, which has 32 chairs and 8 tables.

Five men walk into the bar and sit under the shade of the extension. One of them calls out, "Mr. Correct!" The owner of the bar, middle-aged man in appearance presents himself.

"Big stout and three Heineken, this your pub no dey boom again o. Na wa o!" One of them orders.

"Big customer! You know how the country is. Everything now is bad and this state is even the worst in payment of salaries. So, it will definitely affect business."

"Mr. Correct! God dey... Please my drinks." Mr. Correct rushes inside to get the man's order, returns to drop it when his phone suddenly rings and he picks. After a moment of listening, he responds,

"Who are you sir? No, sir, I did not insult the governor, sir. I only said no payment of salaries sir, so did I do anything wrong in saying that? How did you get my number?"

The phone call cuts. Mr. Correct looks at the phone in disbelief and fear but gains confidence to walk back inside his shop. In less than ten minutes, some huge men in police uniform storm the arena. The drinking men take to their heels, prompting Mr. Correct to rush outside to meet them. No time is given for any explanation as he gets beaten to a pulp. Nearby traders just stand and watch as Mr. Correct is assaulted mercilessly. Striated wounds cover his hands as he bleeds from several locations around his head. The mobile policemen, as popularly called, leave him helpless in a precarious condition, they go straight to OMC. The doctor is summoned and he responds.

"Are you the doctor here?"

"Yes, officer," he answers.

"Good! A man has been beaten. Do not let him enter your hospital. I repeat, do not treat the bastard, or you will be next."

The other officer speaks, "Doctor no dey our dictionary o. You do anyhow, you see anyhow."

The five mobile police officers leave.

Not long after the police officers leave, family members of Mr. Correct rush him to the hospital. The doctor tells them about the threats he had received from the assaulters but they do not listen. He begs them to carry him elsewhere but they respond with several pleas for him to accept their patient. He manages to escape their grip and runs into his office. They refuse to leave, dropping him just outside the entrance of the reception. The nurses come to his door in turns to notify him of recent developments of the situation while he replies with further instructions aimed at encouraging the relatives to leave. The doctor kneels in his office and weeps, thinking of what to do, his oath and the lifeline this patient may have. By the next time another nurse comes to notify him about their stubbornness to stay, he opens his office door, lets them in and begins his treatment.

Three hours into his treatment execution, when everything seems to go well, Mr. Correct gives up. The doctor runs back to his room to weep again, hitting himself in bitterness and regretting why he heeded to the officers' threats. An argument about payment of hospital bills erupts. The relatives insist on not paying but the nurses persist, disallowing every direct link to the doctor. After much quarrels and insults, they pay partly. The nurses notify the doctor and, in reluctance, he allows them to go with their corpse. Some hours later, when he is calm, the doctor goes to the ward to check on the only patient left, Miss Aishat, the victim of ketamine intoxication.

"Good morning, doctor," she greets.

"Good morning, Aishat. How are you today?" He asks.

"So lovely."

"Yeah, I can see that. You look dazzling and pretty."

"Oh come on, doctor. You always flatter me even when it isn't necessary. You are just like my younger sister with words."

"Oh dear, I am not good at flattery. The last time I tried it, two snakes sneezed."

She laughs out loud. "Father in heaven! You are so funny, a kind hearted and very good person. No day passes by that I don't pity you because of what you pass through. You know, I initially carried this mentality that doctors in this country are greedy, mean, selfish and all about the money and reputation, but now I see it differently."

"Thank you, Aishat. You are far too kind."

"Sometimes, I feel you need to leave this profession, but then again, if your type should leave, how are we going to cope?"

"Oh dear! You are now the one leading our counseling session and with so much flattery." Both laugh.

"That shows I am improving, right?"

"Yes, Aishat, your improvement surprises me. I didn't even believe it would be this good. I was told you had a reaction last night."

"Hmmm Doctor, I felt as if I was becoming an imbecile. I thought all the crimes I had committed in my life were coming back to me in one consequence."

"Oh no! Don't believe that. Haloperidol which we used on you for ten days has its own neurogenic side effects. And that is why we tabulated the symptoms and my nurses always asked you some questions and checked on you two-hourly."

"Yeah, doctor. I got so tired and annoyed with that."

He laughs, "they told me, but I encouraged them to encourage you not to get tired. You could feel some restlessness which we call akathisia, some muscular rigidity, blurred vision or even constipation. In your case, it was muscular rigidity and we also noticed some persistent hypotension in your vital signs monitoring which is another possible side effect and one time or another some agitation, increased respiratory rate and dry mouth were recorded, all being side effects of the haloperidol administration. I am surprised your blood-sugar did not go down and there was no episode of seizures or increased sweating."

"Yes, doctor. My mouth was open and stiff, saliva was just coming out like a flowing stream. Two face towels soaked was the last straw."

"Yeah, but after we gave the anti-allergic parenteral treatment, everything became normal in no time and you slept."

"Yes, doctor!"

"Don't worry, we've stopped it now. So, how about urine frequency?"

"Whohoo!" This is the best part. I can stay two hours without emptying my bladder."

"Goodness me! Is this not a miracle?"

"Thank you so much, doctor."

"Oh dear, the pleasure is mine."

"I hope I am still going tomorrow."

"Yeah sure, you will."

"Thank you so much, doctor."

"I am happy you are doing great my noble radio presenter."

"By the way doctor, sorry for the loss today. The evil in Nigeria is becoming something else; I don't just know where this country is heading to. It is clear we are moving backwards instead of forward. How could police officers assault a citizen and stop a medical practitioner not to treat him?"

"Thank you my dear, I am just so tired. So, so tired; but what can I do? There is a reason I am here. I am getting stronger, but with the recent happenings around, I may evolve into a three legged being."

Both laugh as her younger sister walks in. "Doctor, meet Halimat, my sister. Halimat, meet doctor," Aishat introduces. They shake hands as Halimat visually assesses the doctor to his surprise.

"Oh yeah... Oh yeah! I love the impression you give, doctor. Your hidden swagger may be in infra-red but only those with a high degree of sensitivity can notice it," Halimat comments.

The doctor laughs, "thank you, Miss… I can see that it is an erudite family."

Aishat laughs as her sister continues, "yes, doctor. It is. Please, Sir, I'd like to have those songs you gave my sister. I am also depressed." She behaves in a desperately needy manner.

"Just get them from her."

"She told me you have over forty two thousand songs, and I was like, what!"

He laughs, "ladies, have fun spending time together. I've got to go."

"Bye, doctor."

Halimat whispers while he walks away. "He's so young, cute and bold."

"I can hear you loud and clear," he loudly announces, not even looking back as they laugh and watch him leave.

In his office, he sits and writes down some notes when one of his new nurses knocks and enters.

"Sir, there are three girls here seeking to be enrolled in the auxiliary program," the nurse reports.

"Tell them we don't run such programs here."

"I told them, Sir, but they insist on seeing you."

"Just go and tell them you've told me but there's no point."

"Sir, they've been here for the past fifteen minutes and are refusing to leave until they see you."

He sighs. "God! What is this again? Okay, let them in."

The three ladies walk in a straight line. "We will be very brief but you can all sit," the doctor says.

"Thank you, sir," they appreciate harmoniously.

"You are here for auxiliary nursing training right?"

"Yes, sir," they answer in a chorus.

"But we don't run this program anymore." One of them speaks, "please, hear me out sir."

The doctor listens as she begins to tell her entire story from childhood. She talks garrulously with no clear point stated.

"Okay, okay, okay," the doctor cuts in. "I think we are done here. We don't do trainee-programs or auxiliary nursing program here, period."

The three girls get on their knees instantly and begin to beg. The doctor observes with suspicion that someone has inveigled these young ladies into this act as a trap against him.

"Ladies, please leave my office now," the doctor demands.

At this point, he stands up, opens the door for them, but they remain on their knees. He laughs in reaction.

"All this drama is not coming from your guts. Someone is pushing you to do this, right?"

"No, sir! We want to learn. You are the best here and we know we will be good if we learn under you," one of them pleads.

"I don't believe you. If you want me to teach you, tell me the truth and you will train for free under me. Is someone behind this?"

The girls hesitate but finally agree.

"Yes, but sir, we will not tell you who."

"Thank you, ladies. That's all I need to know. Leave my office now before I call the police."

The girls stand up immediately and leave.

Just about the same time, a woman is rushed into the hospital with about fifteen accompanying relatives. She talks irrationally and is very aggressive. The Doctor accepts her and takes her to the amenity ward where all limbs are tied. The crowd is controlled by the nurses and only her two sisters are allowed in. She is in severe respiratory distress and the doctor orders for the nebulizer and corresponding tools to begin her remedy.

"What happened?" He enquires.

"Hmm! Doctor, it is evil spirit o!" One of the women answers.

"Evil spirit?"

"Yes, doctor."

The patient starts groaning as she speaks to the ceiling. "I hate you, I hate you, leave me alone."

"You see! Doctor, you see! It is evil spirit. You will not understand," the patient's relative complains further.

"So, you brought your sister to a person who will not understand her plight for help? Once again, tell me what happened."

Just immediately, a folder is brought to the doctor to record the patient's history, while the relative speaks.

"She has been possessed for twenty years now and we always take her up town for deliverance. We went today and during the session she collapsed. That is why we brought her here," the relative explains.

"She just collapsed? This deliverance you speak of must be an enervating process. If you really want me to help her, then I will have to know exactly all that happened."

"Ah! Doctor, the spiritual leader is in the reception. It is better you go and ask him o."

The doctor goes to the reception and from his appearance, it is easy to guess he is the one. The doctor takes him to another ward and asks him several questions.

"So, I really want to know what you did exactly or gave to her that made her fall so sick, almost to the point of death," the doctor asks.

"Doctor," the hirsute man begins, "I know this is your profession. Just do what you have to do for her, because you will not understand. In fact, no matter what you give to her right now, she won't be able to sleep because of the extent of demonic possession."

"What! So since you understand so well, why did you bring her here then? You are the expert and you know so much, so why are you here? Do you want me to help her or not?"

"Why are you shouting, doctor? Is it because we came here?"

"No, it is because you almost killed someone and you are still taking your actions likely. You still do not understand what you've done. Are you telling me or not?"

"Okay, fine! Normally, we use black seed oil in our sessions. We boiled one and asked her to inhale it. She refused, proving very stubborn, so we forced it on her and a little portion poured into her nose."

"Jesus Christ! You mean to say, you made her take in hot black seed oil via her nose?"

"Stop shouting now, doctor! We do this every day and I've been doing this for the past seventeen years, so no big deal."

"And how many have you killed in these seventeen years?"

"Don't insult me, doctor. I say, don't insult me."

"Okay, thank you for the information. Please, do not go anywhere near her. It is best you stay away."

"But her deliverance is not complete."

"Not in my hospital! When I am through, you can do whatever you want outside this hospital."

"You are arrogant, doctor! Don't insult our customs and beliefs," he speaks contumaciously in confidence.

"You are rebellious, evil man!" The doctor responds and lashes further, "don't insult humanity. Please go outside."

"And if I refuse?"

"I will call the police."

The spiritual leader laughs but goes out.

The thought of what the woman has been passing through for the past twenty years is almost putting him to a breakdown. The deliverer is neither remorseful nor humble, which offends the doctor even more. He goes to his office to pick up some items and when he returns to the amenity ward, he meets a shocking event. The spiritual leader is on the patient's neck, trying to pass some fluid and rub her cheeks with it, against her will as she screams loudly in implacable disapproval. The doctor rushes to her rescue, shouting on top of his lungs.

"Who the hell do you think you are? Get out of this place now!"

The man laughs, leaving the room while informing the doctor that she isn't the one manifesting, but the evil spirit in her. She screams at him in disgust, warning him to leave her alone. The doctor drags the spiritual leader who as well fights back. Several men come to the scene to stop the fight when finally separated, the doctor asks him to leave, and he does. The doctor ensures she is sedated and she is allowed to fall asleep, which she does immediately, contrary to the spiritual leader's assertion.

He goes to the general ward and sits on one of the beds, perplexed and in so much anger. Nurse Fatimat comes around to encourage him.

"Sir, I know this is new to you but it is our culture o. And it is our strong religious belief. Sorry it happened this way, but what just happened to this woman happens to one in like fifty people, so it is normal. The people outside feel offended that you shouted at their spiritual leader like that and they are not happy. So sir, in case of next time, you should know how you will go about dealing with this type of case. I will talk to them and hopefully by tomorrow when the situation is calm, you and the spiritual leader can make amends."

"Thank you, Fatimat," the doctor acknowledges. "Are you also offended?"

"Sir, no, I am not. I understand you and how you feel. I know you're doing this with a good heart, so I am not, Sir."

"Thank you once again, Fatimat."

"The pleasure is mine, Sir."

XXXXXXXXXXXXXXXXXXXXXXXXXXXX

It is seminar day and the reception is gradually getting full with people, well indicated by its obstreperous atmosphere affecting even the surrounding wards and offices. The doctor is in the general ward for males as he talks to a recuperating patient.

"How are you feeling?"

"I am fine now, doctor, no pain again."

"For how long have you been an ulcer patient?"

"For eighteen years now, Sir."

"Have you done an endoscopy to ascertain your diagnosis?"

"Yes, Sir, in Federal Medical Centre, Akure."

"Okay, and since then?"

"I've been taking some drugs and it has been on and off."

"How well do you eat?"

"Well… Well, doctor, I eat. Let's say I eat when I need to eat."

"When do you take breakfast?"

"Like 9 to 10 O'clock."

"And what about dinner?"

"Like 7 to 8 in the evening."

"Hmm! Not good."

"What drugs do you take?"

"Mostly transilicate and gestid."

"Is that all?"

"Yes, doctor."

"Don't you eat in your work place?"

"I am an entrepreneur, sir. I dig boreholes, so I go from place to place."

"Good! You are even in a better position to eat properly."

"Okay, sir."

"You see! The best medicine for you, ulcer patients, is food. A good eating habit is majorly what you need."

"Ehen… Doctor."

"Yes. For instance, I took my dinner by 7pm yesterday and my breakfast by 7am today. Do you know that my stomach has gone twelve hours between meals?"

"That is true o, doctor!"

"So, this is assured to be fasting. Of course, 12 hours without taking a meal is like fasting, isn't it?"

"Yes, doctor."

"And that is why the first meal of the day is called break-fast, you see!"

"Is that so?" The patient gets fascinated.

"Yes, it is. So, imagine I take breakfast by 10 or even 11 or 12pm, or not at all as boarding students do, I would be spending 14, 15 or 18 straight hours without food".

"My God! I am really guilty of this."

"Now, this is a big problem because the stomach is acidic. This medium helps for the digestion of the food you eat and if food isn't there for a long time, the acid wears out the stomach walls until it becomes a wound. The medical name for wound is simply called ulcer."

"Okay! Is that so, doctor?"

"Yes it is. So firstly, you must take your breakfast very early. 7am should not pass without you eating something."

"Okay, doctor."

"Then ensure you do not stay up to seven hours during the day without food. So, let's say you eat every six hours, you should take your lunch by 1pm and dinner by 7pm."

"Jesus! I didn't know this o."

"Finally, you will need to shorten that twelve hours of night without food, so before going to bed, take something light. It doesn't have to be food per se. It can just be tea, pap, fruits, some snacks or slices of bread. Just take something light to cut short that twelve hours of fasting."

"I will do that, doctor."

"Do you have any questions?"

"No, doctor!"

"Good. Please repeat what I just said".

The man felicitously repeats the doctor's instructions to his satisfaction. "Great! I am impressed. See you in a month's time."

"Thank you, doctor. Bye bye, sir."

"Bye bye".

As soon as the man leaves, a group of four elders enter.

"Good, morning Sirs," the doctor greets.

"Good morning, doctor," they reply randomly, then one speaks.

"We are here on behalf of Mama Nuratu."

"Oh, please sit." They sit and he continues, "her husband came the other day to meet your absence. He came to your house and we were made to understand he was not allowed in, so we decided to come here with him to really apologize."

Another man speaks. "I am Mallam Abdulmalik Yusufu, the father to Nuratu. I was very mad when I heard about what she did. It was uncalled for and considering what you've done for our daughter, I am sorry, sir. Please, forgive."

"Thank you, Sirs, for this. She was the last person I ever thought would be intractable to me and just as you've said, considering the time, money and efforts we put into your daughter's case, who was already attracting funeral rites from people, your wife, I must say, showed the height of ingratitude and wickedness. From her quarrels, I noticed she had made up her mind to come here and cheat me since she's aware of others who left this hospital without either paying at all or paying in full. Well, Mallam Abdulmalik, I will tell you to your face that I will not let go that balance of fifteen thousand naira. If you don't want to pay, fine! I do not regret bringing her back to life. I give God the glory for that, but I have the apprehension that if she comes here again, something bad may happen. So, stick to your previous hospital, but pay my balance."

Another who looks desiccated speaks. "Calm down, doctor. They will do everything possible to pay."

Though the doctor does not believe, he replies, "good, I really appreciate that."

"We are all happy you are here and we have heard a lot of testimonies about you.

Please don't be discouraged, don't change. Life has its challenges everywhere, just stay strong. We definitely need you here."

"Thank you very much, sirs."

They conclude, shake hands and leave while he follows as he goes to the reception for his monthly seminar talk.

XXXXXXXXXXXXXXXXXXXXXXXXXXXX

It's 10pm and after checking vital signs, the nurses return to their station to watch the TV set and gossip when nurse Fatimat notices a young man in his early 30s with a left sided facial scar. He is just outside the front door of the reception, inside the hospital compound. Their boisterous talk abruptly ends at the sight of his fierce countenance. He stares at them in truculence, remaining static in the same position for a very long time. Nurse Fatimat gathers some boldness and walks to the door but stays inside.

"Can we help you sir?" She enquires.

He keeps silent.

"Please sir, can we help you?" She asks again, but the young man does not reply. "Sir, if you have nothing to do here, you better leave."

The young man takes an audacious move and begins to walk towards them. The second nurse screams from her station while Fatimat fights her weaknesses to remain bold. She picks her phone and pretends to make a call to the police. The young man stops and walks away. The paucity of confidence is overwhelmingly palpable as both nurses fidget in a heightened sympathetic reaction. They hold each other to give themselves strength even though the shock still electrifies them.

"We need to at least prepare ourselves," Fatimat cautions.

"How?" Medinat responds.

"Let's take some tools which can be weapons for us and keep close by. We have retractors, let's keep two here. There is a hammer in oga's room. Let's take it too, we must learn how to stand."

Medinat looks at Fatimat in awe as she wonders how quixotic that idea is.

"Stop looking at me like that," Fatimat shuns. "Is it not better than staying and doing nothing?"

After a while of starring at each other, they move around to look for weapons.

Hours later, at about 1.30am at night, the boy appears again. Medinat sights him and alerts Fatimat who is already fast asleep. The boy stands in the same position and stares at them the same way. Medinat quickly gives the doctor six missed calls and in about ten minutes, just when the young man is about entering the hospital, the doctor zooms into the compound to the ladies' great relief.

"Young man, how may we help you?" The doctor asks.

He turns and faces the doctor without saying anything.

"Are you okay?" The doctor asks again, but the young man does not reply.

The doctor walks slowly and carefully towards him.

"Okay, whatever you are thinking right now, just pause and evaluate for a second, is it worth it? Am I doing the right thing?"

As he is getting closer, the young man pulls out a kitchen knife to stab the doctor. The doctor swiftly grabs his hand and arm-locks his head. The struggle continues as both bodies move in a tight combat from wall to pillar, then to the doctor's car and finally to the ground. The doctor manages to pin the strange man down to the ground, but the man spits on his eyes. They struggle yet again, this time leaving the knife on the floor, some distance away. As soon as the man is let loose from the doctor's grip, he runs away. The nurses come to help the doctor stand to his feet as they go inside.

"Sorry girls, the new security guard was to commence work tomorrow, so I thought today would just pass with some luck. I guess I was wrong."

"No problem, Sir. We got some retractors and hammer just in case."

He laughs, "nice plan. I will be with you this night.

"Thank you very much, sir."

The doctor calls his wife over the phone and explains everything to her before going inside the bathroom to clean himself up and settle into the night.

At about 6.30am, he leaves for home to prepare and get back to work. And when it is exactly 8.00am, three thugs walk into the reception with a heavily built, pot-bellied man in an arabesque designed kaftan. "Where is the doctor?" the pot-bellied man asks.

"Who are you, Sir?" A nurse confronts.

"Where is the doctor?" The man repeats, ignoring the nurses, he goes to the doctor's office. After a quick search of the hospital premises without finding the doctor, orders for the pharmacy to be ransacked. They storm the pharmacy, breaking the glass partitions and throwing out every drug in it. When individuals from outside notice, they rush to take whatever they could in a serious tussle, clearly showcasing how poverty in the land is seminal to this new struggle for survival. When his pharmacy is already half destroyed, the doctor walks into the compound. As soon as his presence registers, the chaos drastically reduces and individuals with full hands and arms run through the second gate not minding if he cares or not. He walks in, calm and mettlesome to where his drugs have been thrown. The man immediately walks out toward him when a military van of ten soldiers arrives. The man tries to run but is easily grabbed alongside his boys and taken away like a pariah on his way out of the city.

The doctor sits on the stairs of his corridor, just in front of the reception's front door and stares at the sky in deep thoughts. He nods his head periodically as he looks up yet again. "Why has luck been partisan against me? Why?" He continues his wonder and then eventually stands up. "This country is not for me. I'll definitely leave," he concludes.

XXXXXXXXXXXXXXXXXXXXXXXXXXX

Hours later, an unconscious, chubby woman is brought to the hospital and, as always, with an accompanying crowd. The doctor runs to the reception to control the situation. She is taken to the ward and two women narrate the incidence.

"It is her husband o! If you see how he beat her eh, doctor, it was a beating never to forget," the first woman reports.

The second woman adds, "we do not know what happened o! All we started hearing was ehgbim! Ehgbim!" She continues to narrate with very active body gestures, "he nodded her on the face five times, she fell from the stairs and he still rushed her to continue his beating."

The doctor listens in shock to even imagine how heartless this individual is. Her mouth is partially open with blood stains around it and also showing the loss of her incisors. The nurses get busy with intravenous fluids, strong analgesics, sedatives and taking of blood samples.

"So, where is her husband now?" He asks.

"He ran away when we started gathering."

"Interesting!" He walks into the reception to meet the police officers, one of whom asks, "are you the doctor?"

"Yes, officer," he replies.

"We've caught the man. He's in our custody now. Please continue with treatment. We assure you that he must pay every dime."

The doctor laughs, "I don't work based on assurances."

"Oga doctor," the policeman calls, "we are officers of the law and as we have said, we will make sure it happens."

"No, sirs, with all due respect, I will not accept that. This woman is also pregnant and obviously there's no life in her womb. We have checked and no heartbeat. We will need to also evacuate.

Her treatment for now will cost forty eight thousand naira, and as you can see, my pharmacy has been ransacked today. The reality surrounding me now does not even warrant me to be ascetic. This is real. Let her at least pay twenty seven thousand naira upfront for today and tomorrow. I will go and look for the drugs myself. If by tomorrow nothing happens, the relatives can come and carry her. I will not be interested."

One of the officers walks up to him. "Oga doctor, here is my card. Just go ahead and mark my words, you'll get your full pay."
"I'm sorry, officer. This is not enough. It will never be enough."
The other police officer grumbles, "and he was with another woman just after beating his wife to a pulp."
The police officers go outside, rally round the people and tell them about the doctor's position, meanwhile the doctor stops any form of investigations due to unavailability of funds. The mood converts from a noisy one to a saturnine

serenity as the people come in batches to beg him to no avail. Phone calls are made and after some time the deposit is paid for treatment to continue.

The police officer walks in again. "Oga doctor! You see! Please go ahead with treatment. Even if it is hundred thousand naira, it'll be paid for," he boasts.

"Oga officer, once bitten, twice shy. I've been bitten more than fifty times, so right now, I am dead shy. I have started resuscitation and that is the best I can do for now. Once the balance is brought, we shall continue but if nothing comes in by tomorrow, they can take her and go." For the next ten minutes, the officers try all manner of persuasion to no avail, then they leave.

CHAPTER 9

The next morning and it is exactly 6.00am, just when the doctor wakes up from bed, his phone rings. Nurse Medinat speaks.

"Sir, the policemen are here o! They want to speak with you," she reports.

"Okay, hand your phone over to them."

"Good morning, doctor," one of the police officer speaks.

"Good morring, officer. What is so urgent that you come to the hospital this early?"

"Sir, the man placed under our custody escaped in the early hours of this morning."

"What!" The doctor's scream wakes his wife. "How?"

"It is a long story, doctor. We just came to tell you to continue treatment. Don't be discouraged."

"And who will pay? The Police?"

"Oga doctor! Take us for our word."

"In Nigeria? Word here is as heavy as the nitrogen gas. Please, officer, I am closing this case in my hospital. The relatives will come and carry her to wherever they can continue treatment."

"Oga doctor, stop this. You swore an oath o."

"Yes, officer, the oath is meant to save lives, not to be used as a weapon against me. It's an oath for service, not for self-destruction. Why do you people even care? You've not done your own end of the bargain and you are here sweating over mine?"

"No, doctor, don't even insult us…"

The doctor, not minding the continued conversation hisses and hangs up the phone, immediately sending an SMS to Nurse Medinat to ensure that the patient is taken away by relatives before he arrives the hospital.

Later in the day, he walks into an empty hospital with only the nurses present. He sits for several hours and just when he's about to leave, three men walk into the reception.

"Good morning, sir. We believe you are the doctor here," one of them says.

"Yes, sir. How may I help you?"

"We are from the ministry of environment, sir."

One of them hands over an official form to him.

"Wonderful! Just when I thought I've seen it all!"

"Can we see in your office, sir?" The man requests.

"Oh no, Sirs, we can see here," the doctor declines. "You see, not only is this form far from being pellucid, it as well lacks pungency."

"Oga doctor, speak normal English, so that we know if you're insulting us or not."

"Okay, so the ministry of environment is taxing me for gaseous emission and pollution? Is this for real? Am I running a refinery here?"

"See o, oga doctor, this is not us, it is the government. There's nothing we can do about it."

"You guys in this place are really stretching my tenacity. I am learned, you know, and I know what I am doing. I cannot and will not pay any gaseous emission and pollution fee."

"Good! Then the next time we come here, we will close down this place."

The doctor laughs. "And who gave you that authority when you are neither the ministry of health nor the ministry of commerce and Industry? If I am a defaulter, then take me to court, which is the right thing to do. So, the next time you come here, what I will be expecting from you is a court order, nothing more, nothing less." He looks up the ceiling in their presence. "Nawa o! This country is just terrible! I am fed up." They stare at each other and then walk out in annoyance.

Immediately they leave, a set of thirty three people brings a chronically ill patient with a swollen abdomen. The nurses rush to help the patient and the doctor comes around and examines him, asking two of the patient's relatives some questions before going back into his office to put down some notes. He comes back and gives the nurses some instructions while returning to the patient's bed. He orders every relative to move out, he sits on a plastic chair, waiting for the nurses to come around. After a while, the doctor stands up, leaves the ward and is about leaving the hospital premises to abandon the patient with liver cirrhosis when the relatives run around him and as usual beg for a long time. They insist but he persists and, more strikingly, he never utters a word to them. When they notice his seriousness and rigidity, eleven thousand naira is immediately raised. He goes back to the nurses and inquires the total amount for the management of the patient. Being twenty five thousand naira, he opts to go ahead and start treatment. Everything is set and the paracentesis is carried out.

The next day, the doctor comes in at his usual time to resume work when he meets two men standing in front of his door.

"Good morning, sirs," the doctor greets.

"Good morning, doctor," one of the men responds.

"How may I help you?" He asks.

"We are from the board of internal revenue."

He laughs in self-pity, "okay, follow me, please." They follow him to his office and all is seated while the one who seems to act in taciturnity presents their official form to the doctor, and he reads it.

"Thirty thousand naira for sign boards and forty thousand naira for business presence? I thought I had paid the local government for sign boards and adverts."

"Yes, doctor. That is for local government, but this is going to the state."

"Whew!" He sighs, breathing out hard. "Well, as you can see, no patients."

"Yes doctor, but this place is busier when you compare it to other places."

He laughs, "are you people taking data everyday on our businesses?"

"You never know, doctor. Okay, just bring fifty thousand naira and we will go."

"I don't have fifty thousand naira, and besides, I'll have to treat a whole lot of people to get that amount."

"Oga doctor! This tax is for the whole year o. Okay make it forty thousand naira last. That is the best we can do for you."

The doctor stands up, goes to his bag, counts some notes and drops them on the table.

"This is twenty five thousand naira which is all that I have gathered since the last two weeks. I cannot push it. I can't get more anywhere, so are you taking it?"

They look at each other shaking and nodding their heads in silent communication and then, the one who doesn't speak takes the money as the other immediately signs on a receipt.

"Don't worry doctor, we've been hearing about all that is happening to you. Just hang on. Trust me; you have the people's approbation already. They speak highly of you," the one who writes the receipt says, as he hands it over.

The doctor nods in disbelief then replies, "Thank you, sir."

"No, doctor! I mean it. You're well respected here. Don't mind what is happening. We are all struggling to survive, and that is why things are the way they are," he avers.

"Thank you once again," the doctor replies as they stand up and shake hands.

As soon as the men leave, a patient comes in. "Good morning, sir," she greets.

"Ah! Madam Cecelia Johnson, how are you?" He replies.

"Fine, doctor, very fine!" She converses with great pleasure.

"You've been consistent and I like that." She smiles, frequently nodding her head in a tractable fashion, "Yes doctor, anything you say o! It is my life and my marriage."

He bursts into laughter, going through her folder and giving out gestures of a positive impression. "You've been doing well, from 38.8 to 32.3 in ten weeks and then to $29.7Kg/m^2$ in another ten weeks. You are officially not obese, but still overweight. You need to continue your regimen. So, any complain?"

"No, doctor! I can only speak of improvement o! No more seizing breaths at night, no more joint pains, chest pains, audible heart beats and weird breathing."

"Aha! I am happy for you. Even from your body. It is very obvious you've reduced."

"Yes, doctor, but I still have irregularities in my menstruation."

"Okay, Madam Cecelia."

He writes down some detail on her folder, writes again on a drug prescription book, tears the copy he writes on and gives to her. "Our pharmacy has been ransacked, so you can go outside and get these drugs. You can only find them in Chukwudi wholesale store or check Greenfield Medications, just along the express."

She gets on her knees, "thank you, doctor. God will reward you abundantly."

"Stand up Madam Cecelia," he says as he tries pulling her up. "It is our Job to see our patients get well."

"Thank you, doctor. I heard of what happened to your pharmacy. They are just hoodlums from the opposition party."

"But what has that got to do with me? I am just minding my business here and I have tried to avoid any form of political or social association with partisan goals."

"Yes, doctor. Mr. Correct was beaten up from an order perceived to come from the governor himself or someone close to him and they came here to warn you not to attend to him, which you obeyed until it was already too late before you changed your mind. The thugs standing for the opposition aren't happy."

"But is that my fault? Armed mobile policemen came here to threaten me, what should I have done?"

"Doctor, they are not policemen o! They are thugs in police uniform."

"Imagine! Were those guys thugs?"

"Yes, sir."

"So thugs can wear police uniform and cause mayhem?"

"Yes sir, even military uniform too, it is a common problem here."

"Anyway, they still pose so much danger to me. Thank you, Madam Cecelia, for the information."

"Thank you, doctor." She leaves for the next patient to come in.

"Good morning, doctor," the next patient greets.

"Good morning, Mrs. Comfort Emmanuel. How are you?" He asks with a straight face.

"I'm fine, doctor. Sorry, I have not been coming for my checkup."

"Oh no! Don't be, you categorically stated in your testimony in church that you would not be coming for checkup, since the doctor has become the devil's advocate now."

"It's not like that, Sir."

"It is like how? I don't really get it. Is the knowledge of medicine from the devil? Why are we always the bad guys when you give testimonies in church? Despite all we did to salvage your situation, imagine the things you said, all in the name of testimony."

"Doctor, I was so overwhelmed."

"Yeah, madam Comfort, for someone coming out of depression, I was really impressed."

"I am sorry, doctor," she pleads while going down on her knees.

"No, no, no, no! Please don't do that. I am not God. I'm here to serve you and that's exactly what I'll do. But if only you people could appreciate us more, you'd understand the importance of our efforts, and maybe, just maybe, this work would be a lot easier for us, the doctors, and also for you the patients. I guess you waited for the symptoms to surface again before coming here, right?"

"Something like that, doctor."

He shakes his head in pity. "It's okay. So, tell me what the problem is."

The consultation continues for the next thirty minutes. He writes some prescription for her and she leaves, smiling and happy.

He goes to the ward to examine the improvement of the patient with liver cirrhosis who came the previous day. He is very impressed with the patient's improvement and the way he interacts with his family members, but the abdomen has started swelling up again. The doctor informs them of his improvement and the need for another episode of drainage before he goes home the next day. Everyone is happy and full of thanks as he leaves them with the patient.

About three hours later, a twenty four year old woman comes to the hospital in serious abdominal pain. She is quickly taken to the amenity ward and the doctor's attention called. As soon as he arrives, he notices that the part of her wrapper covering her pelvis is soaked with blood.

"Madam, what happened? Tell us the truth because your life is in danger," the doctor enquires.

She speaks in difficulty because of the excruciating pain. "Abortion! Abortion! It's abortion o! I did abortion!"

"Okay, madam, where and how?" The nurses already come around trying to give her some injections.

"My husband! My husband! Please don't tell my husband o! My husband. I did it in the chemist! In the chemist o!"

"When, madam?"

"Yesterday."

The mobile ultrasound machine is set up, a scan quickly done while both the film and scan report are printed out.

"Are you here with any cash?" The doctor asks.

"Yes, doctor. Yes o!"

"But, madam, your husband will need to know. If really you don't want that, then a relative should be here with you. Tell us who to call. We cannot treat you alone here. What if something happens to you?" "No, doctor! No o!"

"Then you should go elsewhere, madam."

"Please, doctor! Please o! I don't want to die! I don't want to die o."

"Okay, give us a number."

"Okay, doctor. Check my phone. Call Solomon. He is my brother. Please o, doctor, help me! Help me! Help me! Help me o!" She speaks in distress with laboured breathing, while the doctor instructs the nurses to call her brother and tell him to come over, immediately. She is then taken on a stretcher to the procedure room. The tools are quickly set up for evacuation and, in no time, the procedure commences. He is assisted by another nurse as the evacuation is carried out.

After the procedure, the doctor pulls off his mask, head gear and apron, washes up and goes to his office to take down some notes when his door is knocked. A nurse comes in.

"Sir, Solomon, her brother is here, but with two policemen."

He gets up and goes to the reception.

"I hope all is well, officers."

"We also hope so, doctor. You are under arrest for carrying out an abortion on a married woman, without the consent of her husband."

"Interesting! And who is responsible for this arrest?"

"Me, sir," her brother, Solomon, alerts as his tawdry chain swings like a pendulum on his neck.

"Okay, one minute gentlemen."

The doctor goes back to his office, takes the folder and checks a little box lying in abeyance on his table. He gets hold of a few complimentary cards and leaves. He gives the nurses a few instructions before following the officers to the station.

In the station, the doctor writes down his statement while the boy who carries a sodden trunk writes his.

"You see doctor! This is a case of abortion which is a very serious one. You have to be under our custody while we carry out further investigations. The doctor reacts in laughter much to their embarrassment.

"I guess you officers are doing your job, so keep up with the good work. Nevertheless, it is paramount you begin your investigations with presenting evidences. I have a scan result which shows products of conception even before I carried out my evacuation. This is indicative of an already done abortion elsewhere. Mine was to evacuate and save her life. What I see now is that I am being arrested for doing my job and saving a life and the so-called upholders of the law have decided to be adamant on the case because they anticipate a little change from this situation," the doctor speaks boldly.

"Hey! Hey! Doctor, don't make us yell at you. Which change? Don't they evacuate during abortion? You evacuated, a relative reported, her husband has not consented. Let us do more findings first, Mr. Man," a police officer yells.

"It is okay. Take your time, but remember, we owe it to our patients to work in confidentiality. Moreover, she's an adult and that was exactly her request.

We are not here to be moral judges or prefects of morality. We are only here to save lives. Can I at least call my lawyer?"

"Yes, sir, but stay here so that we hear all you say."

"Thank you."

The doctor makes a call indicating the region and exact location of the station while also mentioning the names of the officers at the counter."

"Hey! Hey! Oga doctor, enough! I say enough!" One of the officers yells as the doctor pockets his phone. His wife rushes in with their baby on her back.

"Sweetheart, what is the matter?" she asks.

He explains everything to her, even showing his evidence to her and she gets provoked.

"What nonsense, officer? My husband has clearly done nothing wrong and you know it. You just want money for bail, right?"

"Madam, we will either send you out or make you join your husband in jail," the officer at the counter threatens.

"Jail?" She mocks.

"Jail for what?" The doctor asks furiously. "Is this how rotten this country is now? I am here because I was accused of carrying out an abortion. I have brought out clear evidence to show you it was not an abortion, so what is it again? So I should be in jail while you carry out your investigations? I thought I should be innocent until proven guilty. So if I meet your father on the road and accuse him of assault, you will immediately put him behind bars, is that it?"

"See! Oga doctor, that one nah Hollywood o. If you are in Rome, behave like the Romans. Do you want bail or not? Then you know what to do. You're not behind bars because we reverence you as a doctor o! Abortion is a crime in Nigeria, maybe because you trained abroad, you didn't know. Know it now!"

His wife goes out ranting on top of her voice as she calls a lot of people through the phone. Then two men walk in.

"Well, well, well… Who do we have here?" Mr. Abdulfattai, the president of the clinic association speaks. "I can see our honourable doctor is in trouble. What has happened?"

The doctor smiles at their meddlesome antics and responds, "ask this young man here and ask the police."

"Oga doctor, we are not against you. We are not your enemies. We were just passing by when we heard your predicament," Mr. Lookman encourages.

"I'm in no predicament, Mr. Man," the doctor counters.

"Anyway, please tell us what happened. We will be glad to be of good help to you Sir."

The doctor ignores him and looks the other way.

"Oga doctor! Are we quarrelling? Why picking up a fight where there is none?"

Again, he shuns the man, but this time, looking at the ground.

"Okay, doctor. It seems you are not interested in our help." The president smiles once again, sitting down beside the doctor on the bench as he tries giving the doctor some comfort in a manner which is obviously perfidious. He speaks for a while but with no response from the doctor. Mr. Lookman who stands adjacent them also chips in his contributions from time to time, but the doctor stays mute. Mr. Abdulfattai then pats the doctor's back and the doctor abruptly reacts, looking at the association's president in fervid embarrassment.

"You two should leave now," he requests. His wife walks in. "Who are they, honey?"

"They are the so-called clinic association," he replies.

"Please, leave us alone. Just leave us alone," she yells.

Mr. Abdulfatai stands up immediately "Ah! This one na family affair oh. Okay officers, how much is their bail?"

"Oga, it's only twenty five thousand naira," the police officer behind the counter quickly replies.

The doctor looks at the officer in shock and looks at the dramatic men.

"I am not a party to this nonsense. I repeat, I am not a party to this. I do not give my consent and I clearly am not interested in anyone's help."

His wife whispers into his ears and he sighs in relief while Mr. Abdulfatai continues. "Ah'ah! Doctor, twenty five thousand naira is nothing now! We can help you, just let us and we will do it now."

The station's landline rings and one of the police officers picks, but only says "Yes. Okay. Yes." As soon as the officer drops the phone, he calls Mr. Abdulfatai to the side and whispers, "Oga, just help him pay the money so that he can go."

"No! He has to accept our help," Mr. Abdulfatai replies loudly.

The doctor and his wife sit and whisper to each other, not minding what is going on.

"Oga presido, give us the money now or doctor is going nowhere," the officer warns.

"What is it with you, officer? I will not give you the money until the doctor accepts this help. I can't help someone who doesn't need it," Mr. Abdulfatai restates.

"Exactly!" the doctor's wife angrily responds, "We will never accept help from you."

Solomon, the brother to the patient starts panicking and showing signs of unrest when suddenly the DPO walks in.

"Are you still keeping the doctor here? How dare you? So you make the Nigerian Medical Association officials call to threaten me eh?" He yells at his junior officers.

"Oga, sorry sir, these men here in our front planned it. It is them, sir."

The DPO turns around to face them. "Oga Abdulfatai and Oga Lookman," the DPO calls. "Una enter one chance today. You both have bitten more than you can chew. What is your problem with this law abiding citizen? Why can't you leave the young man to his business? He is the actual doctor and you decide to frustrate him?" The DPO faces his officers. "Oya officers, collect forty thousand naira from them or arrest them. I hate crossing paths with lawyers and doctors in my life. Those people know how to gang up and embarrass someone. Oga Abdul, you are my person but I have to do this."

The two men are taken to the reception and asked to sit on a bench, out of respect. The doctor stands up and thanks the DPO, before approaching the men. "As you can see, I do not need your association. I am well protected, even if your weak association is the enemy, I have strong immunity." He walks out of the station with his wife.

XXXXXXXXXXXXXXXXXXXXXXXXXXXX

Now at home, the doctor speaks with his wife while eating on the dining table. "I hate this country," he laments.
"Oh my husband, don't just start," she responds.
"Sweetheart, forget all these talk, nothing is right anymore. Even those who are supposed to uphold the law equivocate

for selfish gains. Nothing is just right anymore. Some other countries are corrupt as well but there is still this sense of an equipoise reality between good and evil. Not in this God-forsaken country."

"Honey, please stop! Don't let your anger take advantage of you."

"I am not angry, my dear wife. I am only lamenting on the fact that we are finished."

"Sweetheart, stop!" She screams.

"Oh, my dear wife, you sound as if I am committing the crime of apostasy. Just check it, no one is guileless anymore? If you stand for what is right, you're a devil. If you're an advocate of due process, then you're Caesar's robber, from leaders to the grassroots…"

She cuts him short, "hope! All we have is hope and the yardstick to having that is life. Are you still living? Yes, then have hope".

"My dear, if all the citizenry has is hope on the future, then they have no future."

"Relax, my ever passionate husband. Hope can exist anywhere — the deepest tunnel, the darkest corner, the tightest space or the hottest environment. Hope can thrive in all these places and, from your position, you are a lot better than millions of people out there, so you have no reason whatsoever not to be hopeful."

"Hmm! You're always my natural analgesia but poetry won't work this time."

She looks at him seductively and smiles. "Really?"

"Yes, my wife."

"Well, speaking about hope, our website has been ready since two weeks ago."

"Wow! Let me have a look."

"Not so fast, boy!" She softly slaps his hand off her laptop. "I've been sending applications to different medical and health-related NGOs to come and partner with us here, since we do not have the capacity to help these people, but out of the forty three mails, five have responded positively."

"Wow! That is lovely. So, what next?"

"In seven months' time, one from Spain called 'Clean Cuts' has accepted to do free surgeries for three months here, using our facility. The good thing is that they will leave all their equipment here when they go back."

"Jesus! Sweetheart, do you know what that means?" He explodes in Joy.

"Yes, my darling husband. I'm negotiating with the second right now. They'll be here immediately after the first one leaves. They want to work for eighteen months on free cervical cancer check and treatment as well as taking the data."

"That would be great, my dear."

"So, you see, my love, there's hope. We can still help this community no matter what the obstacle may be."

He leaves his seat and kisses her, "oh, my darling. You're truly my Angel with a shining light that renews every minute. I love you so much, honey."

"I love you too, my husband. You have a good heart and I do not want anything, any situation or anyone to change that in you."

"Thank you love, we can now start processing our UK visa."

"WHAAAT! Did you hear all I have been saying at all?"

"Yes, darling. The hospital will still run in good hands, as it helps the people, but what about us? Remember, we are in a country where a young doctor dies of Lassa fever and the health minister blames it on our carelessness. Remember we are in a country where if we, the doctors, stand up to fight for our rights, especially when the system is concerned, the populace is quick to judge us wrongly. Remember, we are in a country where dying for the country is an absolute waste of life and devotion. Remember that our own minister is saying that not every doctor may practice or become a specialist; they will not care if I become a medical tailor or carpenter; worst of it all, if I become a corpse. These same people fly out at the slightest symptom they feel and the docile citizens see nothing wrong with it. It is risky if I continue to live here and it is scary if my family remains here. So, we need to help ourselves too. I have a family to take care of and I have the future of my children to worry about and secure, so we are still leaving darling. We must go."

"Okay, darling, I am excited all the same."

"Yeah! God knows I've tried my best. Just look at the downward trend of what is happening. There was a time when our enemy was the government, then a time when our other colleagues in the health sector started fighting us. Then it evolved to the doctors fighting themselves. Now, it is worst because the patients who are the reason we are doctors in the first place are now fighting us. Meanwhile, the previous trends still continue. Individuals now believe their traditionalists, friends, grandmothers, spiritual leaders and even hear-says, but not the doctor anymore. Things are really bad now. Practicing in this country is no longer interesting. The sour taste is even becoming bitter."

"Oh, sweetheart, take it easy. Life is simply testing you as you reach the zenith; you will still do more wherever you go. Don't ever shorten your hands to influence others positively, so please stay optimistic."

He tickles her as she screams playfully. They stay together on the long chair in the sitting room, leaning on the side of the bed as they navigate their new website.

XXXXXXXXXXXXXXXXXXXXXXXXXXXX

It's the next day and the doctor drives to work, but stops at the late Mr. Correct's bar just to observe the current situation of things, and as soon as he enters the frontal shade extension, a young man hurriedly walks out of the main room in a busy mood, carrying crates of empty bottles while giving instructions. The young man is very familiar to the doctor with notable bodily features, especially his left sided facial scar. The doctor soon identifies him when he eventually tries avoiding the doctor by pretending he is running errands. He rushes back into the main office but the doctor follows. "I am not here to fight you, young man. I didn't even know you are related to Mr. Correct," the doctor says.

The man ignores him, still acting busy. "Now, I know why you attacked me the other day. What happened to your father isn't my fault. I was pressurized and intimidated. I needed to make sure I was fine first. I am really sorry."

The young man hesitates, clearly showing his grudge, then speaks. "He is not my father. He's my trade master. He is supposed to release me today to stand on my own, after serving him for six years."

"Oh my God!" The doctor laments.

"But he is no more today. I understand your hands were tied, but I wish you had made your decision to treat him sooner."

"I am sorry, young man."

The young man gives no reply and after about a minute of silence, the doctor leaves.

As soon as the doctor enters the reception of his hospital, his nurses rush to welcome him.

"Sir, the man with the liver cirrhosis is still very much around. They want to go but are yet to pay their debt."

"This is not an issue. Let him remain here until his financial issue is sorted out. The last thing I need now is stress."

"Sir, he requested to go and wash his system. He said he has an appointment for today to wash it."

"Can you imagine this nonsense? So he has some thirty thousand naira to pay for washing his system but cannot pay my balance?"

"Sir, we have talked to him several times but he is adamant and his relatives have been wanting to see you too."

"Nobody should come near my office. I am very busy today and I am not interested in talking about that. Let them pay and go. Is that understood?"

"Yes, sir."

The doctor walks into his office as the first out-patient walks in.

"Good morning, Hajiya Usman."

"Good morning, doctor."

"How are you this morning?"

"I'm great, thank you. Here is the scan result."

She hands over a sealed white envelope to him. He opens it and reads the document in it.

"Good! Very good, Hajiya. I am happy there's no sign of infection. We had to take our prophylaxis seriously and it worked," the doctor comments.

"Thank you, doctor," she says. "I've left my husband."

He looks at her soberly. "I'm so sorry for everything, Hajiya. So far as there is life, there is hope. I'll never advice any victim of domestic violence to stay. A man who can hit you can eventually kill you. Assaulting you till you had a miscarriage was a red flag."

"Exactly, doctor," she agrees. "I had to, though our culture tells us to stay and endure."

"The oldest and broadest culture on earth is humanity and since I don't hold anything against it, I will never be at home with some of these cultures." He goes further to adumbrate the doses of her take-home treatment and encourages her. "I'm happy you listened to me. So, what business have you started?"

"I sell second-hand clothes. I travel to Kano to get them and then sell here. Despite the economic hardship, the business isn't bad, especially children's wear."

"That's good, Hajiya. Economic independence is what the African woman should strive for. In most cases, the Nigerian woman is stuck in the trap of domestic violence because they have nowhere else to run to and are handicapped financially to pick up the pieces and move on."

"Yes, doctor."

"How about your children?"

"They are with me."

"Do you have sons?"

"Yes, doctor. I have three of them and a daughter who's my first child."

"That's good. My next point is very important. Teach your sons to value and respect women. Take this training seriously and don't give any chance for slip-ups, from courtesy to gentleman behaviour toward women and, above all, how to love and keep a woman. How old are they?"

"Who, doctor, my sons?"

"Yes, Hajiya."

"Seven, five and three years old respectively."

"That's good! They're still very young and can be trained. In fact, indoctrinate them to love and appreciate women. Use yourself as a reference point to always bring out that disdain their father created when hurting you and equate it to domestic violence to other women, more emphasis on their potential wives and girlfriends so that it sticks in their heads."

"Thank you very much, doctor. It is a good idea. I've never thought about that."

"Yes. I gave a seminar last week and ninety three women came. I'm working on organizing another one next month."

"Wow! I must attend, doctor. I'll come with three of my friends who are also facing the same problem like I do."

"That's great! Please do. The process of having good men starts from you, their mothers. Instead of spending so much time fighting the men, you can also spare some energy to train the boys under your care to be good men. Women thoroughly teach their daughters to be good wives and even to the point of worshipping the man, but fail completely in training their sons to be responsible and that is why marital chaos still persist in our time."

She laughs, "yes doctor. I like how you said it and I completely agree with you that indoctrinating them is exactly what we should do."

"Finally, and most importantly, you women should learn to protect one another. Stop being a problem to yourselves. You filled out my survey form, right?"

"Yes, doctor."

"Do you know that, out of 341 issues women face, 323 involve their mother-in-laws, their sister-in-laws or both in this community? That's 95%. Also, 266 cases are due to another woman outside the marriage, and that makes another 78%. I have lived here for two years now and I know how women also chase men aggressively, especially married men. I also heard almost every girl below 27 years have the diabolic products used to control the will of men. As much as I still find it hard to believe this, I am seeing how common and popular Garuma products are. Worst of all, is how I see women maltreating their house helps and I can tell you that in the majority of these cases, no living animal would be able to take the pain some of these house helps pass through. Your children, especially your sons see these happenings and naturally learn from them. And you know what? Some of these innocent girls working in these homes are actually the relatives of these women maltreating them. If not a sister's daughter, it is a cousin's daughter and so on. Is this not so unfortunate? You women must also learn to be good mother-in-laws and sister-in-laws and as well, good guardians. Know the limits of your roles in the families of your male loved ones. Don't get too involved in their lives and let their wives be as independent as they should be. Let them be the true managers of their own homes as it ought to be. You women give many problems to yourselves and your own case is no different. Seven sister-in-laws and one mother-in-law against you for the past thirteen years is more or less war, I admire and commend you for surviving this. Now that you've tasted the bitter experience, don't let another woman suffer same. You have three sons, so very soon, you'll be a mother-in-law. Please, take note o." The doctor draws his ear to close his advice.

"Thank you so much, doctor. We are really enjoying you in this place. You're so passionate about your work. You show so much care even in your professionalism. This is unique. We don't enjoy this from other doctors around here. Thank you so much again."

"You are welcome, Hajiya. In addition to our clinical treatments, anything that will ameliorate the sufferings of the people here is what I'm after."

"Thank you so much, doctor. You're a blessed one! I've seen it on your palms. Asides wealth, you'll be a man of global influence. I'm not joking, I mean it, doctor."

He smiles. "Hmm…. Thank you. So, you have the gift of chiromancy?"

"What's that, doctor?"

"The practice of telling what will happen in the future by looking at the lines on someone's palms."

"Oh, I thought it was called palmistry."

"Yes, that also," he agrees. "Thank you for your kind words."

"Thank you too, my doctor." She stands up and leaves.

The doctor is already at his car door, about to enter when a black SUV swerves into the hospital compound. He stops to observe as a woman is brought out of the car, wrapped from head to toe with three wrappers.

"Hello doctor," a young man calls. "We've brought Mrs. Kayode to you."

"For what this time? Two weeks ago, you took her away against medical advice, not even giving us the benefit of the doubt to attempt our treatment plan."

The doctor moves close to the patient and opens the wrapper to see a stressed face having different colours.

"Jesus!" He exclaims. "What happened to her?"

"She used a medicated soap to bathe, which severely irritated her skin. She has been screaming intensely and just stopped a few minutes ago."

"I'm sure you are not coming directly from home."

"Does that even matter, doctor?"

The woman starts groaning again as she writhes in agony, infecting everyone around with fear, even to the doctor. "Please take her to a tertiary health facility. Go to Federal Medical Centre in the capital. I cannot handle this case anymore." Three men immediately drop to their knees and plead. "Please doctor, we know you can help her. We've heard so much about your new tricks on this kind of skin problem."

"Please, my brother, get up. I am the professional here and if I say I cannot help, then I truly cannot. There's really nothing I can do for her now. This is for her own good and even the risk you are asking me to take is bad for me because if anything goes wrong, I'll be held responsible and I know you will ensure of that. Please go and see a specialized doctor." Suddenly, three motorcycles carrying three women arrive at the entrance of the hospital compound. The women come down and run straight to the doctor and join the unpleasant begging choir, "please, doctor, ejo! Please, we're begging you. Forgive us for not trusting you, sir. Help us."

"No, please," he refuses. "This has nothing to do with my ego or vengeance. Her situation has exacerbated. She's worse now. How do you expect me to treat this case?"

The doctor turns around and faces his nurses. "Besides, I've never seen or handled such a case as severe as this before." He faces the pleading women again. "It is obvious she's been bleaching her skin for decades and using more than one harsh method. Please, I'm also begging you, go to a big hospital in the capital city," he directs.

While they deliberate, the female patient continues to groan in pain and suddenly throws off every piece of clothing wrapping her body until she is eventually completely naked, exposing her worn-out skin, slacked with lots of stretch marks and pruritic lesions, all making her skin resemble a dirty squeezed wet paper. She runs around naked screaming while the men chase after her. The doctor quickly goes back to the reception and comes outside wearing a pair of gloves and holding two syringes. She gets captured and immobilized. "Doctor, help us, please! Help this woman!" one of the men screams.

"Yes, I will, but the best way to help her is to send her to a dermatologist. I'm here with sedatives. I'll inject her to calm her down, then you should use the time to get her to the capital city before she recovers. There's nothing more I can do."

"No, doctor. We need admission. We know you have the cream. We don't have enough now but I swear with my life and that of my unborn child that we will pay you completely. We know you are scared of debt. We will pay, doctor. Please, give her the cream with your usual injections. Please, doctor, help us."

He ignores the man's plea and is about giving her the injection when the other man slaps it off his hand. It falls to the ground and he crushes it with his right foot. "Doctor, please, we don't want this. We want treatment."

The doctor gets frustrated, starring at them in rage. "Please take her now before it's too late. I cannot and will not do anything. It is beyond me, I'm sorry."

He walks quickly back to the hospital and rushes to his office and locks the door after entering. Two of the men follow and as soon as they get there, try to open it but cannot. They shout, bang at it and throw so many abusive words insulting him and his hospital. They go about screaming, insulting the nurses and even the patients around. One of them goes to the front door and urinates there. The chaos continues, prompting the police to come in, to rescue the situation. The men are arrested while the sick woman is taken off. The doctor exhales in his office and speaks in a low voice, "God help me. I'm getting frustrated. I'm tired, I'm so tired."

XXXXXXXXXXXXXXXXXXXXXXXXXXXX

It's the next day and there is a knock on the door.

"Who is it?" The doctor asks.

"It's me, Hadiza, sir. We have another serious case waiting sir," Nurse Hadiza reports.

"Have you prepared them to see me?"

"Yes, sir."

"Okay, let them in."

A woman and three men walk in as nurse Hadiza drops a folder for the doctor.

"Morning, doctor," one of the men greets. "Remember us? I'm Mr. Audu Paul and this is Lookman Suleiman. We are both officials of the clinics association."

"Oh yes! I know." They shake hands.

"So, is she your relative?" The doctor asks.

"No, doctor," Audu answers, "she has been in our clinic for the past three days now and her situation isn't getting better."

The second man, Sule, adds, "she has been complaining of severe shoulder pain on her left side for the past 3 weeks. She's always weak and tired. Normally, she stays in her shop from 9am to 7pm, but now there's no stamina to last till afternoon, and since she came to the hospital she hasn't used the toilet. Her case is very complicated for us, which is why we brought her here."

The doctor smiles, "I appreciate your will to do the right thing. You should have just written a referral letter to me and I'd gladly acknowledge it. You shouldn't have stressed yourself coming along," the doctor says.

"We know that, doctor," Audu replies. We just wanted to make sure she is well attended to."

The doctor smiles again, "thank you for your concern over your patient. She's in good hands now. I'll take it from here."

Audu and Sule look at each other, "what are you trying to say, doctor? Are you asking us to leave?" Audu asks and the doctor responds in bewilderment, "it is against medical etiquette for a health officer to be present when another is performing his duty. It's either he's monitoring the other one or stealing from his knowledge. We don't do that to each other, unless colleagues tackle a case together."

Sule answers, "yes, doctor. That is what we want, to tackle this case together."

"No, sir, first of all, we are not colleagues, and secondly, you said you referred her here. So please, I beg you in the name of God, kindly allow me do my job."

The two men look at each other, hiss and leave, banging his door after them. The man who's left is her nephew who is present to help with the interpretation. After about ten minutes of asking several questions, the doctor carries out a physical assessment of the affected shoulder, comparing it to the other, while assessing surrounding muscles as well. He comes back to his seat, writes and continues his questioning.

"Does she carry load on that particular shoulder for a long period of time?" he asks her nephew.

The boy interprets the question in their local dialect. She answers in the same dialect and he answers the doctor in English. "No sir, but when she was in Ado Ekiti three years ago, in her son's place, a wardrobe fell on her back and both shoulders were affected. After taking traditional herbs for three weeks, the pain left her, but two weeks ago, the left shoulder started hurting again."

"Thank you for that information. What about vomiting and some signs of convulsion?"

"No, doctor. I've never noticed it and she said she has never suffered from any of them?"

"What is the colour of her urine?"

"It is normal colour, sir."

"What is normal colour of urine to you?"

"It's like light yellow, sir."

"Have you noticed any changes in the urine colour of late?"

"No, sir."

"What about when the symptom started?"

"Yes sir, the first 5 days of the beginning of the pain."

"How was the colour?"

The woman speaks for a long time and the boy interprets, "In general, sir, she cannot really say."

"Okay, look around and tell her to point at any colour closest to the colour of her urine at that time."

She looks around and observes. After a while, she points at a dark brown material on the window."

"Hmm! Almost like tea-colour," the doctor observes. "I can see that her skin is not uniform in texture, appearance and hygiene. Does she suffer from any skin disease?"

"Yes, doctor. For the past three years now." "And what is she doing about it?"

"She's taking some tablets, sir."

The woman reaches for her bag and brings out a card of tablets. The doctor collects it and reads aloud slowly, "Medroxyprogesterone acetate." He writes on the folder in his hand. After writing further, he explains to them the need to do an ECG and some blood tests. He makes them understand the effect of the progesterone drug on the woman, especially as it affects her serum potassium content. He goes further to tell them she will be admitted for close monitoring and finally recommends additional management in physiotherapy. He becomes even more firm in the kind of diet she may have to stick to, especially if the blood test confirms his initial diagnosis.

"The diet must consist mostly of any leafy vegetable, raw tomatoes, oranges, bananas, avocados or coconut water," the doctor recommends. He calls out for Hadiza, hands the folder over to her and they all leave. He goes out to stretch his legs around the compound when Audu rushes to him.

"You may have the knowledge and skill but not the power. So is it the recommendations of some avocados and coconut water that is making you feel like a superman?" Audu asks discourteously.

The doctor gives a lugubrious looks. "You have no right to read the folder. You're here as a patient relative and nothing more."

"Of course, you even referred to me as a health officer, right?"

"Oh, please educate me, my friend. What are you, a doctor?"

Audu laughs, shaking his head as he walks away. The doctor stumps angrily and walks to his nurses.

"So you now let relatives read patients' folders?" Come to my office now! Angela, you as the receptionist should guard the folders here with all jealousy."

The nurses walk in a line trembling behind him as they enter inside his office. "What's wrong with you? Why can't you be smart for once? Patients' folders are confidential documents. They are evidences to the things we do here. You all know these things," he shows his dissatisfaction. "I'm tired. I'm so tired. Please don't add to those already giving me stress."

They genuflect. "We are sorry sir. It will not repeat itself."

He looks at them with his fading anger. "You can go," dismissing them. After about ten minutes, Hadiza returns. "I'm sorry, sir. I cannot find Samson's folder. I've searched around but couldn't find it."

The doctor looks at her angrily. "Do you know he is due for discharge today?"

"Yes, sir. I just cannot explain it."

"Get out of here!" He screams at her as she hastens out of the office. Almost immediately, a man comes in.

"Good morning, doctor," the man greets. "I am papa Samson. Thank you for all your assistance. He's doing very well now. You're a miracle worker."

"No, sir," the doctor replies in humility, "we thank God for everything. I guess you're ready to go."

"Yes, doctor."

"Great! Just pay your balance with the nurses. And please ensure you still go to the Federal Medical Centre in the capital city. Thyroid crisis for a thirteen year old boy is a bad prognostic factor of the disease."

"Thank you, doctor."

The man goes out and after about three minutes, there is a loud altercation in the reception. The doctor refuses to go out, but when he hears Angela scream, he quickly rushes out, "what's the problem here?" He asks.

"This useless he-goat slapped me," Angela reports, pointing her finger at Papa Samson. The doctor looks at the man in surprise. "Papa Samson, why? You cannot just come here and assault my staff like that," the doctor confronts. The man grumbles before speaking.

"They told me I'm to pay seven thousand five hundred naira. I asked them to show me where it is written."

The doctor gets furious, "but right from the outset, you knew that was your balance. You begged me on bended knees, remember? You paid seventy five thousand naira instead of eighty two thousand five hundred naira, remember?"

The man looks at the doctor. "That's mouth o! That's just mouth and words, doctor. Show us where you wrote it."

"No, we won't. It's a confidential document and we will give you receipt after payment. That's all you should be concerned about."

"Doctor, I'm warning you, just respect yourself. Respect yourself o!"

"What nonsense!" The doctor is enraged "What the hell! If you guys don't want me to be in this town, just say it and I'll leave, but don't come here and be frustrating me. The fact that you're emphasizing on this folder issue clearly means you stole it. Bring back the folder and pay our money or else, Samson, your son is going nowhere."

The man also raises his voice, "if you're a doctor, try it! Foolish man! Try it."

The man's wife comes out of the ward also shouting, "all these fake hospitals with dishonest doctors, God will punish all of you. You're sending us to Federal Medical Centre and you still want to collect more money. God will punish all of you, bastards!" At this point, the doctor knows what he is up against as this is clearly a family gang up, a strategy they have adopted so as not to pay their outstanding fee.

Mrs. Samson tries to leave with her son when the nurses rush to stop her. Seeing this, the man comes to the doctor and holds him by the neck as he shouts "Release my son! I say release my son!" The hospital's security officer comes to the doctor's rescue. The argument goes on and the tussle continues. The security officer overpowers the man, taking him outside and restricting him from getting in. The doctor sights some of the elders who begged for the admission of the boy and asks, "my elders, why are you all quiet now? Didn't we agree you pay the initial fee and pay the rest later? This family always owes me every time they come here. I refused but you did something by advocating for them. Please do something now."

"Oga doctor, there's no money in the country, please bear with us. We are sorry. Please, just let them go. There's nothing we can do also."

Mr. Samson comes back in with three other huge men but the doctor intercepts their movements immediately. "No need for more trouble," the doctor gives in. "You can go with your son." The man takes his family away, succeeding by a dint of extreme violence. The doctor watches in disdain as he relishes on the firsthand experience of recidivism. He comes to the nurses and queries them, "this is your fault. See how you've allowed an idiot run afoul of this hospital. You have until the next hour to find the folder and you should all report in my office after your shift."

Moments later, the patient with liver cirrhosis starts gasping for air. Resuscitating equipment is set, a gastric lavage is done and the oxygen cylinder is placed for the man to breathe. After about fifteen minutes of running around, the man gives up. The doctor comes out of the ward and informs the relatives who are outside the hospital premises. One of them asks about taking the corpse away but the doctor reminds them of the bill of sixteen thousand naira they owe. Series of begging begin, compounded with arguments. The doctor leaves them in anger and goes into his office. Fifteen minutes later, one of the nurses rushes in and reports, "Sir, some men are here and it seems they are performing burial rites on the man o."

"How do you mean?" He asks.

"The corpse has been wrapped in white clothing and they are praying in front of it in the Islamic way."

"So?" He asks curiously.

"Sir, this is bad o. What this means is, after their prayers, they will leave the corpse for us and go. We will then be responsible for the dead body from now on."

"What!"

The doctor springs up from his chair as he rushes to the scene of prayers with the nurse. He tries calling out on the praying men but they do not heed to his distraction. 45 seconds after the prayers, not even one of them says a word to him, despite his persistence to talk to them. They walk out of the hospital and together with the women outside, they all leave. The doctor makes several calls with disappointing results. He reaches out to some of the traditional leaders he knows but they all let him know there is nothing that can be done. He reaches out to some community personalities but encounters similar result. He finally submits to the eventuality and calls out for his nurses and they have a brief meeting about how to bury the abandoned body. He makes more calls and engages in different negotiations. Finally, he comes to an agreement with the diggers and the custodians of a particular cemetery. A Peugeot pick up van arrives with four men who pick up the body as he joins them to the burial site. Digging is immediately done; the body is placed in the hole and covered. He counts thirty five thousand naira and gives the men, giving six thousand naira to the custodians of the cemetery. He hires a bike and goes back to the office deeply frustrated.

Now in his office, he gets even angrier and begins to destroy things while screaming. He pushes the fridge down, flings the files on his table, breaks the lamp stand and brings down the examination bed, still screaming. The noise from the chaos in his office is so audible that those in the reception can hear it loud and clear to the extent, it scares every woman listening.

"Is this how reduced I've become?" He asks himself. "Oh lord, why me? What have I done to deserve this inveterate hostility?" He walks to the middle of his office and falls to his knees, holding his face firmly with his two hands, looking up and screaming.

"I'm messed up! I've been brought so low to this obloquy, why? Why?" He laments out loud, influencing the nurses in the reception to cry as well. Patients' relatives around are not left out as the infective atmosphere from the smoke of his mood catches up with them; evident by the swift change of sadness enveloping everyone as they fall into a sobriety. One of them even confesses, "this doctor has been so good to us. He does not deserve this. We are wicked in this town, very wicked."

Another adds, "I'll curse all these people if he leaves us. He has been a blessing to us. I know the people he has brought back to life from the brink of death. Let's go and encourage him."

Two women and a man walk to his door which is locked but does not stop them from encouraging him through the barrier from the outside as they talk to him in the inside. At a point he seems quiet, only to pour out another outcry again. "I hate this town! I hate this town so much. I'll leave before I'm deracinated," he cries on.

The people look at each other in fear and beg him more. Neighbours begin to gather, the women grinding, the shop keepers and the mechanics around come to the hospital vicinity in depressed moods as they attempt to reach out to him. But the more they attempt, the more he screams and cusses. At a point, he punches the walls of his office, banging the windows and severally throwing the examination bed to the ground; this goes on, three more times and then he finally stops. More people join in the begging, encouraging him in their own ways, even the three patients he has in the wards cry to the heavens for the doctor to stay calm and be strong. The nurses are so scared, holding each other and shading tears as their body fidgets to every terrible sound produced from his office. The scene he creates eventually diffuses around the neighbourhood and those affected sink into a sober mood to share in his pain and fear of what may come next.

After about thirty minutes of tranquillity, he comes out with a dejected outlook and asks his nurses calmly, "have you seen the folder?"

They look at themselves in fear without a reply. He yells at them, "HAVE YOU SEEN THE FOLDER?" They nod in a positive response as Hadiza hands it over to him.

"Where did you find it?"

"On the ground, near the gate, Sir."

He pauses for a moment and angrily looks at them but talks calmly in a hopeless manner, "you three are fired! After this shift, do not return," faces the receptionist, still talking in the same manner, "Angela, ensure that no folder goes missing again. Hand over to the next set of nurses; let me start planning on hiring someone more dedicated. I'll come back in the evening to sort things out."

He walks to his car absent minded as he gives no attention to the patients' relatives and neighbours around who try to give him comfort and the pleas from the nurses who just got fired.

CHAPTER 10

While in the office, writing, nurse Medinat rushes into the room.

"Sir, the Ministry of Health officers are here," she announces.

The doctor stands up, adjusts his lab coat and steps out to meet an invasion of press men and heavily armed, masked policemen. Just as he's trying to come to terms with what is happening in a very slow rate, Dr. Hasi walks up to him and announces, "all the nurses, move to this side," pointing to his left. "Introduce yourselves and tell us where you trained." Starting from Nurse Medinat to the third nurse, they introduce themselves, while the doctor looks around still in shock. Dr. Hasi continues in great passion and at the top of his voice while the cameraman and correspondents focus on him. "I hate mediocrity," Dr. Hasi speaks with contempt. "I hate quackery in my life. I take this business of human lives very seriously. Here is a doctor, a qualified one for that matter, dealing with quacks. He has been stubborn, despite our warnings. He still romances the system of quackery. I will not take this! We will not allow this nonsense to continue here. Are you allowed to do this in your state?"

"Yes, we are allowed to," the doctor replies in a quick reflex.

"Then, you should know that we do not do this in this state. Never!" Dr. Hasi faces the policemen and instructs, "take him! We are going to the capital immediately."

After a few minutes, the doctor smiles and requests to take his phone from his office. They allow him. The doctor goes into his office, takes his phone and comes out to meet them in the reception as Dr. Hasi rants in front of the camera.

"Count yourself lucky because everyone here has begged me to pardon you. Nevertheless, I am closing down this clinic with a seal."

"No need for that, Sir. I am already packing my things. Just give me today to do so," the doctor calmly requests.

Dr. Hasi looks at him in surprise as he signals one of the journalists and both walk to a corner close to his office "You're a journalist, right?" He asks.

"Yes, doctor," the lady in suit answers.

"Are you sure?"

"Of course, doctor."

"Please, give me an opportunity to speak on camera for a fair hearing. Do you believe in a fair hearing?"

"Sure, we do, doctor. I will talk to my boss but be rest assured you will have a chance to speak. I also need to let you know of a little secret," she whispers. "This is all acting. It is an intimidation tactic for you to succumb to whatever demands they want from you. So, you need not bother yourself doctor."

"Okay then, let me play along with the script too. I still need to act my part so that I am not left blank, defeated and condemned as a criminal."

The journalist goes out, while the doctor talks to his wife through the phone. After a series of negotiations, to the strong objections of Dr. Hasi, the journalist agrees and the doctor is summoned outside, just in front of the reception's door for an interview. "So doctor, you've been accused of employing quacks here, what can you say about this?"

"Thank you very much. I appreciate the fact that the ministry is bent on maintaining standards. I am very happy and will always encourage quality, especially when the lives of citizens are involved, but the problem here is the system and I am, unfortunately, a victim and not an offender. When I first came, I opened up vacancies for the nursing job and out of 91 applications, only one is actually a registered nurse. So, where are we going to get these registered nurses? Ship them from other states? The funny thing is we have a school of nursing just at our backyard here but it is either the graduate nurses are not motivated enough to practice, thereby becoming traders like the three neighbours I have on this same street, or due to the very expensive cost of training, most, if not all of them, would prefer larger cities such as

Lagos, Abuja, Akure, Kano, Rivers and even Kaduna instead of settling to work in this small community. So, instead of the ministry to come here and act as a Commando against me or my clinic..." Everyone except Dr. Hasi interrupts with laughter as he continues, "why not do something about the system? You want to ban the importation of rice. It is a good move, but terrible at the same time if you have no plans to boost the local rice production in the country, which is really what the ministry of health is doing right now. Encourage more people to participate in the nursing training program and if possible, give incentives for them to work here. Secondly, all my nurses have trained for at least three years in other peripheral facilities, I didn't train them, I employed them as already trained from elsewhere. So, where has the ministry been all these while? Every hospital here in this community runs with the services of these auxiliaries, Dr. Hasi's inclusive. So, why the singling out of Omega Medical Centre?"

Dr. Hasi tries to challenge him from the background but is objected by everyone around for the doctor to continue. "There are also clinics run by nurses, quacks, so-called trainees with lots of auxiliaries. They, in fact, run the nursing training program as well, so why aren't they arrested all these while? I guess I am a threat or rather a bloody stranger who is also too young to run a health facility in this noble land. Well, I will respect the wishes of the government. If they want me to leave, I will leave. I will not spend my productive years fighting, fighting, fighting and fighting." The doctor now faces Dr. Hasi, "You win!" He turns his face back to the small crowd, "any more questions?"

Dr. Hasi grumbles in the background of the interview, "look at the hospital premise, so much grass."

The journalist asks, "Your surrounding is said to be bushy with grass everywhere, what can you say about it?"

The doctor responds, "oh, so now, the complaint is the grasses in my premises! It is funny how I see something different in the same surrounding you speak of. Nevertheless, cutting grasses is a continuous process and they do not stay at the level you cut them. It is unfortunate you all came when the grasses have supposedly grown, even if I am bad sighted to see what you see."

Everyone laughs as the doctor walks into the hospital. Dr. Hasi unleashes more rants in front of the camera as the doctor's wife sneaks in to meet him in the office. "Darling, how are you?"

"Oh sweetheart! I'm fine. I'm fine, I'm okay, really. I'm fine."

"Sweetheart, I'm happy you're taking it well."

"Yes, love. Do I have a choice?" This is clearly the clinics association's doing. They have won. Now I've grabbed the lesson I was refusing to learn. Nigeria is for everybody, but there are as well land owners even in the Nigeria. It's their land, their business, whether qualified or not, and most importantly, their power. I cannot fight them."

Nurse Medinat rushes in.

"Sir, Nurse Fatimat has collapsed," she reports.

The doctor rushes to the reception where all the nurses are, picks Fatimat up and takes her to the private ward where her vitals are taken and an intravenous fluid administered. All others cry in so much pain, begging the doctor not to give up and leave. After resuscitating the collapsed nurse, he goes back to his office to meets his wife.

"Sweetheart, is she fine now?" His wife asks.

"Yes, love. She'll be."

"So, what next, my love?"

"Isn't it obvious? I am not needed here. The country is just in a total mess right now. We need to leave this place as soon as possible."

"And our website?"

"Yeah, tell the NGOs exactly what happened. If they are still interested in this god-forsaken country, then let them collaborate with the general hospital here. I don't bloody care anymore."

"Honey! I totally agree with you on this one. What about this facility?"

"I'll sell all of it. How long can one stand on one leg? I don't want to end up breaking it. I will also not bow to someone else or allow myself to be bullied, despite being qualified to serve this country in my own capacity. In my own fatherland, I feel like a bastard, I just cannot continue like this anymore. God knows I have contributed my own quota and I am proud of what I have done so far. 4,377 patients, both new and returning, so far, is a good record. So, let's go to the other side of the world and see how far we can go."

"Oh sweetheart. I can't wait, can't wait, can't wait! They kiss and then he goes to the private ward where the nurses are, reveals his next move to their disappointment, while they come together in one heart-felt warm embrace. Nurse Fatimat lies on the bed looking at the sad scene as tears flow nonstop from her eyes.

XXXXXXXXXXXXXXXXXXXXXXXXXXXXX

It is three weeks after the incident. The hospital is locked and its surrounding unkempt. Grasses have already grown back in the vicinity and the background messed up with faeces of different consistency and shapes. The solar panels at the sides of the building have all been dismounted and looted, but the building stays intact with all points of entry heavily locked. A big truck drives in. The doctor comes out from the passenger's seat alongside a friend, while the truck itself comes with three young men in the back.

"So, this is the building, my friend," the doctor points. "This is where Omega Medical Centre operated."

"It's a big place, my friend," the doctor's friend observes. "It's just unfortunate that the people do not value what they have." The doctor opens the lock as everyone goes in. He speaks with the driver and the boys and gives them instructions on how they should pack, before going into his office with his friend.

"Wow! Just look at the facility you have here. You truly invested in this business, my friend."

"My dear, that's how it is for now. I have no regrets either. I've treated thousands of families and thousands of individuals. I think I'm in humanity's good book right now."

His friend pats him on his left shoulder, "Definitely my friend."

There is a knock on the door and the doctor opens it to see the driver.

"What's the problem?" He asks.

"Oga, some people are here to see you. They are preventing us from packing," the driver complains.

"What nonsense!" The doctor reacts and angrily rushes out to meet about forty people, all in a very sad mood. Immediately, he comes out, his mood changes as they come close to beg him.

More than twenty of them get on their knees while the women among them wail, begging him to stay. He informs them of the impossibility of staying and shows them the level of no return he has reached in his decision. One of the men makes a phone call and assures the doctor of a full refund of the money he paid for the packing of his things. Despite the doctor's persistence, the people refuse to back down and by the time he has spent half an hour with them, the compound is full with over one hundred more people. Some complain about how their relatives who were dedicated clients to his hospital had died elsewhere. Some complain about how they are charged about three times more than his price in other facilities. A good fraction of his patients is present as it ignites the softest part of his being.

After some minutes, he looks in surprise as he shares in their pain, even shedding tears without knowing. He looks around to actually notice his own influence in so many lives. He gets so many needy embraces and is pampered with much love but at the same time shaken with supplications and requests to come back to operation. The driver comes to him,

"Oga doctor, what's going on? You didn't tell me we will come for a crying and mourning show. Time is money and we don't have any. If you are no more interested, just pay our balance and we will leave."

One of the men in the crowd comes to him, "Mr. driver, we've gathered fifty thousand naira. How much do you need?"

The doctor comes immediately, "I've paid him thirty thousand naira. He needs thirty eight thousand naira more. Please don't bother about this, I will handle it."

"No, doctor. We will not allow you lose so much money because of us," the man promises and immediately pays the driver who takes his boys and goes back with an empty truck. The doctor looks on, in surprise as his friend walks up to him and says, "You seem surprised."

"Yeah, the same people fighting me to death to avoid paying what is right for me are now the ones gathering money to pay the driver off, on my behalf." He ponders out loud.

"You've told me a lot about your experience here, but from what I see, you're of good standing. The people love you. They've missed you. So I guess there's a missing link somewhere between you and them. Maybe you need to settle down properly to understand them more.

In a short while the place gets more crowded as all the former nurses and auxiliary nurses match to the place in a group. They walk right through the crowd to the doctor and join in the begging. He takes them to the reception where they pour out their minds about how they have missed working with him. While in the reception, a woman and a young boy walk in and when the doctor sees her, he quickly walks up to her for a conversation, while the young man serves as their interpreter.

"Good afternoon ma, you are looking really good," he compliments.

"Good afternoon, my doctor. How are you?" She replies.

"I am fine, and you?"

"I'm doing great. What is this that I'm hearing about you leaving us? Is it because of the few idiots disturbing you?"

"Yes, ma, these few idiots have caused me a lot of problems, significant enough for me to leave. If you remember, you were around when one created his own drama."

"Oh my dear, please do not mind them. They are nothing you should be afraid of and we have all learnt now. We will do everything to protect you here and make you flourish. We need you, we seriously do. See my case, for example. I've gone to the other so-called clinics and hospitals and nothing was done despite taking a lot of money from me, I wonder what would have become of me, if I never met you.

People from neighbouring towns are beginning to know about you, everyone is already embracing you as their own doctor, so please, doctor, don't leave us."

"Okay, ma, I will think about it."

"Thank you, my doctor. Please give it a good thought and consider people like me o. Where would I run to if you leave? I would just die before my time."

"No way! That will never happen." They embrace, she leaves and, immediately, his friend comes to him as he gloats, "that's the fifty four years old woman I shared with you guys on the Whatsapp group."

"The one who came with complaints of myalgia of the sternocleidomastoid muscle?" The friend asks.

"Exactly!" He exclaims in response.

"Is she that woman walking freely and at ease?"

"Yes, my friend."

"So, what was your diagnosis?"

"It was hypokalaemia, secondary to chronic steroid use. We had to treat the hypokalaemia with infusions and diet, then I stopped her from taking the progesterone, with some sessions of massage, before she became okay. I wrote a referral to the dermatologist in the capital and she is taking some alternative drugs."

"Why the dermatologist, was she having any skin issue?" His friend asks.

"Yes, there were some well-circumscribed plaques on one part of her body only, and it was for this reason she was on steroids. I suspected some dermatitis but after she came back from consulting with a dermatologist, lichen simplex chronicus was diagnosed and some topical steroids prescribed."

"I see! And the myalgia?"

"There's great improvement. In fact, the last time we met, during her check-up session, she said the pain had become minimal."

"Great job, bro!"

"Thank you, my friend. You see that man coming in this direction?" He points at a man coming from the entrance. "He was one of those who gave me trouble."

"Then I need to leave you two to trash out your issues," his friend walks away. Papa Samson approaches the doctor's direction and extends his hand for a shake, but the doctor refuses.

"I, in particular, have missed you, my doctor. I truly have."

The doctor laughs, "I hate it when people get facetious like you do now."

"I know you won't believe me and I wish I had listened to you earlier. Samson passed away two weeks ago. We never went to the Federal Medical Centre as you instructed us to, because we were trying to save some money. We felt you didn't really know what you were doing."

The doctor screams, "My God! I'm so sorry about that."

"It's okay, doctor. Can I see you in private?"

"Sure," the doctor leads the man to his office, wipes two dusty seats and they both sit down.

"Doctor," Papa Samson begins. "I'm sorry for all I've done. We are in hard times now and the economy is bad. We, the men, carry the responsibility of the family to ensure it survives and runs well. That is why, sometimes, we just do what we have to do to maintain this survival."

"What an interesting excuse from you! If we all decide to behave like that, civilization will go extinct for the jungle to rule the streets of our dwelling. I can imagine cheating you and later giving you this excuse. Would you understand with me? No matter your explanation, I'll never agree with you. The people here have made it a system not to pay consultation fees and I still went ahead to charge you guys with minimal profits, and funny enough, you all know this. Yet, you come here and act so barbaric and cruel. My generosity has caused me a lot of trouble with my competitors and colleagues, and yet, I get absolutely no encouragement from you. The first time I ever engaged in the bargaining of medical bills is in this town. The first time I've experience being insulted and harassed by my patients is in this town. My blood pressure is gradually rising and you guys have given me a bad taste of my profession. I don't enjoy it anymore, it doesn't interest me like before, I don't feel fulfilled and happy and you still expect me to stay?"

"Sorry doctor, I thought you were leaving because of what the other clinic owners and health officers have done to you."

"Yes, Papa Samson, but that's just a fraction of the reason. Even before that, you people of the town had chased me away with your attitude and ingratitude. I fall mentally ill at least once in three days here and I've developed so much hatred as well. Do you think it's still worth it?"

"Yes, my doctor. Please, doctor, you're a very kind man, understanding and a good Christian. Don't let a few people change who you are and make you neglect the actual people needing your services. Just look around you and you'll see how important you are here. Many have died just because you're not around.

Your methods have exposed a lot of wrong doings perpetrated by the other so-called doctors and health workers. We need you, doctor. Please, don't hate us. If we do not know, now we do. My neighbour who treated his children for malaria and typhoid visited one of the clinics yesterday with the same children for the same reason but ended up paying four times the amount. You're a God-sent here. Please, doctor, don't neglect your calling. I'm begging you in the name of God to consider my request. Also, I owe you seven thousand five hundred naira. I am here to pay double the amount."

"No, Papa Samson., thank you very much. There's no need for that."

"No, sir. I have to pay you, my pastor instructed me to carry out this restitution with you to avoid nemesis."

"So, you had to wait for an unfortunate event and your pastor's instructions before you do the right thing? So you did not regard your doctor, until your pastor told you to do so? You even want to pay double. Wow! No hope for doctors in Nigeria."

"My doctor, no matter what you say or do right now, I'll never get angry with you. I have to give you this money and, please, I beg you in the name of God and your family, accept it."

The man kneels down while the doctor remains standing with each hand resting on its corresponding side of his waist.

After a short while the doctor helps him up. "Stand up, sir, leave my family out of this. I'll accept the money. But for what it's worth, I do not hold anything against you. I've forgiven you since the very day you hurt me."

"Thank you doctor, please, I'm begging you once again, go outside and consider the people you see. We all need you."

"I've heard. I'm thinking about it."

Both men walk out of the office into the compound filled with people, even to the street outside the hospital.

"My God! All these people because of me?" The doctor whispers as Papa Samson pats him at the back.

"I told you, doctor, this is your town now and if you come back, I promise you, without a doubt, you'll be king here. We all know your worth."

The man leaves him to attend to the new people who are just trooping in. The doctor goes round encouraging them as they shed tears. Some come with their test results and he attends to them. His friend watches in awe and assists him in ministering to the people. While this is ongoing, a woman runs into the compound like a mad person, falling on her knees as she wails.

"Doctor, please don't go, please don't go," she begs. "This town belongs to you. Please, don't go."

Some men come to the doctor and take the woman away from him, but as they do so, more wailing women fall on him. More men come to pull him off and securely take him back into the reception of the hospital. One of the nurses collapses as well and the two doctors rush to resuscitate her, leaving her in the cub-webbed-designed ward on intravenous fluid until she becomes stable.

"You see, my friend, it is impossible to run a business dejure and defactor in this country, but from what I've seen so far, you've scaled through that phase of business. If you come back, expect a boom, so I strongly suggest you work things out with these people, redefine your networks in this town and come back in full force. I assure you that you are good to go. You definitely have no qualms in this place. I'll be leaving you now. I'll be in the capital before I move back tomorrow morning. Just go ahead, do your thing and claim this territory. They have handed it over to you with their own hands. You'll be a fool if you don't claim it bro, a big fool."

"Thank you bro, I'll see you tomorrow."

"Nah, take your time. They need you here. I'll be just fine."

The two doctors embrace and then his friend leaves.

The doctor begins to address the nurses and just immediately, a man walks in.

"Good afternoon, doctor. I am Mallam Idris," the man introduces himself.

"Good afternoon, the popular mallam Idris," the doctor greets back. "I've heard so much about you, Sir. How are you?"

"Oh, my doctor, I'm fine. It's really unfortunate that you are even thinking of leaving, but when I came here and saw the people, I was relaxed. What is happening here right now says it all. You can't leave us unless your heart is made of stone. You are now part of us and if not because you're already married, we would have given you not just one but three wives."

The two men laugh and the Mallam continues, "I'm serious o! You cannot leave us, you're just too important to us."

"Thank you, Mallam. I really appreciate it. I'm still processing everything that is going on here. I can't believe it."

The Mallam laughs, "I understand the cruelty you sometimes pass through, but trust me when I say you're not the only one suffering from it, I mean it. The other doctors around suffer same too; even the ones you think are your enemies suffer similar problems. Don't blame the people. They have suffered a lot. When you go through the history of this town and its people, you'll realize that they've been the state's demi-monde for a long time now. The governor may be from here but they've unfortunately enjoyed no benefits from him."

"I understand, sir. I don't want to act on my emotions. I need to take my time."

"Thank you, doctor, but in case you've made up your mind to leave us, estimate the items in your hospital and tell me the final price. I'll buy everything including your diagnostic machines, foetal sounders, laboratory gadgets and electronic amenities. I don't want you to go o, but just in case you've made a final decision to go, sell them to me."

"Okay, sir. I'll think about it. Just drop your number."

They exchange numbers, stand up, shake hands and the man leaves. The crowd outside still persists as the Mallam goes out to meet them with the former nurses. Everyone waits for an assurance from the doctor but he gives them none and for this reason no one is ready to leave. But after some hours have passed with no change of heart from him, the people gradually begin leaving.

In the evening when everywhere is clear, he goes round the compound one more time in deep thoughts, climbs up the building to the third floor and walks to the balcony of the uncompleted apartment to have a good view of the town, but the total blackout makes it impossible. He takes his time to think over what has happened, but remains clueless on the next move to take, calling all sort of holy indignations to come to his rescue. His heart bleeds for the people now and there's no doubt he's needed in the town. He decides to call four people who can influence his decision. He takes his phone and makes the first call.

"Good evening, dad, it's me," the doctor begins. After exchanging pleasantries, he explains his predicament then his father advices from the other end of the phone.

"A people who can assault their own doctor, cheat him and even treat him like trash will do so again. They all rallied round you today not because they truly love you but because it is now clear to them that your services are needed and your absence means those important services of yours become unavailable. They don't miss you. It's the works of your hands they miss and I assure you that nothing will change. Our economy is full of uncertainties and the situation in the country, from insecurity to unemployment, is getting worse. If these are the reasons for their strange attitudes against you, then gear up for more, if you decide to stay."

The second phone call, he makes is to his wife who also tows his father's line, "Honey, count me out of this. Don't be deceived by their fake love. Yes, I know you've seen a huge prospect after today's crocodile tears and you'll surely boom in business if you return, but also remember that you'll be hated the more by your competitors and that puts you more at risk of being eliminated by them. I strongly believe they attacked you spiritually when your leg got stiff in the middle of the highway while crossing, but you did not believe me. They did not succeed spiritually, that's why they are going physical with you. Do you even know they took your matter up in LAMAO FM? You were slandered, insulted and lied against. Three of my friends called to tell me. You might be sleeping one day and a hired assassin could come and finish you up, then what next? Remember the doctor from Bauchi state who was good at removing fibroids? Who remembers him now? Please, honey, I need you, your family needs you. You've taken a decision, and please, it should be irreversible and should stand. Your international English exam came out very good. We've made good steps in moving on, let's continue to move on and leave this country for good. We've given our own contributions and even if no one acknowledges it, God does, and that is good enough for me. Let's go where the government will encourage us, the people appreciate us and the systems propel us to greatness. Please, honey, no going back."

The doctor asks, "but what about the fact that I inspired them here." His question drives her to provocation.

"So, they got inspired only when you decided to leave, eh? How sincere! Don't listen to them! Get out of there, sweetheart! Not only inspire, they can get 'outspired', 'superspired', 'firespired' and even expired if they want. All I care is for you to leave that town for good, honey." She hangs up.

The doctor takes some time to think before calling the next person. This time, it's his doctor friend. After exchanging pleasantries, the doctor friend gives his own advice. "Paul young sang this song," he begins, "'wherever I lay my hat, that's my home.' I believe, in the first two years, you had been trying to lay your head well, but from what I've seen today, you're fully laid in that town. You've found a fertile ground, toiled and moiled, fighting through the harsh weather of challenges and staying strong after all the difficulties. Now, your crops are germinating, so don't be a foolish farmer who walks away. Your competitors may get angrier. Just be very careful and take all precautionary measures to be safe, especially in your home. For now, let your family be away and only let them come back when you're sure you've fully gained grounds, but don't let this opportunity slip off, brother. You've worked for it, and it has come for you. Please go ahead and earn it."

The doctor thanks his friend and the call ends. The last person he calls is his pastor. The man of God advises, "I've always told you, doctor, that this is your land, to be taken over by you. But taking it will not come easy. You're young, bold, brave and non-relenting with an unbelievable level of tenacity and mental stamina. You cannot show all these and back down when the going is about to get smooth for you. Are you scared of what your competitors will do to you? Plans are already underway as the men and youths of the town want to bring these so-called health officers and doctors to book with the warning that if anything happens to you, they will be paraded naked in town and burned alive. People are already standing up for you, doctor, and the whole town is on fire because of your threat to leave. Leave now and see how you'll disappoint an entire town. Please do not judge this place by the sins of a few. Things will change from now on and from what I've seen, things are already changing. Remain in town for now, doctor, we need you."

The doctor thanks his pastor and the call ends.

"My God!" He exclaims. Two people say leave, and the other two say stay. "What should I do?" He thinks to himself, "I love the people, I love my job, but I've also reached my lowest with these people. What should I do?"

It is now dark. The doctor walks around in the darkness, massaging his chin with his phone, and then a call which has an international calling code comes in.

"Hello," the doctor greets.

"Hello, doctor. This is Onyinye," says the voice on the phone.

"What! Onyinye! Where are you?"

She laughs, "I'm in Belgium. The police chief is a very generous man. He enjoyed my company so well and decided to meet my request of sending me here to do my first degree in nursing."

"Wow! The chief, huh? I'm happy for you."

"Don't think otherwise, Sir. I'm a lady, I had to take my chances to further my career."

"You need not explain, Onyinye. I totally understand. As a matter of fact, I'm so happy for you to be doing well for yourself. You know what you want and you've gone for it. Don't come back here o, just remain there." He laughs and cautions, "I'm just kidding though."

"With the happenings around you, Sir, I doubt if I will ever come back to that goddamn country. I heard about what happened and I'm aware of how sensitive your today's visit has been."

"Really?"

"Yes, sir."

"Wow! So my predicament has already travelled abroad? What a small world!"

She laughs, "well Sir, I just called to encourage you. I was there with you and I know the challenges you are facing. Also, I lived with the people and I know how important you are to them. They need you badly and even though they were not aware of it, I think they do now. So, Sir, follow your heart. Think carefully and know what you want. Either way is good for you. Just make sure you do the right thing and take a decision you'll be proud of in the nearest future."

"I'm speechless. Thank you so much, Onyinye. I cannot believe I'm getting encouraged by you."

"Yes, sir. Anything for you sir. You were once my boss and will always be my boss. Count on me anytime you need me."

Both laugh, "you will never change, Onyinye. You are now the boss and I really appreciate your call. Do you know that the doctor who washes systems also came here? I doubt his motive of coming, maybe to see for himself if I am actually leaving."

"What! Some people really have no shame o. But sir, were you able to figure out what he is actually doing?"

"Oh yes. It is so unfortunate. Do you know that this man takes Rifampincin, injects it in saline and administers it to these poor people?" The doctor reveals.

"What! That is fraud! So, since the side effect of rifampincin is heavily coloured urine, he uses that to deceive them?"

"Exactly! Wow! The ever-sharp nurse Onyinye, I am so impressed. That is what he does, my dear. A drug for tuberculosis treatment is what he uses to 'wash' the systems of these people, taking advantage of its side effect as 'evidence' to deceive them."

"Oh my God! And look at how they so much believe in him," Onyinye laments.

"My dear, that is the issue. It is really unfortunate."

They talk a little bit more before they end the call.

Immediately after the call, the power is restored. The doctor continues to walk around on the balcony. He stops, looks around and spots the Muslims praying outside a mosque not too far from his location. The highway is busy with the night life activities that have just begun — hotels engrossed in movements, the park which never sleeps, loud music from some quarters of town, boys in youthful exhibition, walking with their female counterparts in skimpy dresses, chemists and provision stores still providing services, barbers' shops, loud sports viewing centres and lots of bars.

He obviously misses them all as they take him back memory lane, while staying lost in his observation. A cool breeze blows at him, giving him extra comfort, then he sighs in relief and makes a call, "hello, is this Mallam Idris?" He asks.

"Yes," the Mallam affirms.

This is doctor. Everything in my hospital including the diagnostic machines, foetal sounders, laboratory gadgets and electronic amenities is 48.5 million naira and not negotiable."

OTHER BOOKS BY THE AUTHOR

The Soul Talkers
Biblical Love Psychology
The Devil's Orchid
99-1 series: Cry of the middle Belt
99-1 Series: The return of Uthman Danfodio
Tropical 20,000: O & G Module
Tropical 20,000: Paediatric Module
Tropical 20,000: Medicine Module
Tropical 20,000: Surgery Module
Black flower painted
(solution based analysis of the Nigerian public health issues)